THE PLEASURE IN PAIN

THE PLEASURE IN PAIN

A Queer Horrotica Anthology

Roxie Voorhees

The Pleasure in Pain: A Queer Horrotica Anthology is published by Dragon's Roost Press. Copyright © 2024 by Roxie Voorhees

All characters in this book are fictitious. Any resemblance to any persons living, dead, or otherwise animated is strictly coincidental.

All rights reserved. This book or any portion thereof may not be reproduced or used in any manner whatsoever without the express written permission of the publisher except for the use of brief quotations in a book review.

Printed in the United States of America

Print ISBN: 978-1-956824-24-7

Ebook ISBN: 978-1-956824-25-4

Audio ISBN: 978-1-956824-26-1

Dragon's Roost Press

2470 Hunter Rd.

Brighton, MI 48114

thedragonsroost.biz

For all the queers that hide, that pretend, that didn't make it.

Contents

A GIFT SO SWEET Zach Rosenberg	1
REGINA DI SANTANA Grace R. Reynolds	17
CAUGHT IN THE MOMENT Sapphire Lazuli	19
FRANKLIN & JACKSON JB Corso	29
GRAPHITE Amanda M. Blake	33
WHERE TO DRAW THE DOTTED LINES M. Lopes de Silva	49
WRITE MY EULOGY ON THE GLORYHOLE BATHROOM STALL Rae Knowles	51
I WANDER THE EARTH LONGING TO TASTE YOUR BEATING HEART Minh-Anh Vo Dinh	59
THIS LIVING HAND Aleksandra Ugelstad Elnæs	69
MANTIS Dori Lumpkin	71
BITE Arthur DeHart	85
ALPHABET CITY ANACTORIA Rain Corbyn	89
SILICONE TOYS Violet Mourningstarr	99
BY A THREAD Caitlin Marceau	103

HUNGER, THE SEA Charibdys	121
THE ROSES OF HELIOGABALUS Sofia Ajram	127
THE LEATHERMAN Darren Black	143
LITTLE SADDLESLUT GROWS UP Avra Margariti	145
WHITE & WOLF Marisca Pichette	155
A KISS WITH THORNS K. M. Carmien	161
WHAT THEY DON'T TELL YOU ABOUT THE MUMMY'S CURSE Anton Cancre	177
MOTEL POZITIVE j ambrose	183
THE TASTE OF ASH & BLACKBERRY Clar Hart	195
WE'RE ALL FAMILY HERE Shelley Lavigne	199
INVITATION Jessica Swanson	213
Acknowledgments	215
About the Editor	217
About the Authors	219
Dragon's Roost Press	227

A Gift so Sweet
Zach Rosenberg

Captain Temperance Isaac wanted to kill Laurent de Adnet as badly as they had once wanted to fuck him.

They made ample progress toward that goal at the moment. With a hurried oath to Hashem, the *Shrike's* captain evaded a blow from the fine French rapier. Balanced precariously on the rocks, Temperance flashed a grin at their former lover. "Did going Privateer make you slower, Laurent?"

He laughed, like it was one of the games they used to play. Just another set of verbal repartee while sharing a mug of ale from their tavern overlooking the sea. Except now the games were over, and Laurent wore the colors of the Royal French Navy, while Temperance wore only the bounty they earned.

"Surely you'd know I'd make it quick, Temper. Jew or no, I owe you that," his accent still raised the hairs on the back of their neck. The pounding adrenaline in the pirate's head left them flushed and grinning. There was something enticing about facing their former lover like this. Temperance never loved Laurent and always suspected they might have to kill him one day. He was a greedy fellow, treacherous and faithless. It was what made bedding him so enjoyable—no risk of attachment for either of them.

Zach Rosenberg

Temperance felt compelled to kiss him goodbye when they were through. There was something almost romantic about that, something to sing about back in Nassau port. "Oh, Laurent, wasn't that always your problem?" They caught his sword with their own and turned it.

Temperance hoped such a remote island would offer respite from pirate hunters, but Laurent tracked the *Shrike* with alarming persistence. He knew Temperance too well, and became a liability Temperance needed to expunge.

And so they committed themself to the next strike, a full piercing lunge that Laurent struck aside. He parried, as Temperance knew he would. Sensing an opening, he deflected the blade and struck. But Temperance crouched down low. The sword whistled overhead, causing Laurent to extend himself. He recovered too fast for Temperance to strike with their sword. But instead, they shifted their hand down to their boot.

The concealed knife came free. Glinting in the sunlight, it found a new sheath in Laurent's gut. His eyes went wide, mouth hung slack. Temperance smiled at him, leaning forward to brush their lips against his smooth cheek. "I'll say Kaddish for you, Laurent," they murmured.

"Really, Temper," Laurent sagged against them, as his strength fled his limbs. "You piercing me? That's really how this should end?"

"Laurent, be a mensch and die swiftly for me, would you? Don't be a sore loser now. It would be quite unattractive. You've already kept me from my crew for too long."

Laurent's blood flowed from the wound, soaking over Temperance's blade, and to their hand. "They say Jewish pirates from Spain once used this place as a cache," he murmured, his hand over Temperance's own. "Perhaps they left just a bit of magic for you to win this."

"Dear Laurent, you must be delusional with pain." Temperance's voice dripped sympathy like syrup. "Please, allow me to handle that. One cut, I'll make it clean and painless."

"I appreciate that," he managed, swaying unsteadily. Temperance prepared their sword for a blow. "But?"

Laurent lunged at Temperance, seizing them by the neck—too

close for them to bring the sword to bear. Temperance's eyes widened, a sudden sense of panic suffusing them. They struggled in his grip, Laurent's teeth baring in some approximation of a wolfish smile. "If I have to cross the river, Temper, I'll drag you with me."

Temperance twisted, but Laurent refused to unhand them, even when Temperance found themself slipping from atop the vantage point. Temperance struggled to pull away, but the water's impact felt like striking solid stone.

Any breath not throttled by Laurent drove out when hitting the crystal pool below. Laurent's grip loosened, and Temperance, using some hidden reserve, pulled away from him. Their knife was still lodged in his guts, but their sword was lost. Temperance moved to pull the blade free and finish the job. Just when the blade came free, a current seized them, dragging Temperance down in a riptide.

In the past, they appreciated when Laurent took their breath away. A touch of consensual pressure around their throat at just the right time could be enjoyable. But forced underwater, Temperance could only choke and gurgle, scared they'd inhale too much water. The current continued to pull them and any hint of sunlight vanished. The water around them was black, frigid and heavy. Temperance's skin ached from the cold, their chest burning for oxygen. Still the current pulled them, ripping them down.

Painful starbursts flashed against their eyes. They could not see which was which, could not tell up from down. They did not want to die, not when there was so much plunder to be taken, battles to be fought, and men and women to swive. They longed to be back in Nassau with a warm bed, rich wine, hot fish, and a plump and comely barmaid to share their bed.

They didn't want to die. Not like this.

Then, just as abruptly as it had taken them, the current stopped. Temperance clawed at the water, fighting for the surface until their head broke the water and they sucked in mouthfuls of gelid air. Stars faded from their vision and their eyes began to adjust to the darkness.

They were in a cave, resting in some subterranean pool of water. Around them pillars of rock framed a wide open chamber. Temperance dragged themself from the water. Winded, bedraggled, but uninjured, they savored the sweetness of unencumbered oxygen. Something caught their eye as they adjusted to the dark. There, upon closer inspection, up on one stony pillar, the defaced rock bore a resemblance with a number of familiar-seeming symbols. Snake-like figures ran along each side, and a lion stood proud at the top. Its pose, unmistakably a Lion of the Tribe of Judah, a sign of Temperance's faith and heritage.

"Temper," Laurent's voice, a throaty rasp. Temperance turned to see the man washed up against the cave's floor. Soaking wet, he shivered from the cold. The front of his tunic was stained black in the dim light, Temperance's knife still jutting from his flesh. Laurent grew pale, his handsome face twisted in pain. "You're still alive?"

"Despite your best efforts. Hush now, there's something strange here. Give me a moment and I'll put you out of your misery. Don't fight back when I use that knife to slit your throat."

He tried to rise, failed, and sank back down. "Is there a way out?"

Temperance couldn't see one. "Relax, Laurent. I'm not stuck here. I'd eat you, but I doubt people are kosher." They grinned at their own macabre joke, before their gaze pulled to another pillar. There were more carvings, images Temperance would know anywhere.

It was Hebrew. They recognized the words of the Shemot, the names of God. Invoked for prayers, but also for power. Temperance's eyes narrowed to slits, recalling how the water had dragged them down and pulled them along no matter how hard they tried to break free. Almost like it guided them here. Temperance no longer felt the rushing thrill of battle. "Just wait here a moment. I'll kill you soon."

"Take your time, but not too much. This hurts." Laurent sagged back, groaning deeply. His face twisted in pure anguish. "The stomach. Really?"

"Didn't leave me much choice. Hush now." Temperance took in the environment. The cave was massive, with pools of water flooding the area. Some sparkled, shining like luminescent crystals, allowing only hints of daylight through to the other side.

One pool rippled, as though something beneath the glassy surface moved. Just a little tremor, but the ripples spread wider. Faster. Then the next pool shifted, like something great and vast shivered beneath it.

Temperance wished they had their sword. Their teeth worked through their lip, eyes reading the stone carvings. Hebrew letters, although Temperance had not read the language in a long time, they were sure of it. But as far as they could read, it appeared to be some sort of command.

An order for something to remain *within*.

Laurent called Temperance's name. They recalled the only weapon they had was in Laurent's stomach. Stepping toward him, something splashed in the water. Temperance turned to be greeted by that something rising from it.

Its body shone with the same iridescence as the water' like a fish in the blackest depths creating its own illumination; the light glowed from its body as if it were a living thing.

"That can't be human," Laurent managed.

Taller than Temperance, it stepped from the water on clawed feet. Its body was lithe and slender with a long pointed tail. Temperance could make out the formed muscle beneath the silver flesh. The body appeared human. What was more, it appeared female with a larger chest and an emptiness between its thighs. Its face bore an ageless, otherworldly beauty. The lack of human imperfection was harsh, drawing to mind the raging beauty of a hurricane. Some natural force, as much a part of the unforgiving world as the great tides. It raised an arm, a thin membrane like wings or fins between them, a glistening shroud of argent gossamer.

It spoke, its voice a chorus of whalesong. Though Temperance did not read Hebrew well, they recognized it.

"I see the dead and one who hovers between," it sang. Its lips curled, tiny needled fangs in what Temperance considered a smile. It stepped forward, gazing at them with an unblinking, pitiless gaze. The hair, like fire coral, hung to the thing's shoulders. "And I sense one of the B'nai Yisrael before me. Hovering between. Do you not know of the Sheydim when you see them, child of Judah?"

Sheydim. Temperance knew the word from old stories. Creatures of primordial creation, neither human nor angel. Men referred to them as demons, but they were no fallen monsters to occupy some Christian hell. Sheydim were beings who followed their own natures and pleasures. Sometimes to the detriment of humanity.

"My name is Temperance," Temperance murmured. They could not speak Hebrew back, so they relied on Yiddish instead. The Sheydim seemed to understand, cocking its head. "How did you come to be here?"

"Whence sailed your people from Spain with merchants and conquerors, we came with them." The Sheydim drew a sharp nail to its lips, running a crimson tongue across the talon. Laurent groaned weakly, but the creature paid him so mind. "We were *sealed* here for offering our gifts. Across these islands. Though others came to seek us out, honor us. Those dead and in between."

It looked at Laurent, with hunger in its eyes. "I am Naamah," it murmured in Hebrew. "And I offer my gift for release. Tell him."

"It says it has a gift for you, Laurent. Its name is Naamah."

Laurent stared up at Naamah, the Sheydim gazed back, ravenous. "Gift?" the dying man wheezed.

"He is dead. I would ease his parting, take away his pain. In return, I ask only for what he no longer has use for. Not in an unpleasurable manner. But he must *consent.*"

Temperance relayed it again, a sinking feeling grew in the pit of their stomach. But Laurent held no hesitation in his eyes. "I agree."

"Laurent, you don't know what this is—"

"You've already killed me, damn you! I agree. Let it end this. Tell it, Temper. If I ever meant a single thing to you, say the words."

Temperance debated pulling the knife free to cut Laurent's throat. Agony made him stupid. It occurred to Temperance, they stared at a monster from legend. And they should have been more frightened.

But staring at Naamah, the curves of its body, the sharp contours of its form, Temperance was surprised at the intensity of lust that lit beneath their flesh and chased away the cold. Just a glance from Naamah's eyes brought bumps all across their skin. Smiling at Temperance, the Sheydim walked forward. Past them, to Laurent.

One hand closed around the knife in his gut and pulled. Temperance expected a shout of pain as the blade slid free, but Laurent only smiled, enraptured by the Sheydim. Naamah ran a hand along his stomach, the wound sealing without a scar. The blade clattered to the stone, slick with blood.

Raising its hands, Naamah ran them along Laurent, shredding his clothes to mere rags falling from his body. "Your death is assured. But there is sweetness at the end. Naamah's gift." It leaned in and brushed its lips on Laurent's chest. Its teeth closed on his pale skin and he shuddered with a low groan. The sound similar to the way he responded when Temperance did the same.

A lustful heat rose between Temperance's thighs, and they knew all they could do was watch. Watch and wonder why this ancient being was sealed away on such a remote island. Naamah paid them no heed, simply plucking away the torn rags of Laurent's clothes and tossing them aside like peeling a succulent fruit.

Laurent's body held more scars than the last time Temperance saw him naked. His toned body splayed on display, Naamah's talons toyed with his chest hair. Between his legs, his cock grew, standing firm at attention as he groaned at the Sheydim's ministrations. Naamah chuckled, a focused pride evident on its face. The Sheydim leaned across him, leaving behind a small trail of kisses along his body.

"Temper, it feels good," he managed, his hands roaming the silver skin. It rippled, like the surface of a river receiving a small stone at its center. Laurent cupped one of the Sheydim's breasts and squeezed, drawing a soft purr from Naamah.

It helped Laurent sit. "No pain," it murmured. Its hand took hold of his shaft and stroked. Such a terrifying claw, yet it handled his cock with gentleness. Stroking and guiding it, tugging and pulling, as Laurent groaned with more ardor than Temperance ever heard. Beneath the wrappings that bound their chest, their nipples stiffened. Between their thighs, they felt a wet heat. Temperance begged the sensation away, reminding themself the thing before them was a monster. They found the knife on the ground and longed to find the strength to seize it, and plunge it into Naamah's back.

But all they could do was stand and watch as Naamah tilted Laurent's cock up, and mounted him. Legs wrapped on either side of him, as it guided Laurent in. The moans escaping him were inhuman, pleasure bleeding into every note of his voice while the Sheydim rode him.

Slowly, it rocked its hips, the silver scales fading to pale flesh. Purring, eyes half-closed, the Sheydim ground its body into Laurent's own. His hips pushed upward, his own eyes meeting Temperance's. There was a triumph there, as though he sensed Temperance's arousal. He found a prize he did not have to share. Rooted to the spot, Temperance brushed a hand between their own legs, against the seam of their trousers. Pleasure shot through them, sharp as a stabbing blade. They resisted the urge to cry out, fixed upon Naamah riding Laurent.

"We give thanks to Hashem for this. My gift," the Sheydim murmured. It rode Laurent in practiced, quick motions. Pushing down to meet him grind for grind and thrust for thrust. "My grace.

"My food."

It brought a hand to Laurent's neck. Those razor talons flashed and a crimson mark appeared across Luarent's throat. If he was in pain, he gave no sign. If anything, his movements increased in their passions. He drove up into Naamah, moaning. Even as a carmine river flowed from without the side of his neck. Naamah encircled him with arms and wings, driving itself harder and harder upon him. The blood seeped into the stone around them, Temperance's eyes widening as the horror of the situation smashed upon them heavy as a falling mast.

Laurent grew pale and wan, his blood fleeing him. From his body, Naamah carved away a narrow ribbon of flesh. It came away, thin and bloodless like a pale ship's jerky—a cured little strip of Laurent that Naamah placed into its mouth and chewed with hungry relish.

"Temperance. It's so good," Laurent moaned while cupping the Sheydim's rear, pulling himself into it.

"Shhh," Naamah purred. Its body writhed, shimmering like moon-colored fire upon the dying pirate. As he bled away his remaining life, Naamah fucked and feasted upon him. From his body, the Sheydim picked away bloodless flesh with claws and teeth. Naamah's own moans rose from its lips, as though feeding enhanced its ardor. Temperance's legs trembled, but the feeling of arousal refused to fade.

There could be no blood left in Laurent's body, and Temperance knew why. Naamah wielded its claws like a shochet using a knife on a bull. It was hungry, for the Sheydim could not die like humans, but had been locked away for so long. It desired food, to feast upon the dying with their consent. But to feast, it had to prepare its meal, and it would not do for it to ingest blood.

That would not be kosher.

Laurent moaned, trembling out in what Temperance recognized as release. Laurent slumped back, torso picked clean of flesh. Naamah chewed and swallowed, while Laurent smiled, nothing left, but a vacant corpse.

The Sheydim rose off him, letting his limp cock free. The remnants of his seed ran down its leg, and the creature reached down to collect it. Naamah slid the sticky white liquid upon Laurent's thighs and flesh, before lowering its mouth to feast out of Temperance's view. As though it flavored its meat.

Temperance wrenched their gaze away with effort, their mind tossed in a conflicting tempest of emotion and tortured attempts of logic. They needed to escape or they would doubtlessly be next. Their knife laid on the ground. But a mere knife against a Sheydim, a being as old as the world itself?

At least it would be better than dying without resistance. But before Temperance moved, Naamah rose, leaving only the skeletal remains of Laurent. So quick. In its famished ravages, it ate so swift, with inhuman speed. The creature held in its hand one sharp shard of bone, picking its teeth until they were clean.

"You," Naamah sang, "live in between. Death is your companion. It walks with you. Do you wish to yield to it, flee the rigors and pains of this life? Accept my sweet gift?"

Looking into Naamah's eyes, Temperance understood the meaning of its gift. It was release, a passage from this world to the next. Sweetness and pleasure would be their companion, an indescribable bliss.

The way Laurent died.

He'd been good, but not perfect. Once, in a fit of pique, Temperance ground their hips on him so hard, he released long before Temperance began to enjoy themself. He once mishandled

Temperance so carelessly, their skull cracked on the headboard and ruined any chance of their progression. Though they never trusted him, Temperance had enjoyed his lips and his body between their thighs. It felt so wonderfully, humanly imperfect.

Unlike what Naamah offered—an ultimate pleasure to end everything. Laurent surrendered, but he was merely Catholic. Temperance knew endurance the way few others could. They were a Jew in a world that did not allow Jews to exist on their own terms. They were used to fighting.

"You are uncertain." Naamah's hand caressed Temperance's cheek. Their heart threatened to burst. The heat between Temperance's thighs increased and when they tried to speak, only a mewl escaped their throat. The memory of Naamah consuming Laurent only inflamed them, some dark desires hidden even to Temperance until this moment.

"You. You're doing this to me."

"No, I am not. It is only you." Naamah took Temperence's face in its hands and leaned forward. Its lips brushed theirs, tasting of sweet shadow. Naamah's tongue parted Temperance's lips and Temperance kissed the Sheydim back. Hungry, their tongue dueled with Naamah's, their arms encircled one another.

Naamah bore Temperance back to the floor of the cave. "In between," it murmured again, "Yet, living is so painful."

Temperance wanted to let go like nothing else. They could see why the Sheydim had been locked away. One look at its impossible beauty, one taste of its pleasure, and one could barely resist what it offered. Even at the price.

Knowing this and still longing, Temperance let Naamah undo their tunic. Not with the hurried slashes that had torn away Laurent's clothing, but a slow and steady pace. It undid the wrap around Temperance's chest, the captain whimpered in relief, as the breeze touched their dark, stiffening nipples. Naamah teased one, then the other, rolling them between their talons. So sharp, yet the Sheydim was delicate.

Temperance's pants and undergarments followed, leaving them naked and exposed. The knife lay forgotten across from them.

A Gift so Sweet

Naamah perched above the captain like a vast bird of prey. "What do you wish?" It spoke Hebrew still, its tone playful. One hand slid against the dark hair between Temperance's thighs. A sharp talon traced the lips below, running along them. A little prick, almost enough to draw blood, mingling pleasure and sweet pain.

"You," Temperance pulled Naamah down, feeling its soft scales. Running their tongue against the creature's lips. Kissing Naamah, Temperance pressed their bodies together. Temperance's breasts pillowed against the soft scales of Naamah's. The feel of the Sheydim's sex against theirs almost made Temperance climax.

"My gift?" Naamah's nails brushed against their throat. Its body rocked slowly, sparking new fires of ecstasy through Temperance. Give in, and pass from this world, Naamah's eyes said. It smiled with sharp teeth, the passage to eternity.

Temperance thought of the roughness of their cabin on choppy seas. Bad ale, terrible weevil filled biscuits and hard, salted beef. They thought of disappointing lovers and battle wounds. They considered getting seasick after drinking too much grog. So many things were utterly wretched about life.

Temperance now wanted nothing more than to experience all those things again. They were Temperance Isaac, captain of the *Shrike*. There was plunder to take, wonders to see, people to bed.

They would live. Because they were Temperance Isaac. Jewish pirate.

They rolled Naamah back, hooking their leg around the Sheydim. Surprised flickered across Naamah's face, just before Temperance kissed it. Rough as a crashing wave, Temperance wielded their lust as keen as any rapier.

"I want you. And you are mine, now. Do you understand?" They pushed their body against Naamah's, bringing a gasp from the Sheydim

Naamah's eyes flickered with a new emotion. Hunger, but not for flesh. The Sheydim's breath quickened, the creature's lips curving upward.

"Good," Temperance hissed. They kissed, and bit across that soft, scaly skin. "You want to taste me?"

They pushed themself up, not a great bird of prey, but a lithe and agile predator. A shrike, they thought with triumph. Temperance rose to straddle the Sheydim's face. "Then do so. Captain's order."

Temperance's back arched, an involuntary groan escaped their lips when Naamah leaned up to obey. They rocked themself upon the Sheydim's face, feeling its tongue stab into them. Curling, flexing within Temperance's body as though designed so perfectly to reach every center of pleasure. Naamah's claws fixed to Temperance's thighs, holding them in place as the Sheydim feasted.

"Yield," Naamah purred. Yield to death, to that erotic feasting Laurent succumbed to. Temperance threaded their hand into their own hair and pulled hard to feel a rough sting. The pain felt good, enhancing the sensation of pleasure. But it also kept them focused. As though sensing Temperance's preference, the Sheydim slapped their rear, making Temperance grind harder on its face.

Naamah twisted, shifting them. Pulled to their side, Temperance met the gift between the Sheydim's thighs, a leg locking around their head. Its tail slithered about Temperance's head, pulling them into the pale silver lips. Naamah's rough feasting upon the captain spurred their own hunger.

Temperance leaned in, taking in the salty, sweet scent from the Sheydim's core. They ran their tongue into Naamah, feeling the Sheydim rock and grind to their own mouth. Seizing the soft rear of their would-be executioner, Temperance pulled Naamah in. Drowning on a low tide of pleasure, Temperance moaned freely into Naamah, hearing it gasp with them. They shifted their head, tasting the Sheydim's clit, and on a sudden impulse, gently ran their teeth upon the silvery pearl. Naamah bucked wildly, hissing in a language that sounded older than Hebrew.

Temperance never allowed an opportunity to pass them. They fixed their mouth there, licking, sucking. This was less sex and more a duel between them. Naamah slapped Temperance's ass, digging in their claws. The pain was a sweetness heightening Temperance's desire, but again, anchored themself from Naamah's temptation.

Naamah came first. The rush of heat drenched Temperance's lips.

Wanting to come more than anything, Temperance resisted and pulled their mouth from the Sheydim, and pushed Naamah again to its back. They slid two fingers into the climaxing body of the ancient monster below them. Temperance kissed Naamah, wanting to taste themselves upon the Sheydim's lips but also desiring to give Naamah a taste of itself. Their tongues touched again and Temperance bit Naamah's firmly. The Sheydim's eyes burned with a lust identical to Temperance's own

"Tail," Temperance whispered, voice thick with lust. Naamah understood. The silver limb flexed and bent, teasing about Temperance's legs before slipping between them, letting Temperance grind against it. They began to time the movement of their hips to the motions of their hand between the Sheydim's thighs. They felt the tightness, the contractions of Naamah's body. "You come when I say so," Temperance whispered. They felt the press of the tail to their own clit, wanting to come so bad it almost hurt. "And I finish when I say. My life, my pleasure, is *mine.*"

Naamah smiled and raised their hips, panting freely. "Yes," it breathed out, eyes half-lidded and a smile fixed upon its face. Temperance seized it by the chin.

"I am not your prey. My name is Temperance. Say it. Say it and you can come again."

"Temperance," Naamah whispered, one gleaming hand closing upon Temperance's wrist and holding tight.

"Louder." Temperance hooked their pumper fingers.

"Temperance!" Naamah all but cried it out as they climaxed against Temperance's fingers.

Temperance was a pirate, a damned good one, and they wanted Naamah well and truly plundered. As its body tightened about Temperance's fingers, they pushed their fingers harder, playing with the most sensitive places. When Naamah relaxed, Temperance pushed down against the tail, sliding upon it and once more mounting Naamah's face.

This time the Sheydim submitted with no resistance or complaint, tongue doing its work. Temperance shut their eyes, feeling Naamah's mouth do its work. A smile spread across their face while they thrust their hips down, the heat of pleasure building. Temperance stiffened, eyes fluttering behind closed lids.

When they came, it was not a cry of submission, but one of pure triumph.

They sagged down, sweating and panting. Naamah slid out from underneath Temperance and shifted behind them. They reached out to the only weapon at hand, finding the discarded shard of bone from Laurent's body. It might do no good, but Temperance would fight to the last.

Instead, Naamah enfolded them in an embrace with arms and tail. Its teeth grazed Temperance's neck, fastening there and sucking firm. "This victory," it murmured, "is yours. You are not for my gift. But you've taken something sweeter: a triumph.

"Live, Temperance Isaac. Daughter of Judea. I give you the world."

Temperance, drained of energy, sagged back into the embrace of Naamah. Warm, content.

Victorious.

"Captain!" The shout made Temperance's eyes snap open. Lying in a pool of water, their cheek pressed against the warm sand. "Captain!" The shout came again.

A hand seized Temperance, bearing them up from the water. They caught themself, legs weak and leaden. Eyes focused, they saw familiar faces about them. Their bosun, Akewe, peered at them, concern all across his handsome face.

"We won," he said. "Laurent?"

Temperance glanced back at the water, suddenly aware of something in their hand. They looked down to a glistening shard of bone. A memory rushed back to them, bringing a bevy of emotion. Temperance dropped the bone to the ground. "Dead."

"By the seas, captain, you're a hard one," one man murmured. He looked at Temperance. "We've been searching for you after his men broke away. Feared the worst after the bastard pulled you off."

"Aye, glad for the loyalty. Todah rabah," Temperance said. The

Hebrew drew a chuckle from Akewe. The men might not be Jewish, but Temperance never heard complaints. They'd won loyalty in blood before. "Losses?"

"Only a few," another man said. He frowned. "Still, good men all."

"Aye," Temperance agreed. They looked out. "We'll bury them at sea. Get back to the *Shrike*. I want off this island now. Back to Nassau. We'll get new crew, sell our cargo." And vanish inside with a plump barmaid for a few days, they added in their mind.

"Captain, are you alright? On your neck?" Akewe said. "There's a mark."

Temperance clapped a hand there, the memories all returning. Naamah, its smile, its taste. For a moment, Temperance felt a deep longing to go back, to surrender to the embrace. Or to dominate the Sheydim anew and receive even more pleasure from it.

So they forced themself on, away from the pool and toward their ship, not speaking for a long moment. "Captain?" Akewe called. "What was it?"

"This?" Temperance rubbed their neck, remembering the bladed kiss of the Sheydim. Despite themself, they smiled.

"Just a memory of something sweet."

Regina di Santana
Grace R. Reynolds

Two hands. One bow. A ribbon of sinew pulls from muscle with every strum of the cello straddled between our thighs. This is our exposition. This is the last movement of our sonata, a concerto of love, lust, pain, and ecstasy. A corps de ballet of lost souls that will end in blood.

We were made for this.

I love them. They are the baritone to my contralto, and together, we sound our opening note triumphant in agony. Red blooms on white, I am a crimson silhouette of organza, and still, I push the bow with my hand on theirs. No longer is my clavicle protected by a veil of skin—the bone exposed, yet they plant a kiss in the crook anyway. I reach my hand behind to pull their head closer and press their breasts to my back.

Spezzami la spina dorsale.

Claws dig into my abdomen. As they wind up my entrails into their fist, they hold a fermata—leaving me breathless. My toes trace their cloven hooves, I choke—bury my nose into their fur. Salt, copper, cinder, and smoke; I am intoxicated by their taste and smell. They release, and I glide the bow into a legato to create our vibrato.

From the audience, we must sound like a singular note, an aria of sorrow for all that was, all that will never be. Cast out of Eden and

Grace R. Reynolds

Heaven, our love was never meant to exist in this world. So, shall we strum our final staccato with violence and fervor.

Let them hear the paroxysm of suffering. Let them watch on, voyeurists of brutal euphoria, and tell me there is no beauty in destruction. Tell me there is no pleasure in letting the world fall away to experience the limits of sensation.

Tell me we were not made for this.

A semiquaver of malice and my deltoids peel away. Rhythmic panting, their penis erect, the recapitulation of our debridement pushes us to the edge—they penetrate my ribcage. I can feel a talon stroke the exterior of my heart as it threatens to burst.

I push my chest harder into their arm, forcing their hand to grip my sternum. No one has ever known me this way. Not Adam, Samuel, or any other that proclaims themselves holy. I do not want to be holy; I do not want to be subservient to the teachings of God and man. I want to be equal.

I want to be free.

Distruggimi amore così cadiamo a pezzi insieme.

Their free hand moves on top of mine, the bow ricocheting under their touch. Droplets dance on strings, covering the cello in a thick lacquer of blood and the saliva dripping from my lips. I gag, then plead for release as they chop sixteenth notes like mallets against a timpani, but their focus is relentless. With the little strength I have left, I lift my hands and grab the horns protruding from their skull. They growl my name, their breath hot against my ear,

"*Lilith.*"

My rib cage extricates from the prison of my chest, and our coda ends in a short, guttural scream. They are my demon, and I their deity. A gift bestowed to me by the Othered. Through death, I am reborn.

Condannami all'inferno.

Caught in the Moment
Sapphire Lazuli

The canvas, a toy for the artist's dazzling surgery, is rarely considered in a discussion of the pain in creation. Sure, the artist's mindscape is licked at by thieving tongues as a portrait, a film, poetry are all thrust forth for outer eyes, but the canvas is merely a medium through which these pieces may be shown. A middle place. Placid and alone. Lain between happening and observing. So rarely is the canvas respected as a part of the artful indulgence. So rarely is the medium explored further than the paint dares to touch.

So rarely does the heart feel between the fibers of their dearest's bits.

The studio is dark, as always, an empty, unused organ unaware that it will soon become a womb for something so fresh. *So deliciously new.* A flurry of red and amber hair twirls through the doorway, nearly exploding thanks to the force at which it opened. Bodies. Pressed. Intertwined as lovers become. Even in these early moments, where artistry has yet to begin, there is so much on display. A passion of the flesh. Its pieces. Its every last moment. Queenie and Constance are both the match and the kindling. Igniting. Ignited. Craving the touch of each other and their art.

In rare calms between the storm that is their passion, the pair makes the room as it is needed for the next phase. A platform is slowly edged, between edging of a more yummy flavor, toward the center of the room. Erected, perhaps. Queenie tries to straighten the wooden thing, but their arm is caught under Constance's hand and pressed hard against the floor. Constance thinks to have trapped Queenie, Queenie thinks this is where they'd hoped to find themself. *Underneath her.*

Endless moments pass between moving the stage and angling the lights. Moments spent, instead, angling sensitivity against lusting *lips*. Feeling what will become their canvases. Learning the touch of the material. Dreaming of the artwork that will be created. Feeling. And feeling. *And feeling.*

Queenie, unable to contain themself, and rationalizing a need to first prime their canvas, covers Constance's chest with a gift of their roaring desire as the two roll along the studio floor. Their cheeks turn the color of their hair, embarrassed to have lacked any restraint. Constance, barely containing her own come, takes Queenie's cheek in her hand and presses a kiss. As both lovers giggle and squirm, they look around to find themselves now upon that wooden stage. Lights angled perfectly. Tools at the ready. Words go unspoken, but both lovers understand. Though they crave to never cease this glorious, lascivious moment. Though they lust, and need, and love. This moment is spent.

Now it is time for a *new* flavor of sex.

Forgoing a brush, Queenie slathers, with eyes of adoration, their endless love upon the canvas they call *lover*. Constance. Dripping. Painting with her own eyes in a likened fashion. These two, laborious artists of the heart's entrenched affliction, create now with each other as their medium. Teething on undug delights. Whispering. Loving. Desiring.

A sharp color in the blank void of the studio, Constance engorges—with a brush—upon Queenie's left shoulder, capturing their flesh in a ribbon of azure. With it, drizzling behind the bristles, Constance unwinds so unlike she had mere moments prior. Delicately. Slowly. Savoring every moment of skin with the thousand bristles at the end of her tool. Watching on, one might only see blue, but in this gentle moment, Queenie hears the whispers Constance intends.

"This here is a moment that, after uncovering my withered corpse from the ground a million years from now, would still be found playing through my decayed gray matter. Not repeating, not a cloudy memory, just slow. Slow in case, for a fleeting moment, I blink and miss an instance of your skin that I'll not have the privilege to meet later. On account of my being dead, that is.

"I should like to think there is not an instance of you I won't see, as I trace this azure brush. Your shoulder and on to your arms. Touching you. Knowing you. As the bristles slip into your palm that I know so intimately, I think I might become ravished with jealousy. To know that the pigment can be within that place that has held me, and soothed me, *and pleased me*, and nurtured me. To know that that pigment might come to know, as I have, that your hands are tools for a creation unlike any other—I won't stop them, though my chest will surely tighten."

Queenie is, as forever within the comfort of Constance's memory, a canvas artwork that is so fresh. Not a medium. Not a place for ink to lie, but a crucial piece of the creation in progress. Intent. Constance's eyes press so closely to where her brush glides. Edging over the shoulder now. Edging–excitement. Dripping. Recent memories of her time at the neck and the flavors it teases envigorate her mind. She makes a note to return here with her tongue when her blue pigment is spent.

The girl does not blink. Eyes watering. Rolling. Tears wetting the flesh of her lover.

Other art unfolds too. Queenie, with her free arm, peels the layers of lace that still try to hide Constance's flesh. Depriving and giving in one movement. For this deprivation of attempted modesty unfurls another place for creation. Constance's back gleams in the beams of the studio's single light. Poised against aching lovers. One blue, one nude. Both bare and exposed to each other in ways indescribable by a pen.

So, hands will do it instead—*Queenie's tools for creation.* One such thing crawls onto the exposed canvas, stroking, pressing, touching.

Sapphire Lazuli

Queenie kneads Constance's back and her head recoils as they do; eyes still poised to watch the slipping brush. As though clay, they mold their lover's back into shapes anew. Pushing. Pushing. The sound of Constance's moans are swallowed by the squishy elasticity of her flesh. Queenie, barely containing their own lascivious song, writes in a language only learnt through the action of love.

> Tis' such darling exploration, this.
> You, my moment in yours, in blue and in clay.
> I find it such bliss to know of your moments as you are learning of mine.
> Here would be a fine place to die. Safe. Cherished.
> Known. That is how it feels to be under your touch,
> Known for my intricate nothings that you expand outward as substance.
> My love, if I should be found, like you, buried in the soil,
> If eons pass and my body is but a memory in your gray.
> Know that this kneading I have taken to your back will still,
> In some movement I've no modern words to define,
> Take place in my hand as the painting will in your mind.
>
> O' the goddesses that have tinkered with our flesh!
> Surely, dear, you feel them too.
> The mechanisms,
> Wrought throughout.
> The need for moments is written in our tools, your brush, my hands. Blue and clay.
> I shan't like to think of what moments I am missing.
> Kneading reveals much,
> Needing hides much more.
>
> Have you secret fragments that hide beneath the clay?
> Dripping with synovial delicacies. Under the crust, so to say.
> I mean not to accuse you of lying, rather I wish only to ask,
> When you are turned crimson outward, my dearest love, may I take my hands to touch moments in your secret clay?

Caught in the Moment

Bristles freeze as they kiss blue to Queenie's bicep. Stagnant painting. Constance's gaze does not move, and yet her eyes are anywhere but on the flesh. It would seem that they are swimming. Feverishly. A skyward tumble splashes into the pits of a lover. Queenie, too, is frozen. Hands held firmly against their back-borne artwork, tightening, quietly. Their fingernails, once gently gliding alongside the kneading, turn slowly inward. Toward the flesh.

Toward the flesh. Yes, that is the current attitude. Both parties practically salivate at the thought of it. The undercurrent. The tunnels. The untold truths of a forbidden, sticky place. All waiting for a movement of either azure or clay.

The studio becomes so still. So dark. And yet these visceral moments are alight with a raw, unfiltered intention.

Art.

Attraction.

Both defined as each other in an attempt to know the true name of a lover.

It is hard to tell which happens first. Queenie's arm, inverted, sliced through so that the inner lining may breathe fresh air, dripping not with blood, but azure paint. Humerus cowering in the center. Ivory—*Not yet blue.*

Or upon Constance's back, a bulbous explosion of flesh and bone raining down from a hole where once was kneading. Or at least, it had rained for a moment before the hole was plugged. Reaching digits delve into the inner places.

As Queenie's fingers scamper inside Constance, the carnal artist shivers with a luxurious sensation. Queenie drags their intruder deep to familiar entrances, stroking. Coaxing the orgasmic melody. Lust. Discovering a moment of absolute, pure pleasure from where it sprouts. Constance explodes. Delighted. *Endlessly aroused.* The black studio walls become an ocean and she, a fish. Swimming. Drifting. Gentle touches of seaweed stroke the inner parts of her thighs as she swims by. Though, not the inner parts presented to outward eyes. No. The inner parts that swim in with her own liquids of rouge and crimson.

The girl is dripping.

23

Sapphire Lazuli

Dripping.

Either with blood or pleasure. In this moment, both options are equals.

Constance feels also, sliding into newly crafted folds of her lover's left arm. Their once dark flesh now the color of their hair. Constance thinks of the arm as a bottle, dripping, feeding her an endless onslaught of internal moments. She milks the arm for all it has and paints in azure to mark her place. Queenie is alight at the touch of their lover's delving. Dripping, as is she. Coming. Their bleeding, agonized arm screams at the same decibel as their orgasmically inclined throat. Constance delights at this. She delves further. Feels more of her dearest love.

Humerus shivers, as a cold touch lines its likeness with pigment. Intently. Deliberately. This painting is not explorative, but a delivery. Queenie feels the intended message slither into their nerve fibers. Their lips shake as the syllables caress their inner lining.

"I'd not thought that my dear Azure could be filled with such striking crimson. Love, within these folds you are so warm. So welcoming. The nights I've spent inside of you—if I'd known it could feel like this. Deep. Entrenched. An orgasm feels a mediocre reaction to this moment you've gifted me.

"But then…

"I do fear, am I cold? Is it that sensation that makes you shiver, or does such movement derive from the searing pain coursing through your body? I can feel it. The way you shake and stir. As my bristles touch each stolen secret, I know the mechanistic movements that convulse in your Agony's wake. Though, perhaps it is not Agony. I merely feel these mobile moments of yours; what I would give to hear the music each vibration sings to your inner ears. Your vessels and fibers are but strings to a magnificent harp. Harmonizing. Creating. I am neither the conductor nor the audience, and yet I feverishly twirl through your cavernous auditorium. Spilling my paint, so to say.

"And thus, as this music is forbidden to me, I wish to share with you the melody I do hear. As I pluck away delicate strands of you, digging, delving, taking pleasure in your nearest parts as I feel you do inside of my skin, I hear the adjacent roar of your beating heart.

Queenie, I hear. Kicking. The muscular drum of a fleshy symphony. I'm not sure how to describe exactly how, but the sound is so distinctly yours. As though the vibrations in the air have taken your azure hue. Will you know what this means? To hear a sound so familiar to the eyes? I am uncertain.

"I only hope my feeble attempt at description will capture the true majesty I am experiencing. Oh, to share it with you truly.

"My Deep Azure, you are an instrument to whose maker I will now worship. To be your musician, creating these symphonies of lust that no lyrics could possibly accompany. To feel your vibrations, and humming, and thrumming, and thumping, Queenie, I want to feel you like this until my nerves stop sensing and even then I wish to delve deeper and deeper into the insides of you. Queenie. Please have me, my Deep Azure. Let our music never cease.

"My Deep Azure.

"My Deep Azure."

Queenie, their head still recoiling and lips still speaking the song of new sex, unloads with Constance's deep touch. Every minute movement convulses their body, sending familiarly unfamiliar sensations into the core. Whoever described love as electric, Queenie thinks, has not known the true touch of intimacy. This is not electric. No. This sensation, gifted so gracefully, so agonizingly with love, this sensation is raw. Raw.

Raw. The uncooked meat of Constance slides between Queenie's fingers, twirling secret ribbons, testing new waters. Rising. They think this intrusion of the meat walks known paths, a tensile spot that they have spent countless nights exploring. But then, those ribbons kiss them more gently than any carnal passage.

And Constance's movements—just that is enough to drain Queenie of all they've to offer.

Moan is an unfit word. As is scream. Shake. Come. Even sex feels inadequate to describe this experience between two artists. This act is of knowing. Learning. Exploring. Deeper than a coital thrust, than the slip of a tongue, deeper than any lover could know of the other.

This act is alive. It is beautiful.

It is music. Music. *Queenie hears no music.*

Sapphire Lazuli

Lifting their arm out of the inquisitive flesh pit, hearing Constance's message, the song tempts Queenie. But they pause. Staring at the prod they'd bored with. Feeling. Something. Grown. Along the rims of their fingers, perhaps, are those not nails, but shards of sharp bone protruding from the end of their finger? At the ready for what must come next.

As their lover paints more blue in the dank, red place that has becomer their arm, Queenie lunges at Constance's ears. Talons bared. Queenie questions for a moment if these bone shards are theirs or Constance's; either suffices as they tears at their lover's ears.

Ripping. Delicately mutilating. Needing them. Needing them. No. Kneading them.

Queenie remolds Constance's ears so that they are theirs and not hers. Clay pieces slathered in blood become a part of the invasive audience that Constance described. The broken painter keeps tracing her blue, scarlet ribbons rushing violently from her unplugged hole. As this inner sludge dribbles and sullies the already damp studio floor, Queenie takes their stolen prize and presses it so gently to their lips. Tasting. Teasing. A devout tongue opens out to lick the ears. Devour their flavors. The ones promised by an explorative lover.

Upon the ears, a damp metallic appetizer before it, Queenie is granted a band of marching indulgences down their throat. The beat is felt through their every cavern. As they taste, Queenie wonders if Constance hears the music through their broken arm bits. Quiet tears slipping down her cheek give no clear answer.

Catching these tears with their whispers, Queenie enters Constance's broken ears with lines of unheard prose. Begging for reassurance. Hoping. Silent. The ears detach, the message, unheard.

So.

Siding up through bodily dribbles, Queenie drags their hand gently back through its piercing. Tickling the secret ribbons again. Feeling. Touching. Knowing truths that their lover teased. Whispering in ways even the pit would frown upon.

Lover. Lover, o' mine hear me.
For I hear you, your music, that which you'd hoped I would.

Caught in the Moment

Lover, you're wet in rouge and crystal,
I fear I am at fault.
I hope I am at fault.
I hear.
I feel.
I fear.
Yet, despite this apparent fear,
That my exploration has broken purposefully erected walls,
Has delved further than intended by any angel's piercing arrow.
Despite the dankwetted blood canvas that will not dry.
Lover, I am inside of you and I feel at of such privilege.
Is this your gift?
A million wet ribbons grafted into my knowledge of you.
Your inner moments.

Dear, we've spent years indulging the usual clay of being,
Weaving. Molding. Painting.
Lusting. Oh, have we lusted.
The artwork we've created of each other's being has been delicious.
But this. *Gods, this.*
It is here now that our love transcends the outer shell—
The things I wish to whisper into your ear as I delve.
As I touch.
As I learn passageways even your blood has not discovered.
Constance, my dearest love, it pains me to have deafened you.
I am sorry.
Truly.
But your music, the temptation. The will it took to resist.
I suppose I lacked the strength.
So, now I create in your flesh the poetry your ears refuse to hear.
Molding in secret clay.
I do hope you can forgive me.
I do hope you'll still love me.

Sapphire Lazuli

Joining Constance's likeness, tears leak from Queenie's eyes and marinate on their lover's back. The explorer is shoulder deep in Constance's back now. Feeling everything. *Feeling everything.*

Queenie no longer inquisitively touches, but rather manically searches. Desperate. Their fingers trying to find a final moment of warmth within Constance's meat.

The studio is so still. So dark. So full of visceral intention.

And yet, as the last dribbles of blood spill from the place her ears once were, gentle droplets on her cheek replaced with leakings of red, Constance, frozen, still in this final creation. Slumped. Her insides ravaged, her outsides stained. Her ears are gone, and yet Queenie keeps pleading. Needing. Queenie keeps kneading the inner chambers of their lover.

Constance's bristles stopped moving hours prior.

Upon the bone, a final message written in blue.

"Were my words not enough?"

Franklin & Jackson
JB Corso

Franklin kissed the small of his lover's neck. "This will be our last time together. Let's make it count."

"Maybe it won't be." Jackson's heavy breathing broke the words into verbal packets of lust.

"Maybe they'll leave us alone."

"No, no. It will be. They told me last night."

"Will it hurt?"

"Baby, I'm going to give you such ecstasy that whatever they do won't matter." Franklin stroked his partner. "I think the danger makes you hard, doesn't it?

"How much time do we have?"

"Shh. Don't worry about time. Focus on climaxing for me."

"I don't think that'll be possible. You already took me there twice. I don't know if I'll be able to."

Franklin giggled as he layered soft kisses on Jackson's muscular neck. "Oh, you'll cum. This is the important one. You want it. I want it. They want it."

The young husband's toes curled as his lover planted rows of soft kisses.

"Invite them in. Ask them to watch. Ask them to participate."

Jackson rebelled against the request, hoping to delay something he didn't yet fully understand.

"Do it, my sexy concubine, or I'll be forced to stop." Franklin held his hand still at Jackson's rigid base. He gyrated his hips, hoping to continue the glorious pleasure.

"No, no. That's cheating." Franklin let go.

"Please, I can't invite them. I don't know what'll happen."

"I don't think you want to climax. Maybe you don't even love me." The older lover teased.

"Baby, I love you and I so want to get off, but this seems so different from anything I'm used to."

"Concentrate on us being together. It's our time." Franklin peppered his partner's chest with light kisses, moving his efforts closer to Jackson's left nipple. "Think back to this morning when I sucked you off while your wife showered. Sneaking in the front door like you asked, you on your couch, and swallowed everything before she finished. When she walked out, I was in my car with your taste all over my tongue. Do it, baby."

Franklin's lips grazed Jackson's nipple. Tantalizing sensations rippled across his body.

"Okay, I'll do it. Just don't stop."

"I don't plan to, my sweet one." Franklin held his lips over Jackson's nipple, staring into his eyes with burning anticipation.

"I summon the dead and tormented into this room. Do as you like, as you need to make your eternal afterlife more bearable."

"Perfect," Franklin said with a smile. He lightly sucked Jackson's nipple, eliciting a deep moan. Several cool breezes passed over the men. "They're here. Keep focusing on us, keep your eyes closed, and I promise to take you places you've never experienced."

The scent of burnt lilacs filled their noses. Jackson arched his back as Franklin's mouth explored his chest.

Jackson felt pressure against his legs and arms, as if being held down by weights rolling over his body inch by inch.

"Shh. Don't move. Focus on my mouth." Franklin's kisses moved lower down Jackson's stomach. "I'm going to do that thing you like so much if you promise to seal your eyes until you climax."

"I... I promise."

"Good."

Jackson moaned as Franklin explored the hard length with his tongue. The increasing pressure spread as if he was slowly being covered in sand. The sensations radiated down his legs towards his ankles. His hands felt weighed down by ten-pound weights. A bucking anxiety rattled his thoughts.

"They've arrived, Jackson, my sweet. Keep focusing on me. Don't worry, this is how it's supposed to feel. It's normal to be nervous. I was scared, too, when I was alive."

Franklin sucked with enthusiasm. The heavy sensations along Jackson's limbs crippled his desire to touch Franklin's head. He bucked his hips, climaxing into Franklin's awaiting mouth. His lover continued the pressure as Jackson moaned through the last moments of elation.

"That's what I needed," Franklin said, licking his lips. "You can look now."

Jackson eased his eyes open with post-climactic glee. Swirling masses of dense, dark oranges and greens blocked out the wall lights. He panicked at the confusion, struggling against the pressure.

Franklin sat up. "Now, my love, since your body is free from all but trace amounts of cum, they're ready to feed."

"No, this can't be happening." Stiff gusts blew over his naked skin. His attempts to move were stifled by the unseen forces. Franklin pushed a hand on Jackson's chest.

"Oh, it's happening. When your wife gets home from her night out, she'll walk into the bedroom, possibly hoping to find you waiting for her. She might even get wet at the idea."

Franklin stood up into the swirling vortex. The top half of his body mixed into the visual confusion. "In reality, she's going to see a bloody mess that'll permanently scar her."

His words arrived to Jackson muffled, as if standing in a windstorm. "If she doesn't land in a crazy ward, she's definitely never having another intimate thought in her head again."

Franklin laughed. "The amount of guts and blood and human carnage is going to be insane. I don't know if more than a couple of inches of this room will be free of your splatter. We're going to put your guts all over the carpet. What's left of your organs against the door. Maybe bits of your legs throughout the closet, and what's left of your head will drip behind your bed."

Jackson screamed. Franklin's legs and feet ascended into the vortex.

"Time to die, my love." His words echoed with a sinister chuckle. The cloud descended onto the bed. Jackson's screams were replaced by visceral splattering like a writhing body fed through a wood-chipper.

Susan arrived home several hours later to their bedroom light on. Excitement lingered in her panties as she wondered if Jackson was pleasuring himself. Susan's thoughts wandered through several new positions she wanted them to try.

Graphite
Amanda M. Blake

If it were October, you'd have to keep a keener eye out for nosy neighbors looking for a reason to call down the sirens, but it's February degrees outside; no one's sitting that close to a cold window. With a hammer and a penchant for sneaking into places you don't belong, you pry the plywood off the back door and break your way into the house. It's almost as cold inside as outside, but adrenaline rushes warm through your chest, if not your fingers and toes.

The Hoffman House has been on your bucket list for years—the subject of many a graffiti ghost story and hashtagged creepypasta by physical media artists, vandals to bizarre illustrators. It's famous with a small enough group that the house, plastered 'condemned' on its doors by the city, doesn't go out of its way to discourage devoted trespassers.

Layers upon layers of largely undisturbed dust tickles your nose, because you disturb it with every step on the disintegrating carpet and distorted hardwoods; every breath a moth-wing draft to swirl the hovering motes. When you sneeze, the cobwebs sway. But in the cold, there's a clinical cleanliness to the atmosphere, as though the dust is frost—no mustiness, and with the windows boarded, timeless.

The stories take you to soft wooden stairs. You grasp the railing because it looks solid. It groans under your grip, which does nothing to comfort you. You keep to the sides so the weight of your body and the things you carry with you doesn't strain the rot.

On the second-floor landing, light spills through grimy stained glass in splashes of color, cold from winter sun despite what should have been warm saturation. For a moment, you are watercolor on gray, all gray, blending into the time-sapped colorlessness of the house. Then you switch on your phone's flashlight and go deeper down the hallway to an unpainted wooden door leading to the attic.

You are a spook yourself, a shadow in the corner of eyes, a haunt in spaces people don't want to go and prefer to forget. You're unable to stay in one place, but leave pieces of yourself wherever you go—petty graffiti, more who you are than footprints and what's captured by other people's photographs. You aren't afraid of ghosts, and aside from others like you, you've never met one. The only chills or goosebumps you experience are annoyingly practical.

You consume creepypasta in great, gulping swallows, visit sites of supernatural occurrences, sleep in haunted hotels between roadside diners. But you're not afraid of this house, despite its reputation, because you've never crossed paths with an inhuman monster. Every spirit is a dust mote, and all you get from haunted hotels is a restful night's sleep. You love the lore, but don't expect anything more substantial. The atmosphere feeds you well enough. If you can leave your mark in a place like this, you become part of legend both undeniably old yet unmistakably modern, given new life in a digital age.

The attic stairs are sturdier, but they creak a jagged melody, announcing your arrival into the cathedral of Willard Hoffman's study. These are the only windows with a view. Sunlight as gray as the dull floors and walls beam almost blindingly bright after the boarded darkness of the mausoleum below. Outside appears dead instead of dormant; skeleton branches shiver with the northern wind, kindling grass the same hue as the concrete delineating the deteriorating subdivision. The Hoffman House is condemned, but the rest look little better. Generously vintage cars crouch in involuntary, furtive hibernation. Blank windows stare with suspicion at the condemned

Graphite

without self-awareness or reflection. You don't feel seen, so you step away from the window.

Most of the room has been picked clean by looters and other pilgrims, but the walls have been left undamaged, although you cannot say untouched. No one would damage Hoffman's walls any more than they'd harm the ceiling of the Sistine Chapel. There are as many naked bodies here as at the Apostolic Palace—arguably more, and with as much reverence for the human form, although these illustrations would never find themselves on hallowed ground.

The blandest of wallpaper is covered floor to chair rail, chair rail to ceiling, with hundreds of drawings. And it's not the dust that makes them filthy.

Hoffman was a professional cartoonist and illustrator, but he also inked pornographic pamphlets under the name Harold Grandstanding. Notoriously reclusive despite his uncommon prolificacy, he eventually retreated from public life entirely. The sheer number of small illustrations that cover this most sacred of unsacred spaces supports the hypergraphia theory, for what else could he do with himself when he no longer needed to draw more wholesome fare for newspapers and folios? Although these, too, have their devotees, deservedly so. You devoured them when you were younger, then graduated to his more adult fare in your twenties, inspired by your own dirty doodling.

You start at one corner, where you recognize his style. It's rougher than both sides of his professional work—hastily jotted notes like the margins of your papers and notebooks throughout high school and college, to the exasperation and occasional amusement of your teachers.

The thing that helped you focus, sometimes also distracted you, not least because your occasional subject sat a knight's move ahead of you in history classes, with a spinner's skein of golden hair. When it was loose, you could smell her shampoo and dreamed of burying your face in its spread. Then, in college, even more people you wanted to get to know better surrounded you, but for the longest time, you could express it only in speech bubbles.

After college, in your shiftless days and nights, you've drawn your dirty little pictures in the digital sphere, the filthy bathroom stalls, in marginalia occasionally real—affairs as torrid as the places you seek out, ephemeral as unsealed pencil on paper. There isn't enough time, space, or foundation for permanence—not yet. Perhaps that's why you like ghost stories and stay at haunted hotels—ghosts are liminal, but the stories themselves are knots on bullet-ridden tree trunks, insidious splinters shared finger to finger.

Hoffman's drawings are quick and compulsive, sometimes little more than sketch marks, but in other areas, he shades the figures into stunning reality, a sea of shuttlecocks and pussywillow.

Hoffman was a queer ahead of his time. His blue drawings are mercilessly pansexual in nature, although amateur historians only seem aware of his female conquests—despite a best chum with whom he spent many of his years in a completely heterosexual fashion. The reasons for his variety were left to speculation, whether he suffered unexplored desires or simply found other people's attractions as intriguing as his own.

Despite your own sapphic proclivities, you, too, are intrigued by erections great and small, near or buried in asses, pussies, mouths, ear canals, gaping wounds, eye sockets. Although Hoffman was a family-friendly cartoonist as well as a standard pornographer, some of his rarer pieces took a decidedly darker slant, and these attic drawings—intended for his eyes alone—show the shadows teeming through his mind, the ones he could not share so generously, yet reached a grail-like status among trespassers.

Strange, with all the pilgrimages to this reliquary, no one has ever taken photographs for posterity. There should be a record, something to preserve his prodigious work in its massive gabled sanctuary—something more than legend. These illustrations are in pencil, not ink, although both fade with the erosion and chemistry of time.

Take only photographs, leave only footprints, as the signs say. But that's not what people are supposed to take here, nor leave. Because Hoffman died before he could complete his work, this massive orgiastic undertaking of his own making, if not his own volition.

No photographs flood the digital sphere, except of other people's works added on, their additions to the story. Sometimes the

Graphite

illustrations are of themselves, sometimes of others, sometimes in color, sometimes in ink, sometimes in pencil, sometimes photorealistic, sometimes a more cartoonish or manga style. Deeper to the shadow-ridden back of the room, you find the transition from Hoffman's recognizable styles to those distinct from him. You even recognize a few from the creepypasta and from artists with whom you've crossed paths as shiftless as your own, with whom you've left delible marks—artists known only by their work and never seen, but that's not strange. It's a great wide world with many empty walls.

Hovering your fingers over the unmoving writhe of bodies, naked or partially clothed, you follow the path of the story—the decadence and darkness, the eroticism and horror, the beauty and carnal ugliness, heaven and hell, ecstasy and despair. You don't touch it, because there's no sealant here, nothing to preserve the art except decades of reverence by those who know better than to ruin something true, something real. No one wants to break the chain; everyone just wants to add their lock to the bridge.

This is as important and valuable as the Sistine Chapel, at least to you. So what if it's cheap? All the best things should be, even if they aren't. So what if it's low? Everything that's high only got there because of the things below it. The other pilgrims to this place of worship understood the value, because the house still stands, the illustrations enhanced rather than painted over or wallpaper torn away. And despite demand, none of its grail elements are shared far and wide, for they are meant to be found, like a cartoon sex act under the fake phone number in a bathroom stall.

Maybe the real grail is all the gloryholes we decorate with ironic daisy chains along the way.

In the dim back of the room, where his desk chair left grooves in the thin rug, clouds of blank wallpaper billow above where artists forged their links to Hoffman's. Difficult to believe there can be any empty space, when so many more artists than you could have imagined have contributed, although the stories say those who add their self illustrations to Hoffman's compulsions are never heard from again, like the man himself, who didn't die so much as disappear without a trace.

Amanda M. Blake

In your experience, people like Hoffman who disappear without a trace simply don't want to be found. Investigations into his financials don't indicate debt, so you doubt concrete boots pin him to the lake floor. Perhaps he's chasing the perfect illustration or running from his compulsions. By virtue of birthdate, he might be dead by now, but foul play seems unlikely.

And if artists who add their illustrations disappear without a trace, too, it begs the question how the story spreads. You've seen snaps not of Hoffman's illustrations but of people's contributions, like carving initials into a sacred tree.

But have you seen anything from them afterward?

You pause with your hand deep in your backpack pocket as you rack your brain for posts to follow. You honestly don't know. Timelines all meld together without context, and it's not like you hoped to ever see them again, if you even saw them before. They're just addendums to a mythology, footnotes to the warnings, glittering confetti of mystique that sold you on the pilgrimage that brought you here.

Instead of a pen or marker, you pull out your 6B pencil—darker and softer, easy to shade, easy to smear. You aren't looking for immortality. You just want to be a part of his story, a lesbian transient raising her voice to join the chorus he started, because he was one of the people who taught you how to use that voice—and more importantly, why.

Within the orgy, you draw yourself. It's rough, sketchy rather than clean, because that's your style, recognizable on squatter's walls across the country, on baseboards and subway tile, occasionally viral in certain circles, even if no one knows your name because you include no signature beyond style itself.

You don't like to draw yourself, at least not where other people can see, but it's tradition here. Hoffman's self-portraits in a variety of imaginative sexual acts appear in multitudes on his walls. The sex here isn't about pretty; it's about desire, drawn because it's unspoken and unseen by more than a few. And those few come here not to laugh but to moan, pressing against the engorgement of flesh—male and female and everything in between and outside alike. Desire is blood and thickening and mess, a wonderful, grunting ugliness made beautiful with bursts of oxytocin.

Licking your lips you acknowledge your lumps and folds, your heaviness, your broadness, your age, remember when others found it worthy of brief worship and gratefully accepted your sacrifices at their altar in return. You draw yourself like you've always wished to be drawn by a less crude hand—on a settee like one moldering in the parlor below, flanked by lusciously fat women, a feast feasted upon, filled and filling, one more platter in this wall-to-wall banquet.

Your hands are charred by the time you step back. You've left smudges on the wallpaper canvas, but you don't erase them. Art is never truly independent of the artist.

Not quite athanasia, but it might still last longer than you, like the rest of what you've left behind, children of lead and ink instead of anything between your thighs. That's only been for pleasure and a little bit of pain. You never nurture for long.

You consider leaving immediately, but the cold light outside the window submerges into twilight, and streetlights and moonbeams on the frost reflect brighter than sky. You needed your phone's flashlight just to finish your drawing. Too dark, too cold. Nothing wrong with the sturdy roof over your head, and your sleeping bag insulates. You've slept in worse.

You descend the attic stairs and carefully continue to the first floor, somehow surviving each soft stair again.

After turning out a folded blanket found a linen closet that moths but not dust could reach, you cover the sofa across from the settee that inspired you, then unroll your sleeping bag and tuck your numb feet inside. You chew on protein bars and dream of a hot breakfast.

While drawing, you blissfully forget everything, including hunger —even more when you draw desire, because why return to reality when this is the one you return to? Warm and full aren't guaranteed with the way you need to live, the way you need to be, but your imagination is almost as good, and perhaps fortune will smile on you tomorrow, the next day, or the next.

You burrow into the sleeping bag, breathe and burn until the air warms and the shivers stop and you sink into deep, dark hibernation, and wish not to wake until spring.

You open your eyes to flickering light and humid heat, even though you didn't build a fire in the ashy, dusty, feather-ridden, shit-strewn fireplace to avoid attracting attention.

Dead of winter, you lay tits up and out on the settee. Without dust, the emerald fabric is as rich and deep as new. But although the settee is the same as in the parlor where you fell asleep, you are no longer in the house, at least not as you know it. The ceilings scale too high to see the crown molding, the rooms too large to find corners, and through openings and doorways, the house stretches beyond the blueprints, beyond the property line, beyond neighborhood borders.

You went to sleep able to see your breath, but now inhale a thick, redolent hothouse. Your mouth waters before the perfume's origins solidify in your disoriented semi-dream state.

The fireplace is five times the size as before, but its fire does nothing to dry the heat in the room. Sweat beads on your back, dampens the upholstered settee, rolls down your temples to your scissor-shorn hair, gathers underneath the press of your tits against your upper abdomen.

You are not alone.

All around, on the floor, on the couch you were just sleeping on but which has been reinvigorated as though new, on furniture you've never seen before, on beds in other rooms, on tables, on thrones, among, amid, above, between, you are surrounded by people, and it's from them that the humidity and heat emanates, from them that the perfume rises—of sweat old and new, of pre-cum and semen and other fluids, some foul and some a sweet nectar to you, all mingled together into something both repulsive and divine that brings your still-stained hand to your lips to catch saliva before it slithers down your chin.

Before you completely comprehend the sight, you understand the sounds, a symphony even more intoxicating than the multilayered perfume. Cacophonic grunts, groans, and moans, high and low, guttural and melodic, crawl vibration over your skin, gooseflesh for something other than cold.

Despite the senselessness of your surroundings and company, clarity sharpens the three-hundred-sixty-degree panorama of desperate fucking, a bacchanal without shame or self-consciousness, unrehearsed and raw, too real to be lovely.

Once you fully realize you're naked, too, you try to cover yourself —inadequately, for you are full and take up space, and your hands cannot hope to contain you. You flip from one side to the other looking for your clothes, for context, for an exit, but you find none of these, just bodies and the things that they want regardless of whether they should. There's nowhere you can hide, not even under the settee, where two thin men tangle their skeletons as one of them tops the other with frantic grunts, as though he has a gun's bore against his temple. The boarded window above the couch is gone, nothing but drapes where it used to be. Where the back door was before is a blank wall fused by a man and woman to fuck against, blending into the fire-strewn shadows as though they're part of the plaster.

Even in your disorientation, everything seems familiar, like déjà vu, although all the people are strangers. Still, you've drawn so many faces that you never forget one.

Yes. That's where you've seen those skeletal men. That's where you've seen the three women getting absolutely railed by a dude with very busy hands and dick. That's where you've seen that woman with the inflatable boobs bouncing them painfully over the helpless man beneath her, his cheeks red from being soft-punched in the face.

And on one of the other couches, a man, his unmistakable wide eyes and furred gut recognizable from his cartoon profile, fucks a woman whose arms twist like a balloon animal behind her back.

In the other room, you recognize him again, strangled with curtain rope and suffocating beneath the massive, fleshy woman who nearly subsumes him, except for the thin space between her legs as she braces herself over him and works his cock. It seems so small in comparison to her, but moans suggest it serves her well.

You notice Hoffman again on the stairs, clinging to the railing as he fucks himself with the rounded top of the newel post while a woman lashes his back with a welting black leather flogger.

You've seen all these strangers before—lining the walls of Hoffman's attic study. No matter how simple the sketch, how exaggerated or sparse the features, the artists drew more than mere impressions. You overlay what you see now with the configurations in the attic, double vision sliding together seamlessly.

It makes no sense, but you don't make a habit of doubting what you see. Your only vice is alcohol when you can get it, and right now you can't. Even fever dreams aren't this vivid.

You push yourself up on the settee, still trying to cover yourself, but everyone is too occupied to notice much of you. Even when they do, they're just as imperfect, but it doesn't stop the wet, doesn't stop the heat, doesn't stop the need. They slip, helpless, beneath the bruises of their collective drawn desire.

Cool hands slide over your shoulders, but although you jump, you're not necessarily surprised. Why would you be? You know what you drew.

A woman presses her breasts against the back of your head, while another woman crawls toward you from the foot of the settee, nails digging into the tufted fabric. She stares at you like you're a dessert platter, which isn't usually such an immediate reaction.

You can't say that you've never had strangers before or that you always know their names when you wrap yourself around them, when you make yourself and her feel good for a night and maybe a morning.

You don't know these women at all, though, haven't met across a dilapidated floor and decided without words to keep each other warm for the evening. You're not even sure if they're real, because the women you drew on the wall with you are an amalgamation of people you've met or would like to meet.

But they feel real; hands on your shoulders, on your ankles, cool skin quickly warming where flesh meets flesh.

You erase your hair with dull scissors, but you love long, loose hair on other women. The woman behind you leans over the back of the settee. Her breasts press against the jagged chop, and God, her wavy red hair spills like silken copper over you with the beautiful scent of

Graphite

fresh dark herbal shampoo, even though you can't draw scent with pencil.

You pillow your head against the soft breasts, close your eyes, and inhale the clean and sweet through the hothouse created by fire and bodies. The hair curtains your face, but leaning back like this presents your body now—with its dimples, lumps, and spider veins—with the others. As you rest your cheek on her milk-white, translucent, achingly smooth skin, you're less inclined to care. Your arm shifts away from censoring your nipples—because covering your breasts is a fool's errand—and your other hand twitches, fingers curling to knot against pubic bone, digging into nerves that jolt through you like winter static.

The woman at your feet is black-haired like you, but a thicker black. Skin burnished gold in the firelight, it's darker than yours, where you compare her delicate-fingered hands to your calves as you emerge from between the copper curtains. She still gulps in the sight of you with unsettling light green eyes, like faded river glass except for the gleam beneath, of life rather than semblance.

Whether or not she was real an hour ago, she is no mannequin. She has density, give, with spark and flame, not a mere figment. Which is why you let those delicate fingers creep over your thighs. You cry out when the strength beneath the black-haired woman's own softness yanks you down onto your back again, tits flattened and brown nipples wrinkled and taut as though they still know winter.

The redhead sways around the settee to sit next to you. Her bush is auburn, her leg hair the finest light ginger. She guides your mouth to her flushed, pink nipples before she even kisses you. You respect a woman who knows what she wants and what you want at the same time.

You fondle her sweet, soft belly as you gather her breast heavy on your lips, on your tongue. Those who've never known the comfort of a fat woman don't know what they're missing. But that's okay, because you do know what they're missing and get to have it, and get to give it, too.

Your hands remain graphite-stained. You smear the redhead's white skin like the wallpaper. You shade her paleness, taste and tighten until

Amanda M. Blake

hers are just another chorister's notes in the unending song around you. She finally climbs over your hips and lets you sink back with her kisses, the coquetry of her hair alluding privacy.

All the while, the black-haired woman kisses up your thighs, leaving indentations of her teeth to part your legs wider, until they hang over either side of the settee. The woman settles on her belly before the spread, her breath warmer than the air, but cool against your wet. You feel when her breath quickens; your clit twitches with the knowledge that you are deeply and undeniably seen, in bright enough light for detailed work. Not just seen but perused for pursual, that you are as desirable as you desire, low and pulsing in the heavy cradle of your pelvis.

You grasp the redhead's ass in double fistfuls as she licks the seam of your lips, and the black-haired woman does the same below.

Wait, you try to say. Wait.

But you don't really want to say it, would rather sink under the surface of this impossibility before it realizes its own likelihood. You keep kissing ginger, the other woman's black hair draped over your thighs as she holds you open and sucks from the salt of your lips, then up to latch mercilessly to your clit. All three of you sing now, or at least hum—muffled.

With the right partner, you will make out for hours. With the right partner, you will come seven times. You are partnered with the right women. Under their onslaught, you give everything you can to the redhead, but there's little you can give to the black-haired woman. Even so, she seems content enough to feast upon you when you come, lapping the salt honey of her labors, and she shakes the settee as she rubs herself, moaning long and high when she comes on her own.

After the second leaves you trickling, the redhead brings your mouth to her breasts again, smothers you in a way you would gladly die as much as Hoffman. Pulling herself up by the back of the settee, she lowers herself over your mouth—another perfect death. She rides your face for miles, but it seems to be more for you, for the smear of her juices on your chin and your tongue, for the pleasure of her moans to the distant ceiling.

It's never been like this before, never this hot, never this sweet,

Graphite

never all about you, because even as a selfish lover, the good lays are transactional in the exchange of bodily fluids.

These are priestesses in the strange, small, sybaritic religion of you, relentless and insatiable in their devotion. You wear out before they do, sometimes just rest there with the redhead's pussy grinding over your tired tongue and the black-haired woman's mouth a beautiful suction over your clit. Lust sweeps over you in waves as you revel in fresh carnal scent, in thick thighs on either side of your head, in the bruises on your own thighs, in the ache between your nipples and your clit, in the impulse to rise and fall and sleep and dream and come, this seductive, insidious cycle that bleeds together like watercolors—not your usual medium, although you sometimes play with tea and coffee, sepia tones over your rougher grays. But you don't fall back asleep; desire keeps you on the edge of an unhoned blade, and you know this scenario isn't finished. This wasn't what you drew, not quite—not yet.

The black-haired woman releases your thighs, slides her fingertips center to stroke along your labia. You jerk, pussy clenching, as she probes the slick entrance. No resistance, given that you've lost count of climaxes. She doesn't bother going slow. You keen against the redhead's clit as the black-haired woman slides three fingers in and curls.

As you clutch at the redhead's hip, you reach down to grab a tangle of thick, gorgeous black hair in your fist. You know where this is going, yearn for where this is going.

You double down on the redhead as the black-haired woman doubles down on you, excruciating suction as she takes you with four fanning fingers, spreading and stretching before fingering you relentlessly, making you come again, clenching hard against the pressure of knuckles. Your stomach growls, but you feast upon the redhead instead, laving deep within before returning to her clit and making her croon, grind, crush your skull between her thighs. The other woman plunders deep, five fingers now, not in and out but just moving inside, your entrance a bangle on her wrist that she licks around. She finds the place again that makes you twist and arch and flood her tongue.

You never quite understand how two people become one with sex. Even when it's good, it's still two people, and simultaneous orgasm is almost a myth, sex more like a relay than a dance in your experience. But sometimes…sometimes…when a woman is deep inside you, when you're so thin and tight around her, clenching and clutching almost too tightly for her to escape…sometimes you get close to feeling like part of someone else, connected as thread to fabric, as though you'll never feel alone again. It can't last, but when it's there and when it's good, your eyes roll back and your whole body shudders through another low rolling orgasm and aftershock.

You never want it to end, don't want to go back to isolating in the confinement of your body again. You cling graphite dust deep in the crevices you create in the redhead's curves.

But when you release the woman's black hair to caress the redhead's breasts again, tighten her nipples to twitch her engorged clit against your tongue, your leaden hand leaves not gray smudges but dark charcoal prints on white skin.

You pull the redhead's thighs away from your head so that you can hear, see, think, although she continues to grind against your mouth.

The choir of pleasure around you sounds more like sobs and overstimulated screams, yet backs and buttocks continue to flex as cocks and fingers and tongues plunge deep again and again, thrusts not tireless but ceaseless. Sweat no longer smells fresh, and the other scents of sex ferment sour in the heavy air. Bruises bloom black, smudges of fingerprints, amid scratches like tears of paper over skin where blood drips like ink. Faces contort, but whether in pain or pleasure is unclear. Calves and feet cramp in harsh-relief contractions.

The woman Hoffman fucks on the couch has been knotted into more impossible angles, a twist of rubber and torn ligaments, his fingers spider legs in her mouth as he moves her over his macerated, blue-black engorged penis. In the other room, the large woman's hair plasters to her skull and shoulders with sweat. She pants with exhaustion, but cannot stop taking him into her, even as he wails at her elbow smashing into his half-crushed skull, bloody teeth on the carpet. On the stairwell, he continues to post himself, his back in shreds as he drips ink and candle wax down the spindles. Even the boys beneath you, who you can't see, sound miserable within their moans, despite their steady rhythm jostling the settee.

Graphite

Deep goes the fist, although you clench around it for new reasons. The redhead shakes her head, grinding harder and harder against the bony jut of your chin for some kind of stimulation. Hot tears carve through the soft charcoal and dot her stomach, and fall upon your cheeks. You try to get her off your face so that you can sit up, take a breath, take a minute, but she slides forward onto your tongue once more, and you're compelled to slither it back up to her full, flushed clit, even though that isn't what you meant to do, isn't what you want.

You release her thighs and instead stretch out in front of you to grab hold of the black-haired woman, push at her head, push at her shoulders, whatever you can reach, but graphite dust grits through the sweat on her body and yours. She's caught in your pussy, latched to your clit, groaning with an animal's hunger.

You throb with deadened ache but come again anyway, because you're slave to biology and compulsion, to your self-imposed isolation and dream of connection under the tip of a pencil.

The fire gutters out, replaced by beams of winter sun off snow through an attic window, but without origin, just gray light on gray skin under black shadow, black hair, smudges, and crosshatch.

The house is full yet empty, endless yet condemned, rotting beneath what survives, with an attic of quiet desperation scratched where no one is supposed to see.

Everyone sighs still, finally, frozen within the fireless, motionless winter chill. A naïf would confuse intermission with relief, but you and they are only paused, unchanging—at least until the next pilgrim draws an addendum to the long-sought legend, until all the spaces are filled, or they pull the house down and burn and bury the bones.

Whichever comes first.

where to draw the dotted lines
M. Lopes de Silva

hare bloody
strung up viands
the wind violins through meat
softly, adagio
her fingers parse the meaning
of offal like pearl onions (shining, neat)
she roasts raw muscle
puts a promise between my lips
before I know what it is
I swallow
she strings me up
pretends she knows
how to butcher me (shining, neat)
her knife tip nicking
dots she draws along the way
softly, adagio
I moan for her

Write My Eulogy on the Gloryhole Bathroom Stall
Rae Knowles

I met god in the men's room at the corner of 4th and Broadway. I don't make a habit of using the men's room, but rain was coming in sideways, landing like bee stings onto my ear and neck. Did a quick one-two look. Didn't see the ladies'. So, I ducked inside, wanting a respite long enough to phone a rideshare.

My first fear—that I'd find a line of dudes, dicks out, piss streaming—was unfounded. The bathroom sat empty. Empty except for the smell. I slapped my palm to my face but couldn't cover it, urea and shit and stagnant water so thick it turned the air viscous. I whipped out my phone, determined to get the fuck out of there, but moving too quick, I flung it. Of course I fucking flung it. And it went careening across the nicotined tile, little one inch squares framed by more filth than grout. It slid into the corner stall, and I wiggled my fingers after I caught up to it, as if I might get ahead of the germs I was about to touch, shake 'em off before they clung to me.

Overhead, the fluorescent bulb flickered: one, two, three. It was eerie, in that horror-movie-gearing-up-to-the-killing-scene sort of way. But I wrote the goosebumps off to the lasting chill of freezing rain, averted my eyes from the abomination in the toilet–mustard yellow soft serve sprinkled with ruptured hemorrhoid–and squished into that too cramped corner where my phone glowed.

Looking back, it must've been god that dropped the deuce in there. Face turned away from the thing responsible for one third of the smell, I was eye to eye with the wall. And if not for that, I wouldn't have found it.

A hole.

It was about the size of a fist. Inside was that black-black, that absence of light black, where you can't tell how far it goes. Could've been Mariana's fucking trench in there. I don't know what it was, a calling maybe, but something made me reach. While my left hand secured my phone in my jeans pocket, my right slipped into the hole, careful not to touch the sides. I felt for a stud, insulation, something, but I was halfway to my elbow and when a pinch on my hand made me yank it back. A bug, a spider, a snake, maybe? Three red divots on my knuckle and a pulsing feeling. I'd been bit, and I would've gotten the hell out of there, I would've, if not for what followed.

What began as a twinge of pain, rolling to my elbow then armpit, wrapped around my neck and spread through my core. I didn't realize I'd landed on my ass until my hands braced me from sprawling; but even as I felt mystery grime flake beneath my fingernails, I didn't care.

To call it a *high* would be to trivialize it.

There are seven wonders of the world, people say, and I became the eighth. For the first time, the creator of the universe looked right at me, looked right at me *approvingly*. The rain outside became the constant heartbeat of the world, the fear of germs faded with the recognition that no lifeform was truly apart from myself.

Time slipped; the separation between the atoms of my flesh and air around me dissipated. My body and spirit swelled with peace and warmth, enveloping and smothering every painful thing. It was a state of being so close to how I'd heard religious folk imagine heaven, and yet, the comparison falls short. And I sat alone beside the gloryhole bathroom stall, alone with god, and it was certainly good.

Write My Eulogy on the Gloryhole Bathroom Stall

My phone was dead and the rain had stopped when reality returned. If anyone came in, I didn't notice. Meeting god must've stretched me somewhere inside, because while I didn't have the dull ache in my head of a hangover, I had the prickling anxiety of a new space opened up beneath my rib cage, a birth of absence, and the vacancy there itched deeper than skin and nerve.

I didn't catch a ride share. I walked the three miles home.

Night air blew cool and crisp. The storm had dumped all the humidity from the air into the streets. My breaths flowed easy but shallow. Each step drew me further from 4th and Broadway. I stopped several times. Considered going back. But I figured Alyssa would be worried, a notion confirmed when I slipped through our apartment door to her pacing, frantic.

"Where the *fuck* have you been? I've been calling."

I held up my phone screen, rapidly pressing the buttons to no effect.

"Shit, I was worried."

"Sorry, I—"

"What happened to your hand?"

I glanced down to find the bite marks had turned from red pricks to angry, purple vines clutched around my palm. "Bug bite, or something. I think." My voice sounded distant, and Alyssa pressed.

I tried to explain god.

"You must've gotten stuck by a needle. Lucky as shit you didn't overdose. Actually, Sam, we should get you checked out, just in case." She moved to where her coat hung on the wall.

"No, no." I dropped my purse on the counter. "I'm fine, just need some sleep."

She argued for five minutes more before surrendering to the bathroom to brush her teeth. I rehearsed lines over and over in my head, but couldn't come up with a way to get her to go back with me, not tonight. The empty space beneath my ribs hummed as I settled into bed. I had to go back. To be with god. To feel unburdened and wholly seen. But I told myself it could wait until tomorrow, after Alyssa rested her curiosity might get the best of her.

Uneasily, we slept.

53

In the men's room at 4th and Broadway, Alyssa clutched her hand over her nose, just like I had.

"Christ, Sam."

"Just look."

I tugged her by her shirt sleeve, candy pink against the jittery fluorescent glow of dying bulbs and grime-yellow tile. She squinted to read the graffiti surrounding the hole.

"*Margret Ashbury is a whore. Dylan: Fridays 6-7pm, suck & fuck.* Very nice, Sam."

A flash of impatience made me bite back a retort, but my eye caught the words scribbled in red sharpie beneath the gloryhole. *The devil made me cum.*

"I see it, okay? Your hand looks…"

Purple tendrils shot from an indigo center, swelling that pulsed offbeat from my pumping blood.

"We need to get you to a doctor. What if a black widow was hiding in there? You could have sepsis or something."

"Please, just try it. I can't explain it. There's no way you can understand unless you—"

"Hep C. HIV. Sam, no fucking chance I'm putting my hand in there. I humored you, alright? I came, I smelled, I saw it. Let's fucking go."

The vacant space inside my ribs expanded like heated air, a void that screamed without sound. I wanted to reach behind the wall, to grasp for more, but I let Alyssa walk me out, even agreed to lunch and half-listened when she brought up that coworker who steals snacks from the communal fridge again. Better if she didn't realize, I figured. Would make it easier to sneak back.

The thirty-five minute lunch stretched on, an infinite purgatory of watching my lover butter bread, draw soup to her lips spoonful by too-small spoonful, sip Sprite, ice cubes clinking against her teeth.

"I'm not hungry, really," I told Alyssa, I told the waitress.

I offered my card before the waitress brought the bill, and as I

Write My Eulogy on the Gloryhole Bathroom Stall

signed the check, the lie came out like a song. "Totally forgot, promised to head into work for a few."

Suspicion crinkled her freckled nose. "Thought you were off today."

"I am." I got up. "New hire, helping to get him oriented. Rob, lives with his mom type, not gonna last."

Alyssa shrugged and her expression relaxed. I leaned across the table for a parting kiss, half wondering how I conjured Rob so quickly, half walking the route back to 4th and Broadway in my mind.

The walk was an impatient blur. When my fingers met the metal door handle, the aching void in my sternum nearly ripped my breastbone in half. I rolled my flannel sleeve to the elbow, coy flicks of my wrist, cherishing the moments before my fist disappeared into the dark. Seconds ticked by like sludge as I waited, eager for the little prick and the ecstasy that followed.

Then, the slice made me cry out. I yanked my arm back out of instinct, but bliss gobbled me up before I had time to observe the injury. And it didn't matter anymore. I floated. Everything was fine. God spoke.

Does it hurt? He asked. *You're doing so well. Does it hurt?*

"Yes," I mumbled.

A slump brought me flat down, my sandal sliding off my foot.

I want more, god said.

"Of me?" The words rolled over my lolling tongue.

Give me more of you.

I dragged myself across the tile, inch by impossible inch, eyes rolling and vision blurred. My head grew too heavy, flopped to one side. I tossed a crooked arm toward the hole, and almost thought I saw empty space where the tip of my pinky usually was.

I probably saw it.

But it didn't matter.

My aim floundered, hand missing the hole entirely, but my elbow made it into the black, and no sooner had I offered it did god accept it, hot agony racing up my nerves, fingertip to armpit.

The most delicious emptiness chased all thoughts and pain away. Only a throbbing remained. It traveled through my blood. It gathered in my center. It congealed between my thighs. God wanted me, intimately, vulnerably. And I wanted to offer myself. In the flickering fluorescent light, I removed my top, let it fall, and when the hem dipped into the toilet, my fingers raced to my pussy instead of saving it. I pressed my left breast against the hole, working myself into a frenzy. I thought of god's teeth. I thought of razored bicuspids, sharpened as only a deity's might be, piercing my areola, shredding the membranes beneath.

I moaned.

The slickness of my pussy lips let my hand slip inside, slowed only by the constraints of my jeans.

"Come on," I said, breathy, impatient, arching my back to press my breast further into the hole. The pressure built with the anticipation, wetness bleeding through my jeans as I kept the rhythm, anxiously awaiting the slice.

Is this a gift?

"Yes," came out like a plea.

I'd already started coming when god freed my nipple from the bounds of my flesh.

There was everything, then: The stinging, the soul-wracking climax, the gentle oblivion.

I collapsed onto the tile. Life-warmth poured down my stomach, my jeans stained burgundy, and I checked my hand to find my little finger missing, gore flowing from elbow to wrist.

But it didn't matter.

I took a deep breath.

I laid flat.

I studied the water stains on the ceiling.

I let my fingers trace the graffiti.

I hooked my nail into a hardened piece of gum affixed to the toilet paper dispenser.

"Can I stay like this forever?" My voice sounded dreamy, and god didn't answer. I let myself be held by something which had called to me. Maybe all my life it had called to me. And I knew that nothing had ever felt right until this.

I didn't go back to Alyssa's.

Write My Eulogy on the Gloryhole Bathroom Stall

My remaining days were hazy. Alyssa kept calling, my parents kept calling, my boss kept calling. Alyssa texted. She said lots of things. Things about losing. Losing her. She named a lot of other things, which didn't matter.

There was knocking sometimes, and I got good at being quiet. Very quiet, until it stopped.

Then nobody was calling. Or texting. Or knocking. And that was good.

The first time god fucked me, he wasn't gentle. It wasn't a romance in any way I'd seen or experienced, but the seduction burned hot and fast and desperate. I'd pulled my jeans and panties down, and pressed my pussy right up against the hole like a dog. I wanted to feel god's tongue. I wanted it to plunge inside me, to rip out my cervix with its barbed tip, to gush come and blood until the writing on the bathroom stall was washed away with my liquid, depraved pleasure.

God took my other nipple, my left thumb, my right hand to the wrist.

God had a fat cock and a warm pussy.

I fucked and I got fucked, I gave and I got and I gave pieces away. The pain was gone, even as the blood soaked through my tattered clothing, dried and crusted and flaked off every part of me. I came so hard I pissed myself. Even when hunger had me so weak I passed out, it didn't matter. God was all I needed, god's gifts were abundant and if there was still a world outside that heavy metal door, it didn't need me anymore. And I didn't need it. I'd given Alyssa a chance. I'd tried to show her. Yes, it wasn't my fault she couldn't see. And now she'd never know. She'd never know *him*. She'd never know the fullness of being empty.

Fuck Alyssa.

I squatted in front of god's hole and gave him my ass.

I knew the freedom of giving myself selflessly, of receiving gratefully, of lightening as I was unburdened of my intestines. They made the sound of slop as they coiled onto the yellow tile. God slurped them up like spaghetti. One long pull and they raced into the gloryhole like a speedy toy train, leaving a slick trail behind like smudged tracks. I'd never been so savored, my body like a sweet wine, ripe for consumption.

I dipped my fingers in dark liquid. On the bathroom door I scribbled, *Resplendent suffering.*

We had braided, god and pain and the cosmos and completion and never-having-been and my throbbing clitoris. And my flesh could not be parsed from the most intimate particles of the universe. No separation stood between me and the oldest suffering and the first pleasure. God fucked me into nothingness. I consumed carnality in its purest form as god drew my head to the glory hole and beyond it, took me into her pussy as his cock penetrated my throat. Clenching and thrusting and a kind, contented knowing.

God came.

And I blinked from being. A snap in which I relived my many years of existence and my very few days of living. I came to this one reflection:

If I'd known that first rainy day what I know now. If I'd realized what would happen, how Alyssa would spend her birthday crying, how dad would never again hear a phone ring without a stitch of anxiety, that my body would rot on the yellow tiled floor for six days before anyone found me, that the insects would've chewed through my sclera, that shit leaked from my gaping anus at the end, and the mortician felt embarrassed for me and had to tell his wife about it just to throw off some of the shame, my shame. If I'd have known on that first rainy day, I would've shoved my hand into that hole even faster. I would've never taken it out.

I WANDER THE EARTH LONGING TO TASTE YOUR BEATING HEART
Minh-Anh Vo Dinh

I wander the Earth longing to taste your beating heart. I scour every corner of this decaying planet we call home to satisfy the hunger that overtakes my senses. I breathe in the filthy air flooding my lungs hoping to smell your scent, a mixture of cheap convenience store shampoo and body wash those roadside motels stock in tiny bottles. Your breath is of minty fresh toothpaste, the cheapest dollar store variant, which does the bare minimum to hide the stench.

The average person won't be able to tell, but I'm not an average person. I'm barely a person at all. Underneath all the tacky hygienic products you slather all over yourself, I can smell the heavenly mixture of death and fresh raw meat resting on your lips, their remnants still hanging in the corners of your teeth no matter how many times you brush, stuck underneath your fingernails. They're all over you, invisible to the naked eye and nose. But I see and smell them. The scent of death engulfs you, and from across the club, you glow like an angel. In this moment, you are the most beautiful boy in the world.

I first saw you in the city. I walked through the gay village, feeling immense sorrow at the barrenness of the neighborhood, populated with roaming ghosts, a sad pitiful shell of what it once was. I doubt you can even imagine what this place used to be. But I imagine the barrenness is what attracts you. Those who remain here are a forgotten part of history desperately grasping onto a rotting piece of memorabilia that has no value anymore. Once popular bars are now a miserable reminder of the golden era of true queer joy, where we all disappeared from this godforsaken world for a night and lifted ourselves to high heavens, pumping our bodies with drugs and alcohol until our minds went numb. But you don't care about that.

You wander the Earth longing for meaning. When you're not looking for pretty boys to feast on, you get high off substances. You rarely go for older men because they remind you of mortality, of a future you won't have. My heart aches, knowing that someone like you has already accepted the bleakness of his destiny. You are still a boy, so lost and desperate for normality.

You have always known you were meant to be an outcast, at the age of fifteen when you first kissed your classmate Riley. His mouth tasted of boxed dinner and hot dogs. And seconds after, it tasted like fresh blood. When your lips parted from Riley's face, so did his. You knew when you ate him down to the bones. It was your first time eating anyone, but not your first time sampling human flesh. Lonely young men sought a warm body to touch, and you sought warm flesh to feed. They're new, strangers to the city and to this queer wide world. Like stupid little children at the carnival, everything tempted them and they couldn't stop themselves.

Did you feel sorry for them when you took their lives? I want to ask you that, so bad. I hope to have the chance to find out.

It's been on my mind ever since I first saw you leave the derelict building on the verge of collapsing. I remember the stench so well. In the dead of night, it filled the air like fresh grass on a cool summer day. Most people wouldn't describe it that way. Most people would describe it as earth-shatteringly vile. Funny enough, that's what I heard from a passerby.

"What is that earth-shatteringly vile smell?" she cried.

What a melodramatic way to describe something so beautiful. Not vile, heavenly. Not vile, gorgeous. Not vile, exquisite. But I'm not most people and neither are you. You were coated in flesh and blood, drenched in sweat that glistened against your brown skin and

I WANDER THE EARTH LONGING TO TASTE YOUR BEATING HEART

accentuated your exposed chest. Your polo ripped open, presumably from a struggle. It was too loose for your thin frame, the front lazily tucked into your jeans and the rest dangling in the wind. You were a walking piece of art that I must have. A hunger burst inside me, so violent that I thought it would turn me inside out.

I wander the Earth longing to feel your warmth against my cold, dead skin. Would you take me for who I am? There could only be one answer.

If you were to reject me, I'd fling myself toward the sun and burn for eternity, my ashes scattered across the atmosphere, pieces of me raining over you so I could be with you forever. I've been alive for generations, long before your grandparents immigrated to this country, long before the concept of someone like you entered this world.

Have you figured out what I am yet?

You must by now. You must have read stories about my kind growing up, creatures of the night that stalked unsuspecting innocents to quench their thirst for blood. Like you, I'm a predator. We want the same thing: to survive. Beings like us are born in the dark, bound to a life outside perceived normality, our existence extraordinary and inconceivable to the dull folks confined to the prison they've created for themselves.

And yet, they have someone to share that prison with. What is liberation if you haven't a companion to share it with?

You're too young to understand eternal loneliness. I see you enter the club with the confidence of someone who is still ignorant of how big the world is, to how much it has to offer. You feel invincible, but arrogance will corrode you. I can steer you away from that. I can be your mentor, your maker, your eternal. It does not matter what you wish, I will devote myself to you all the same.

You will never know that I went inside the apartment after you'd taken off. I know it's not right, what a person consumes is a matter of privacy, I imagine. But I want to see what you left behind. The smell of blood filled my nostrils the closer I got. You left the door ajar. How careless, I thought.

I remember being careless when I first turned. I would leave trails everywhere, causing mass panic among the village folks. Dried up corpses in bed, behind an old tavern, resting against a tree at the edge of the forest. Did I want them to be found? In a way, yes. I wanted humans to marvel at my works.

Perhaps you are the same as I.

These thoughts continued to swirl in my mind until I pushed the door open and beheld the sight in front of me. You were messy, incredibly so. There was blood smeared all over the walls, on the floor, under every slit of the tiles. The smell sent a tremor through my body. I told myself I must not disrupt the scene, you'd created it like this for a reason. I wouldn't dare disrespect you. But I so badly wanted a taste, knowing the drops of blood there have been touched by you. I wanted to know what it was like to be the speck of flesh that was on your tongue.

What was once a young man was now barely a man. Half of his face was gone, his lower jaws exposed with flesh dangling from the corner. I leaned closer and stared into the empty blue eyes looking back at me. What were his thoughts in his final moments? His parents? A cherished memory? I barely remembered what flashed into my head as I died.

When I drink, I get glimpses of the person's life, random flashes, insignificant and significant simultaneously. Only when I drain completely do I get to see it all. The memories stay with me, practically mine. Centuries and thousands of souls live within me, bad people, good people. I've learned not to discriminate. You'll only drive yourself insane if you let your conscience eat you up.

For a brief second, I contemplated burying my fangs into the young man's neck just for a chance to see you through his eyes. I still see the marks all over his body. You were violent, so fucking violent. You ripped his throat open. Chunks of his shoulder, chest, and arms are missing. This was a spur of the moment. You needed a quick fix. The dark messy gash on his throat was like an inviting abyss calling my name, painted by blood like an abstract painting.

I realized I was trembling. Why, I did not know. I've encountered many horrors throughout my lifetime, and committed acts so grotesque that your nightmare's nightmare would have to look away.

I WANDER THE EARTH LONGING TO TASTE YOUR BEATING HEART

Nothing could faze me, not even what I'm looking at right now. And yet, I'm shaking with fear.

I wander the Earth…

There was a softness as I sank my fingers into the gash. I swirled inside the throat to get as much on my fingers as possible. Like digging for the last of the ketchup with a fry. The random image got a laugh out of me. What a fucked up comparison to make.

As I pulled my fingers out, the wetness sent a vibration through my body. My fingers looked like tiny crimson snakes dancing in the air, hypnotizing me. Then I swallowed the snakes, savoring the mouth-watering combination of blood, flesh, and remnants of your saliva. I tasted you.

I wanted more, and I allowed myself to have more. Peeling the dangling flesh of the dead boy's exposed jaws, I realized I have never enjoyed human meat before. Everything other than blood did not quench my thirst, they were like empty calories. I looked at the flesh in my hands, so thin and moist. Without wasting another second, I chewed.

The flesh was delicate and went down easily. And once again, remnants of you were present. That was the first time I tasted you, and I have been following you ever since. I have tasted you through every boy you've eaten. I have come to know you.

You wander the Earth longing for acceptance. There are no sanctuaries for boys with a craving for human flesh. Your first experience was biting a neighborhood kid on your sixth birthday. You sucked the flesh off his finger bone like the skin off a drumstick. Your father was repulsed by your actions, and your mother slipped into denial because she always loved you. But eventually, she pushed you away as well.

How that infuriates me. I'd welcome you into my arms, and apologize for how cruel this world treated you.

You live the life of a drifter, moving from motel to motel, never staying in the same town for more than a week, sometimes even less. There were times you slept on benches, on the side of the road. I would give up immortality if it meant providing you warmth for the remainder of our days. I can be your sanctuary. Let my frozen corpse be your home. Let me…

A slim boy with thick wavy hair approaches you. He reeks of shitty tequila. I can see the immediate interest in your eyes. The two of you strike a conversation. Tired of having to shout into each other's ears, you suggest going somewhere quiet. The slim boy suggests the beach, which is a ten minute walk from here. And just like that, you vanish into the crowd and out of my sight.

It's not my first time watching you walk away. You rarely make the first move, it's always boys who come to you. There's an air of mystique to you, partly because you're an out-of-towner. The locals like fresh meat. Oh, the irony of it all.

You're straight to the point, never giving more information than you need to. You don't care for connections beyond the collision of flesh against each other, whether it be a feeding or fucking. You deem it pointless to know a stranger that you'll never see again. Queer men will always worship the flesh but never the soul. What's the difference between feasting on a man and feeling a man inside you?

They both end in catharsis, a release that floods the void within both of you. Queer desire will always override common sense. Does the risk of death matter if it means they get to hold another man against them, to feel the semen seeping out of his cock as it traverses into their open hungry mouth? The answer will be a shrug. Numbness, apathy, indifference. Silly little queer boys. Silly little lambs willingly parade into the slaughterhouse.

Something's wrong. I can feel the franticness in your aura as I near the beach. You have never gotten scared before, but you are afraid. The saltiness of the ocean masks the stench of death in the air. The presence of blood is overwhelming. It wasn't just the boy. There were more. Did it get out of control? You might be careless, but never greedy.

At the top of the sandhill, I peer down at the dying corpse of the slim boy. You have slit his throat with something sharp, probably the pocket knife you always carry, and you have taken a big bite out of his neck. He twitches and wheezes as waves climb over him and retreat into the dark, his blood swimming with the current.

You didn't finish him. Something interrupted you. There is a trail

I WANDER THE EARTH LONGING TO TASTE YOUR BEATING HEART

of footsteps, not just yours. Someone saw you. I follow the trail as it leads to a beach house. The overwhelming blood I smelled comes from inside the house.

A tremendous struggle occurred. A woman in her forties lays in between the side porch and the living room. The glass door exploded when you slammed her through it. Shards everywhere, mixed with her blood and yours. The smell of roasting human meat waffs from the kitchen.

Seeing no apparent missing bits from her, I continue into the kitchen. A giant man rests against a flaming stove. This must be her husband. A few steps in and I almost slip on the blood. It's your blood and his. You've stabbed him with kitchen cutlery, torn at him with your teeth. Blood and bits splatter across the room.

What did he do to you?

He's twice your size, it's a miracle that it isn't your face pressed against the burner. And yet you managed to triumph. You are a survivor, after all. Ribbons of stringy flesh stretch as I pull the man's face off the stove. His eye melted into its socket.

You're tired and wounded now. And nearby.

The front door is open, so I head there. As I pass the staircase, a little boy stands at the top. Poor little newly orphaned boy.

"Is that the smell of bacon?" he asks.

I glance at the kitchen. Do I protect his innocence? The little one skips down the staircase, unfazed by my presence, and straight to the kitchen. I expect a scream, but there's just silence. He's not shocked, I can feel it. He's assessing and wondering.

There's a flashing of red and blue along with a siren's wail. The husband must have called the police before you got to him. I saunter out the front door and there you are.

"You don't look so good," is the first thing that exits my lips as our eyes meet.

I will confess to you that I wish I had said something more profound for our first encounter, and you will laugh at me for even thinking of something so hackneyed. Your gorgeous brown eyes stare at me. There's confusion, but I read something else. Astonishment. You sense what I am, a predator like you. I know that you know.

Minh-Anh Vo Dinh

Tiny glass shards pierce your beautiful skin. Your breathing is haggard, the smell of iron surrounds you. You have never looked so helpless. There's panic in your eyes, the same kind of panic that renders a deer immobile as it waits for the wolves to devour it. You are prey, about to face a beast in blue with a hideous mark embedded against its chest, one that it flashes with pride to display its pure unadulterated cruelty.

The cop draws his gun and barks threats at you. He looks about your age. He's inexperienced and full of rage, fiercely determined to kill without question. As his finger slowly squeezes against the trigger, I saunter toward him and stretch his jaws with both my hands. He never saw it coming. I hear you gasp as I drop him to the ground.

For the first time in your life, you're shocked beyond words. I turn to you and kneel so we're on eye level. There's a slight fear on your face. I understand your reaction, but in that brief moment, it hurts me. I would never think to harm you. My darling boy, I will devour the world to keep you safe.

Silence fills the air. Your breathing calms, but your eyes remain on me. I look down as the cop's blood slithers past my fingers. I stretch out my hand and press it against the red pool, then I offer it to you. Hesitation lingers, but intrigue slowly overrides you. Shivering against the night chills and exhaustion, you reach out and take my hand, the blood smearing against your skin. If I could breathe, I'd hold my breath. You flinch at the iciness of my touch, and I melt at the warmness of yours.

You don't let go, so I entangle my fingers into yours. I hear your heart thump in your chest, I feel the blood course through your veins as you return my grasp with your delicate fingers. Slowly, I bring them toward my mouth and graze them against my fangs. Once again, your eyes widen. I let go of your hand and you continue my fangs with child-like wonderment.

Now you unquestionably know what I am. And you are not afraid. You are fearless.

I remove your hands, walk over to the corpse and drink from it. I want you to see me. After a few sips, I take a bite of his tangly meat as you watch. Your body shudders at my hand running up your back and

I WANDER THE EARTH LONGING TO TASTE YOUR BEATING HEART

behind your neck. I pull you closer and your lips finally touch mine. My tongue slips into your mouth along with the meat and you take it with vigorous hunger. Your breath is warm and your lips soft. As you pull away with the string of flesh leaving my mouth, I tell you my name.

"Call me Anton," I tell you. I feel the tension deflate across your body. I wish all those made-up lore about my kind being able to read minds were true, I so desperately want to get inside your heart right now. What are you thinking? What are you feeling? I feel your eyes study my body, hungering to explore it the only way you know how.

In the history of vampkind, there has never been a documented account of our kind being consumed like food. We're dead meat, already rotted for centuries. I can't imagine the foulness that would assault the tongue.

But you are not afraid. It excites you. I take your hands again and place them against my shirt, guiding you to remove the buttons and peel off the fabric. Unlike you, any complexion has been washed away. My once tanned Asian skin tone is now as pale as a phantom, exposed for you to see.

"Taste me."

So you do. I wince as your teeth penetrate my skin and extract a piece of my chest. So this is what it feels like to be consumed. I study your eyes. There's amusement on your face as you savor me. Then you chew, hard and fast. As you wash me down, I know you want more.

I want to surrender my flesh and soul to you completely. I want to hold you tight in my arms as we consume each other until we cease to exist. If this is my last time with you, as brief as it may be, I'll be satisfied nonetheless. Whether it be seconds or millennia, eternal is this moment.

My existence has built up to this. Take me as much as you'd like. Let me fill you up with my broken parts and bring you life, let me bring you into the darkness and away from the light corroding your soul. Devour me, make love to me, be with me. We can keep on until time ceases to exist, until we're the last remaining souls in this world, until time washes you away and the sun turns me to ashes.

Whatever we change into in our next life, I will never lose you. If

Minh-Anh Vo Dinh

you're reborn in another realm, I will tear through every dimension until the universe collapses. If you're reborn as a rock on the ground, I will scan every single inch of this world until I can keep you safe in my pocket. If we're reduced to molecules, we will wander the galaxies until we find each other again.

You catch your breath, and finally, you speak.

You are an angel sent from the depths of my depravity, a drifter yearning for a home, and the most beautiful boy in the world.

"Leon."

Your name is Leon.

My Leon.

My eternal.

This Living Hand
Aleksandra Ugelstad Elnæs

It was offered to me at a price significantly lower than its value, due to a small fracture in the glass. It is not a remarkable object, in fact it is quite typical of its kind, the gold band evokes the perpetuity of memory, of a love everlasting, and a small compartment carries the pleated lock of someone's beloved, long since laid to rest. The setting is finished with a circle of pearls, and although these are still bright, the accumulated dust of centuries obscures the glass itself and the hair below, giving it the appearance of something long submerged and only recently salvaged.

A set of initials were once engraved on the band in an extravagant cursive, but these are now tarnished and indecipherable, suggesting that it must often have been worn, removed and redonned, perhaps even passed down through the generations, since its creation sometime in the latter part of the eighteenth century. Whether it is a treasure adrift, as suggested by its shipwrecked appearance, or a failed relic purposefully discarded when the wearer ceased to believe in its virtue, I knew at first glance that I could not afford to refuse such a token of loving commemoration, even obtained second hand.

I like to think that it once belonged to a clever and industrious hand, busy with letter-writing and botanical watercolors, with the mounting of shell-work onto picture frames and the stitching of black-work onto samplers; a neat little hand resting upon gathered skirts, remembering a time when the now matted lock was still accessible to touch and might be smoothed or tousled according to mood and opportunity, rather than gazed at through that little convex glass, that distorts the thing it preserves.

It is the only piece of jewelry I wear, for it has a talent for spoiling its companions; portrait cameos appear sullen and sallow faced, and it reduces the most precious collier to a mere junk shop trinket. It is my constant companion, though this has less to do with preference than with the arthritis running in my family, which causes pain if I try to ease it from my finger.

It likes to reside close at hand and at night it sleeps upon my skin, beneath the covers, where it grows warm and lovely, the hair slick and taut, the pearls a luminous grin in the darkness. I have discarded the leather box it came in, despite it being gold-embossed and antique, for it seemed to me so much like a small coffin that I did not like to look at it; in the faltering light the lining appeared threadbare and discolored, like the pillowcase of someone sick and long bedridden.

I presently have reason to believe that the ring belongs to a hand less diligent and more distrustful than I initially gave it credit for, a hand liable to dole out a prescription of nocturnal kisses, each one precisely indented as if made by a mouth of small, even teeth. It is a cruel hand, but it seems to love me too, for when the door is locked and the lamp has grown cold, I can feel it traveling across my body, beneath the bedclothes, increasing its pressure until I gasp for breath, two fingers on the nape of my neck, thumb against my throat.

Mantis
Dori Lumpkin

The rule was that we could never kiss, and you were fine with that. Skin across skin, fingers and teeth and tongues with legs entwined, but never your mouth against mine. I wanted to keep you as long as I possibly could like this; legs open, mouth wide. You were beautiful. And you let me do whatever I wanted.

Collecting you was simple. Almost easier than any of the others had been.

The bar was sticky, a mess of spilled drinks and ruined intentions, and before I had even fully introduced myself, the words came tumbling out of your mouth.

Do you want to go home with me?

A bit forward, and quite brave of you, I have to admit.

I liked it though. And I agreed, with the caveat that we go back to my place, not yours. You were eager enough, giving absolutely no consideration that you were going home with a stranger. Not even trying to get to know me, though you probably should have.

Your fingers twisted between mine on the way home, and I explained to you my proposition.

Again, you agreed. So, so quickly. As if you had nothing to lose, and your entire existence was tied to forgetting yourself against my body.

Dori Lumpkin

I watched you pick at your nails as we approached my front door.

I asked you to keep an open mind, to maybe consider doing some things you never would have thought of before.

You couldn't have predicted what that meant.

You liked it either way.

The door swung open, and I pulled you inside.

Ever since I was young, I liked to destroy things. I never thought about it as destruction, really, but I suppose that's what it was. And what it always had been. I thought it was beautiful, right? To know that I had the power to entirely consume and corrupt another person, with little more than my hands. Even before my mother told me about our family curse, I was the sort of kid who enjoyed watching people squirm. I liked the idea that someone could be uncomfortable for my benefit. It was a simple thing, to take pleasure in someone else's pain. To enjoy the beauty that came from a smear of blood across the floor, and the simple perfection of a scream.

It began when I was about eight. Again, before the curse, before I knew anything. I used to sit by the side of the road and count the passing cars. I wasn't a particularly interesting child, but I was a patient one.

Red car. Green car. Second red car. Black car.

And so on, until I got bored. We lived by a busier street, so it took me a while to get bored, but it was inevitable. Most things are.

The day that it happened, though, I had gotten bored early. There weren't a lot of cars. My attention had shifted to a small pair of squirrels across the street, squabbling over what I assumed to be acorns. Oak trees populated most of the area, so it was relatively common. No matter. The point was that I couldn't pull my eyes away from them.

I couldn't put my finger on exactly why, but the squirrels disgusted me. They reminded me of people. Of the woman my mother had argued with at the grocery store, of the man at the bank who yelled into his phone.

Mantis

Looking back on it now, the joke is obvious. I'm tired of this place, these people. You get it, I'm sure.

Anyway, it got to the point where the squirrels were chasing each other, right? They were running around, yelling that stupid squirrel yell that made eight-year-old me want to clap my hands right over my ears.

It lasted until one of them ran out into the street, heading my direction. It had almost made it all the way across the road until—

Black car number two. A perfect collision. The squirrel wasn't plastered to the front of the car, but nicked by one of the wheels, enough to maim, but not instantly kill. Black car number two drove off without noticing the squirrel. But I did.

I walked to the edge of the road and examined the dark red blood stain on the asphalt. It was beautiful. The way the squirrel's body twisted—so small. So helpless. Parts of it still wiggled. Struggled to die.

I wanted to step on it. Not to put it out of its misery—I wouldn't dream of being so empathetic. I wanted to know what it would feel like to crush the skull underneath my foot. I wanted to know that I held the power to ruin something; to make it even more beautiful than it had been when it was alive.

I kept that secret inside of me. But it had to go somewhere, of course. I was twelve when my mother sat me down and explained the family's curse.

"Mantis," she said when the talk began. That wasn't my name at the time, but for the purposes of this, that's what I'll call myself. "You're old enough now to begin an interest in boys, so we need to have an important talk."

She was wrong about a few things, back then. My name, as I've already mentioned. Also, the idea of being interested in boys at all; it absolutely disgusted me. I was more fascinated with my female classmates; from their strawberry scented shampoo to the urge to cut their eyes out and hang them on a necklace. Beauty was a thing worth collecting.

I assumed she wanted to have some sort of convoluted sex talk with me. I assumed she would teach me about my body, and the wonders of the menstruation cycle.

She didn't. Instead, she sat me down and told me that no matter how much I tried, our family—me included—was cursed forever. Every single person I kissed was doomed to die within a matter of minutes. Regardless of gender, regardless of relationship or age, anyone whose lips met mine would turn into a sizzling, acidic pile of body mush.

I thought of the way the squirrel looked on the side of the road, head half-smashed and struggling final breaths. I wondered if the people I kissed would end up like that—the epitome of pure beauty.

It couldn't have been more perfect. I wasn't cursed. I was *blessed*.

My first kiss was in the catacombs outside the city, where the open-eyed sockets of the dead watched my every move. I had lured the girl there under the guise of exploration. We were sixteen. I had saved it—the kiss, I mean—for the perfect person. I wanted it to be exactly right. Wanted *her* to be exactly beautiful.

And it was. Shame I can't remember her name. What I do remember, though, was the sound of her screams as the bones dissolved inside of her, as blood became acidic and the very thing that brought her so much life betrayed her. I wanted to bottle that scream and keep it forever, to open whenever I got sad, like it would bring me some form of cheer.

Afterwards, I cried to my mother and told her what happened. It wasn't real, of course, but I had to tell her what I had done so that someone knew.

She assumed I had rebelled—that I didn't believe her, and had acted out on my own. Still, she forgave me. She held me as I cried my false-tears, and warned me never to do it again. To be wary.

But she did not know what had been created that day. I died alongside the girl in the catacombs, and I emerged as my true self. As Mantis.

I never listened to my mother. If I had been someone else, maybe I would have gotten scared. Ran away, perhaps. Locked myself in a tower and existed without that transcendental beauty I came so close to. I didn't. I kept on kissing people and watching them die. Sue me for liking the thrill, I guess.

I liked you best on your knees. Sometimes, if you were desperate enough, you could convince me to put my fingers in your mouth and entertain you for just a moment. You'd close your eyes and run your tongue across the length of them. I didn't know what you were imagining, and I didn't ask. It was perfect silence. And then after, a lot of begging; from you, to me. Desperate and empty. Lips parted and glossy with your own saliva.

When you were especially lucky, I would pull your head between my thighs and let you do whatever you wanted there, sometimes for hours at a time. It was your favorite sort of worship. You looked pathetic like that; like you needed nothing more than to please me whenever I wanted, and that your brain couldn't come up with anything beyond that.

There aren't words to describe how perfect you looked in those moments. Every so often, your hands would wander between your own thighs. It was innocent. Exploratory. You didn't mean anything by it.

But still, it was never something you were supposed to do.

It was an act that demanded punishment, and you knew that.

I wasn't the one to decide whether or not you did it on purpose, but perhaps you did. Perhaps you wanted to feel the harsh smack of my hand across your cheek, a reminder that you had not asked for permission. Perhaps you craved the punishment, willing me silently to go farther, push more, hurt you again and again and again.

Were you begging for death?

You couldn't have known.

But it wasn't time yet.

Of course, I have my low moments. It couldn't all be wild thrill and killing people, that wouldn't be realistic. So let me get vulnerable for just a moment, okay? And then we'll get back to the good stuff.

Dori Lumpkin

I was seventeen when it happened. I feel like it's pretty obvious to say that when you're a teenager you have a metric fuck-ton of feelings you never expected, right? And then add on the fact that technically speaking, you'll never find anyone you can have a genuine romantic attraction with because you can't actually kiss them. I'm not a monster, you know. I do feel romantic attraction. It would be a lie if I told you I didn't want to kiss anyone for non-murder-related reasons. But I couldn't. I never would.

It's a difficult thing to be asked to deal with, especially at such a young age. I guess I can say that seventeen was a young age. It wasn't that long ago, really, but it feels like forever. I don't really want to linger on this part, so I'll get to the point.

I wanted to kill myself.

Something about the impossible weight of not knowing how to proceed, the crushing feeling of knowing that I could never kiss anyone. It's a little bit embarrassing to talk about now, but it felt like the world would end back then.

I remember the day I decided to do it. I spent a long time staring at myself in the mirror, analyzing myself. The way my jaw curved and how my eyes seemed dull. Lifeless. It was prom season. Isn't that so stupid? That *prom* was the thing that did me in? Anyway, I figured if I had to kill myself, it couldn't be any normal sort of way. I would never be caught dead with my wrists slit or with vomit all over my face. I wanted to still be pretty. I wanted for whoever found my body to be so stricken by my beauty that they wouldn't know how to react. So, the first thing I tried was to kiss my own reflection.

I know. I know. I'll hold for laughter, just for a second.

Are you over it yet?

Good.

Obviously it didn't work. It was my fucking reflection. All that happened was I got lipstick on the mirror and it made me feel cold and gross inside. But not in an imminent death way, more in like an *I can't believe I fucking did that* way. Honestly, I can't believe I'm telling you this right now at all. It was just… a lot.

I couldn't tell you how I got to my next idea, it just seemed like the next natural move after kissing my reflection didn't work. I assumed that it had to do with sex, right? Like maybe it wasn't just the kiss, but it was the idea of sex as a whole. (I knew that it wasn't. I was being an idiot. No more questions, please.) Or maybe I decided it was related to my spit. It's a little bit blurry at this point, but I guess sex and spit are inherently related, so it could go either way (I have since learned that it isn't a spit thing either, as if this wasn't enough. Only so many times could I spit in someone's mouth without them dying before I finally understood.)

The point of the matter was, if I took the saliva from my own lips and used it to get myself off, then theoretically, whatever poison existed in my kiss could be used to commit suicide. Call it autoerotic poisoning, I guess.

I took it all the way to the end, too. Just me, my hand, and whatever was between my lips.

Only, it didn't work. And I sat there, naked on the floor of my own bathroom, embarrassed as all fuck that I could kill whoever I wanted as long as it wasn't myself (in the way that I wanted to die, at least.)

After that failure, I couldn't take it anymore. I threw a little bit of a tantrum in the bathroom, and then I waltzed downstairs and kissed my mother square on the lips.

Watching her die was enough to bring me back to reality. It reminded me that there are more important things in life than silly high school crushes and kisses under the moonlight. I never regretted killing her, even when the dirt from her grave caked under my nails.

You looked up at me, eyes wide and wondering, and asked if I planned on setting you free anytime soon. It took a lot of my energy not to laugh. Instead, I brushed my hand over your cheek, shoving two fingers in your mouth. That was enough of a distraction, I thought.

Why would you ever want to leave? I asked, pushing your mouth open wider, feeling lips and tongue and teeth.

I didn't try to imagine how your lips would feel against mine. It wasn't worth the trouble. You sighed around my hand, eyes fluttering closed.

Once, you asked me if I did this with all the girls I brought home.

Dori Lumpkin

I did laugh that time, as I tied your wrists to the bed frame and placed a blindfold over your eyes. You looked so beautiful, so helpless. Happy to serve and excited for whatever new surprise I presented you with.

Wouldn't you have liked to know.

Most girls, *I responded,* don't make it as long as you have.

You took pride in that. I could see your cheeks flush; a beautiful scarlet. I wondered how easy it would be to make them stay that color forever. You didn't need to know that the girls didn't make it because I ensured they wouldn't. That it wasn't their lack of commitment, but my constant search for true beauty.

You're beautiful, *I told you, and you spread your legs beneath me.*

I know, *you responded, and the moment felt suspended forever.*

A few years after my mother's death, after the much more important upset of briefly disappointing myself, I decided it was time for therapy. It wasn't something I thought I needed at that point, but it seemed like a reasonable next step. So I did the thing. I made the appointments, I sat in the chairs, I cried the fake tears, and then I made an important decision. I decided I wasn't really getting anything out of the whole therapy situation, but everyone I talked to would make excellent victims.

And really, you'd be surprised how easy it is to seduce your therapist.

The chairs never were that comfortable anyway. And the routine stayed the same pretty much every time. Tell the poor soul sitting with the notebook how my mother tragically murdered my father, and how I am terrified of being doomed to the same fate.

And then compliment their shirt.

And then their shoes.

And then show up after hours, where I know they'll be because I've watched them for a decent amount of time before actually starting sessions with them.

Honestly, the kiss was the easiest part, after all of that work. They were usually surprised enough that they just took it, at first. And by then, it was too late.

By the time we'd swapped spit, my mouth lingering against their lips, them thinking *it's fine, I'm fine, just a crazy client*, they might as well have already been dead. Their bones were already dissolving inside of their bodies, and all they could do was froth and moan and twist and ask me so, so many questions. Usually a lot of *what's happening*, with some *why would you do this* thrown in. The funnest ones screamed. I liked to watch the screams, because, most of the time, they would screech their fucking throats raw until they choked on their own blood, which was just as fun.

I saw a priest, once. I thought that maybe it would be different from the therapy.

It wasn't.

I repented for my sins, sure, whatever, that was pretty okay. But it all went downhill when they asked me to try to imagine the face of God. I'm pretty sure they aren't supposed to do that, but whatever. He looked so earnest, like he actually wanted to help. So I tried.

At first, God was the face of an old white man. Pretty basic, I know. He didn't exactly… inspire anything deep within my soul, you know? It was all sort of…meh. I think that if God were sexier, there would be a lot more Christians.

I killed him, and then took that with me. *Imagine the face of God. Let him power your decision-making, and trust him with your life and soul.*

Bullshit.

But I did like to imagine I worked towards something, even if the Lord Above wasn't exactly what got me off.

So I let my perception of God change—just the slightest. I need to be clear, I still didn't believe in God. I thought the whole act of it was a waste of time.

But it was really, *really* easy to imagine myself in His shoes. With His power. Making my own rules and living my own life, disappointing absolutely no one and knowing that I was the one it all came back to.

After that, it became so much easier to pray, to exist—to *kill*—

when I was the one on the other end of the line. When it was Mantis who got the majority of my attention—no, my faith. Mantis was someone I could believe in, more than I could believe in my mother or any sort of god presented before me.

And now that I killed in the name of something, it felt free. I didn't really need to justify it before, but I especially didn't need to now. I think that what I do is a sort of a gift, you know? Not the kissing, exactly—that is a gift in its own right, but I mean the killing. It is beautiful. I am blessed with the ability to ruin things from the inside out.

I would step on the head of the squirrel, and the blood would stain the street beneath my feet.

It didn't take me long to consider you nearly perfect. Longer than the rest, though they never made it as far as you. They never got quite there before I gave up. You, though. You were a work of art; and I the artist who molded you. You took everything so perfectly, without consideration of your own safety. It was never about you. It was always about exactly what I wanted from you. That was always enough.

You asked more questions the longer you stayed. You became braver, more curious. It made me hesitate, on occasion, as I tied you in place, forcing your legs open, and twisting my fingers through your tangled hair.

I considered what it would mean to actually keep you.

Forever.

What would that look like?

To suspend you within your current state of beauty; almost at perfection, but not quite making it. To let you ask your questions, to listen to you scream whenever I wanted, in whatever way I wanted.

You trusted me, and that contained more power than I had ever felt.

I wondered this often—mostly as I touched you, hands exploring skin, pulling new sounds from your throat as you begged for more and more and more.

In another life, I might've loved you. That was more dangerous than

anything else. To know that there might've been some comfort, some form of domesticity between us, twisted as it would have to have been.
Moments like that made me realize that you terrified me.
Moments like that made me realize I enjoyed it.

You thought I changed with that last little bit, didn't you? That's cute, that you'd have hope like that. Despite all of the god talk earlier, I don't think I'm really someone that you should have faith in, you know?

I've never not wanted to kill someone, is the thing. It grounds me. It's a peaceful feeling. The destruction. The ruination. Absolution, in a way. It's what brings me back to reality every single time. My freakout in the catacombs. My attempted suicide. Each time, the image of a body on the ground, blood leaking from every orifice, light long since left the eyes, comforted me. I tend to forget who I am a lot, you know? When I find someone who piques my interest in such a way, who makes me want to consider that my future could be something other than watching people die. It's easy to lose focus.

I almost lost focus. But I couldn't let myself.

When times like this occur, I like to bring myself back to the squirrel in the street. Instead of stepping on it though, as I often wished, I imagine myself picking it up. Feeling its tiny body in my grasp. Watching the blood drip between my fingers.

In these moments, the squirrel still has a heartbeat. A soft one, but present. Fluttering, like any small animal. Instead of stepping on it, I close my fist. The squirrel becomes nothing but pulp in my hand; a mound of muscle and blood and skin and fur. It reminds me who I am, the power I have to allow others to become.

They should thank me, really. No matter how many times I slip, how many times I almost forget myself and descend into tragedy, I always circle back to what exists at my core, and there's something important about that.

I don't try to make sense of it anymore. Any of it, really. I did that a lot when I was younger, trying to understand exactly why I have a

Dori Lumpkin

gift like this, or why my family was allowed to be this way. For that brief period of time, it was why I was cursed, why I would never be able to properly love.

But maybe *love* looks different for me. Maybe I don't need to worry about letting people stay, or finding the perfect one. Maybe everything is exactly how it was always supposed to be, and I was never meant to wonder. I can love whoever I please, in my own personal way, and whether or not others learn to accept that as love isn't up to me. It never was. All I can do is give. To destroy, and stand, admiring the wreckage I leave behind. That's what I'm meant to provide.

It's on you to accept it. To embrace it.

Do you think you can do that?

Your lips were softer than I expected. Like cracked velvet; chapped, but pursed and waiting. You wanted me to kiss you so badly; what could I do but give in? Your hands on my body, your mouth on my throat. You were everything.

And so was watching you die.

It was like my first time, the very first time, back in the catacombs. Like being a nervous teenager, unsure of what to do with my teeth and my fingers. I thought my hands would go numb, I was so excited.

You fell back on the bed, eyes wide like they were just hours earlier. It was pain this time that led you to such a pristine expression. Not wonder. You wanted to hate me, I could tell. You wanted to reach up and rip me apart for doing this to you. But also, you were at peace. You achieved perfection. You knew it, and so did I.

I chose not to ask how you felt, at that moment. It was best, I assumed, to let you keep some things secret in your final moments.

I traced your body with my eyes, as I had so many times before; the gentle curve of your thigh to hip, your sloped nose just above the lips that ruined everything for you. You struggled. Tried to say something. Quantify your pain, maybe? I didn't assume, nor did I ask. The blood had already pooled underneath your skin, causing deep red blooms to press across your arms and legs, flowering up your neck in some sort of dreadful bouquet.

Mantis

You died brutally, and beautifully. I think you were my favorite of any death so far, and I doubted anyone would surpass you anytime soon.

I pressed a kiss to your cheek once you were finally gone. I don't know why; maybe I thought it would complete the image. Your body was a vision in red, so the kiss was mostly for me.

I left your body for someone else to find. A surreal painting—a woman made more beautiful than humanity could ever comprehend.

You were finally complete.

Time for the next.

Bite
Arthur DeHart

The festival neon was high, and so was Devin Miller. The EDM raged on, and he couldn't help how many glances he stole from the man to his far right. He was scantily clad since it was a rave; tight fishnets and a tank top exposing his entire chest. He was cool with his tits being out since the rave was in the middle of nowhere and more accepting than not. It was a cool night and his pierced nipples were rock hard. The man danced in the tightest and shortest shorts Devin had ever seen.

Both men alone, they cast glances at each other.

Devin watched as the man ran his hands through his own hair then looked his body up and down. It was the first time he didn't feel dysphoric because the man Devin had been watching had light top surgery scars still healing on his chest.

Devin felt his clit throb and he wanted to get laid. The weed, molly and, acid combination started to hit and the sweat in Devin's boxers consisted of more cum than anything else.

He slyly danced near the other man. Slowly he spun like he was in a movie. The acid made the world sharper and his skin tingled. The dancing turned from a silent invitation to arms around a thick, sweaty neck and rhythmic ass grabbing. Devin ground against the stranger's leg, rubbing his throbbing clit while the stranger nipped at his ear.

Devin leaned in and moaned softly in the man's ear making the stranger take Devin by the hips and move him.

"Follow me," the stranger whispered.

Devin followed with a simple nod. He grabbed the stranger's hand and was led into the woods behind the rave. It was dark without too many stars in the sky. The acid kicked in and Devin only thought about how the trees breathed. Everything felt just a little too sharp.

The stranger led him into the dark woods that were glowing with star light. It was a contradiction, but Devin didn't care. Once the two arrived at a clearing, the stranger's lips crashed onto Devin. The man held Devin tightly in his arms and not sure if it was the acid or not, but he felt stronger than Devin expected. Sure, his arms were bigger but, Devin felt that he was much stronger than he seemed. The moon shone down on him and he moaned into the stranger's mouth. He really didn't care if he was going to be murdered at this point. He needed him inside of him, now.

The stranger ran his hands up and down Devin's body sending tiny waves of lightning. Devin's skin prickled under the man's touch. The stranger pushed Devin to the ground, hard. It didn't even hurt as Devin spread his legs open and started touching himself. He rubbed his clit through his shorts in small circles and looked into the man's dark eyes. He was ready to be destroyed, and he didn't care how.

"Take me," Devin whispered.

"I want to taste you first," the stranger replied. He took Devin's shirt off and felt his tits. Usually hating when people touched his chest, this time he didn't mind. The stranger kissed down Devin's neck and licked his pink nipples. He put each one in his mouth and softly bit down, showing them both the attention they deserved. Devin moaned and squirmed uncontrollably.

The stranger kissed down his stomach and took his thick thighs in both hands. He licked his lips and kissed both of his thighs, right near his pussy.

"Beg for it, baby," the stranger whispered with a smirk.

Bite

"Please." It came out as a whisper and Devin could feel the wetness only grow between his legs.

"Sorry, I didn't hear you," the stranger said, kissing his thighs again.

"Please," Devin said it louder this time, bucking his hips.

"One more time, baby."

"Please! Goddamn it! Please," Devin cried out. He was flooded.

"Good boy." The stranger put his mouth to Devin's cunt. He sucked on his pink clit and moved his tongue in circles.

"God, you taste good," the stranger mumbled into his pussy.

Devin couldn't help the moans coming out of his mouth. He knew no one would be able to hear him. When he looked into the stranger's eyes, they'd turned to slits. He made eye contact with Devin and just decided that it was the acid fucking with his brain.

Without warning, tiny pin pricks shock his inner thigh. To his horror and pleasure, his legs bled crimson down his pink pussy onto the stranger's face.

His face contorted in shock and horror, but it felt great. An orgasm was close and felt his ejaculation build inside. He needed the release and the stranger kept going. His tongue felt like sandpaper, and it was surprisingly the most enjoyable and painful experience Devin ever felt.

"I'm close," Devin whispered, bucking his hips.

"Cum for me, baby," the stranger said, licking the blood from Devin's thighs.

Devin obeyed, unable to hold back any longer. He felt himself release into the stranger's mouth. He moaned and raised up on his elbows, his face was red with embarrassment.

"Good boy," the stranger said, wiping the blood from his mouth.

"I'm bleeding."

"You taste wonderful."

Something rustled in the woods. Leaves crunched followed by laughing. When Devin looked up the stranger was gone without a trace and Devin was almost sure that he made up the whole experience.

Alphabet City Anactoria
Rain Corbyn

A few years before the orgy, Zoe read about the cannibal cave that allowed itself to be discovered in Cheddar Gorge, England. When the six geologists entered, they found cave paintings depicting small, black-eyed humanoids eating larger people, and without much thought, proceeded deeper into the caves. Many would later say the paintings were all the warning they needed to keep out, but if you don't know you're part of a horror story, you ignore the ominous signs. Surely, your woes are too mundane for genre. However, when nobody had emerged hours later, more were sent in; no one returned.

Two weeks and an international media frenzy later, armed forces found the only survivor—the winner, who'd eaten every part of the others but the bones. Her insides had burst from her glutting, the others' semi-digested flesh flowered from her every hole.

For nauseous amounts of money, a nationless oligarch bought the cave—not the rock around it, not the dust, not the paintings: just the hole itself, the void. He planted the hole in a vacant lot in Alphabet City, Manhattan, where Avenue A is for adventurous, B is for bold, C is for crazy, D is for dead. What Avenue F stands for, he figured, buying the land on that street, would reveal itself. A dozen crust punks with trust funds, puzzled by the sight of a crane dropping seemingly nothing into the lot, moved in that very day, and turned on each other.

Around midnight, a lost bar crawler found the only survivor—the winner, and recorded him. Quickly dubbed, "The Crackibal," the man sat on a pile of human bones, tearing flesh with his teeth while his ass evacuated to make room for the feast, became news, then a meme, then the controversial name of a $25 fried chicken sandwich joint.

Looking to hide the hole that could not be buried, the oligarch built a dummy nightclub over it, then a flower shop around the club, then a dive bar around the flower shop, and a rarely open rare bookstore around the flower shop. And the hole waited.

Zoe had read all about this when it happened but had forgotten a hundred more important things than that by the time she stood in front of the bookstore, pulled out her phone, and rehearsed the passwords one more time. She had gotten these instructions from an aging fairy (is there anything sadder?) at the Queen Vic, in between lunchtime warm well gin shots, and had felt guilty when she said, no, she wouldn't let him suck her girldick in exchange for his nonsense, then felt guilty for feeling guilty. After all, the miserable old queen hadn't offered this knowledge with any terms or conditions, no more than the back and forth maudlin chatter expected between daytime gaybar chatterboxes, anyway. She didn't owe him shit, she thought, why did she feel guilty? Now, she shivered, fixed her hair and cleavage in the greasy window, and went in.

"Hekkk-ahem, sorry. Hey. I was wondering if you have anything by Spenser. I was told-"

"Yup. Through here."

In a private reading room, she quickly located a canvas-covered copy of Spenser's *The Faerie Queene*, and tried to take it from the shelf. Sure enough, it tripped a switch recessing the shelf, revealing an old oak door engraved with vines, caves, pixies, and satyrs.

Once through, she recited, "Hi. Um, I'd like a Death in the Afternoon please. Hemingway sucks, but the man knew his booze."

A mustachioed vest poured dull green absinthe into a wide champagne glass. The spirit turned cloudy as he poured champagne over it. The bubbles carried woody licorice up her nose, and she stifled a belch as the tincture hit her empty stomach. She was guided to a pivoting grass-covered wall, and into the flower shop. She found the foxgloves as instructed, plucked one and placed it on the tip of her left ring finger, then, chagrined, spoke the last magic words as confidently as she could to the clerk: "Literally fucking kill me, Daddy." The final door opened for her, into darkness.

She considered, Zoe's bottom surgery was soon, and she felt that a topping at a gloryhole was a missing faggot achievement she needed to unlock while still had the gear. After a long string of referrals, ending with the man at the Vic, here she was. Plus, she figured, the experience would clarify some things for her: did she hate her royal scepter itself, or the pressure to be a wrathful king?

After several steps into the black, the door closed loudly behind her, echoing into the void. An anxious moment later, a featureless wall came into focus, and her eyes drifted down. There it was: the hole. A handspan across, with black gaffer tape smoothing its edges, at just the perfect height for her. Suddenly, she realized she didn't know enough about glory hole etiquette. She assumed she could take cues from the others here, maybe even ask someone, but there was nobody to be found. She put her bag down and pulled out lube, condoms, and a signalless phone. She jumped when a velvet-gloved hand emerged from the hole, curled a come-hither gesture, then withdrew. Clear enough. She unhooked her kilt and flinched as a buckle bounced off of her filling dick, then again as the fabric slid slick past her leg stubble on the way to the floor. She stepped out of it and looked around. There was nothing but the wall and its opposite: the hole.

She took her shirt and bra off, figuring the bottomless Winnie-the-Pooh look wasn't terribly sexy. She stepped towards the wall and a shock of euphoria, or at least a lack of dysphoria, hit as her breasts touched the cold surface before her half-hard dick reached the hole. Her nipples hardened at the chill. Stone? It was smooth under her hands, pleasant against her cheek and beneath her soles. A hunger prickled in her guts. She had been worrying about an expectation to reciprocate or transgressing some other cruising rule obvious to everyone but her. It wouldn't be the first time she felt like a queer impostor for not grokking some aspect of the codes and culture. Her aversion to recreational cruelty when she was a gay man; her monogamous inclinations when she was a pan enby; and now as a trans woman, there was no end to the fear of being thought a trickster, a spy, an invader.

An even gentle touch shocked her out of her anxious spiral. A firm gloved grip held the base of her dick, now fully unrolling like a butterfly mouth. The hand coaxed it and her balls through the hole, stroking assertively. Familiar sounds: the crack and splurt of a bottle of lube, soft coos from beyond the hole, the slick crinkle of goo warmed between bare palms.

Somewhere distant, a gruff transmasc voice barked, "Slut, bitchboy, good boy." He repeated between grunting thrusts; a songbird that can only sing its own name.

Two bare lubed hands replaced the gloved one on Zoe's cock, fuller and harder than it had been in months, maybe years. The anonymity circumvented so many of her usual anxieties. To the person across this thin wall, this endless galaxy of space, her dick wasn't a man's, a woman's, something else's, it wasn't even hers. It just was, and it was wanted.

A condom was rolled over it, followed by a tongue, then lips, then throat. She must get out of her own head and enjoy this experience. It used to annoy her to no end when her partners would say that scoldingly, but, or because it was true, you can't shame a boner jam into coming unstuck.

The wall pulled her closer like a magnet, squashing her breasts and belly against it. She worried about the pressure on her new ample chest. Her mind filled with paranoid fantasies of a fuckbuddy popping her tits during sex more brutal than typical wear and tear the implants were made to withstand. With a thrill, she distracted herself by theorizing what caused this pull toward the wall? She was horizontal now, she realized, and the force pulling her against the wall was just good old gravity. She remembered what to do if you're buried in an avalanche: carve out a little hole and spit. The direction your spit falls shows you which way is down, and you dig the other way. She pulled her cheek off of the wall and watched the longest part of her undercut dangle in front of her, confirming that while her feet held her upright, in front of her was also down.

Oh for fuck's sake, Zo, she thought, you're literally getting the last blowjob of your life and you're miles away in a fictional ski accident. As if to answer, the person on the other side of nothing picked up the pace of sputtering, droning quacks around her cock. Truth be told, she usually liked her sex a little porny, but here the showy sounds broke the bottom's featureless anonymity and that pissed her off. This experience was supposed to be the ur-fellatio, the Platonic ideal of disembodied cocksucking, but now once witnessed, the other person had traits that could be pinned down, and thus they (probably he) was definite: Schrodinger's cocksucker. *Stuck in my head while getting head*, she thought, and sighed in familiar resignation as her erection retreated, ashamed of her anxiety, shitty pun, and confirmed every deep dark feeling about herself, even those she could usually hide from in sex.

Two topless femme torsos approached from in front/below. She still felt supported by the wall, but when she looked down the length of her body, she could not see herself, even as the droning slurps sang against the base of her cock. Other than the pallor making the torsos visible against the weightless dark, they couldn't have been more different. The rolls, folds, and squish of one made Zoe do unconscious grabby motions with her hands, while the shiny abs and sinew of the other threatened to ruin her life. Cooperating once again, her dick filled, and her balls ached under the persistence of lips, tongue, and fist.

Both a large and small breast pressed against each of her cheeks. One was the champagne-glass breast of fin de siècle smut, the other the big-ass fucking tiddy of OnlyFans dirty talk. She was asked to choose her favorite, and she regretted her choice immediately, having overthought and answered what she thought they thought was right. But still, she was given both. She licked, then kissed, then sucked, then opened wide, jaw unhinging to swallow an entire breast. First, it was firm flesh on her tongue, then the soft sponge of a steamed bun, then the fast-dissolving panic of cotton candy—a dream being forgotten.

As the pink-tasting slime ran down her throat, seasons bloomed on

Rain Corbyn

Zoe's skin. Spring born baby birds burst from mounds all over her body, their human-baby screams quickly drowned in sourceless white liquid before they flew off, nourished, leaving lotus-pod abscesses. Summer rains filled these holes with warm water, and tiny bear-gays used the new pools for bathhouse cruising, their chest-fur matting with her pus and their tiny spit. They were still blowing each other when she scabbed over them and healed, sealing them in. Autumn turned her blonde hair, ginger, into scarlet, then all hair fell from her entire body, leaving her a bald Jizzferatu sharing her candy bucket with any costumed visitor that asked nicely. Winter clothed her in a spiderweb snowflake gown, and she was severe, ethereal, powerful. She held out an imperious arm, extended a hand to be kissed, and startled as the hand was severed by a diamond edge, flopping stupidly to the floor next to the finally-visible creature that had been sucking her off.

They looked up at Zoe, tears flooding from their solid black eyes, giggled through drool, and took her deep, their nose pressing against her pubis as she came in pulses matching the blood marching from her hand. Small winged beings scrambled for her severed hand, stripping the flesh from it like time lapse rot, then moving on, leaving an absurd novelty prop skeleton hand behind. There was no pain, but panic needled at her full-body numbness, a hot pepper testing the limits of ketamine-frozen gums. The being below Zoe kept suckling, but split into three blobby pseudopods at the shoulders. Each of these shaped themselves into rough humanoid forms while the first head continued washing her dick with a swirling, churning tongue. A mouth bloomed on each of the new pseudopods, and one lampreyed itself to each of her balls. The left mouth laved her sack like a winter tide; the right tugged and slurped like a novice with a poorly shucked oyster. The creature's head on her dick stayed latched to her, while another appeared behind it, and moved through it, ghostly pistoning in the same space as the first head. Another such head joined it, and another, each ring of lips running relays along her length at once, until she was concrete again.

Strong hands parted her cheeks, and a mouth surrounded by a coarse beard planted itself against her asshole and solemnly tongued slow circles. She reached behind to touch the head attached to that mouth, but now, there was no hand on that arm either. Looking at the perfectly healed nubs, she thought of the fisting possibilities, and as if she manifested it, a disembodied vulva appeared before her. Its luxurious lips, dark gray fading to beet-red at the center, made her mouth water, and before she knew it, her nose nudged the swollen, mighty Testosterone-juiced clit above. Invisible thighs crushed her head as she sang pleasure into the pussy and silenced all around her except for a womb-like pulse in her ears: bow pow bow pow.

Another orgasm stalked her, and with her nubs she tapped twice against the outside of the ethereal thighs, gasping for breath as they released her. She laid on her back now, still weightless. Words sprayed in cum on her belly, and carved painlessly into her chest: Whore, Goddess, Chalice, Cumdump.

As the vulva fucked itself on her nub, she felt a million eyes on her, the uncanny falling sensation of a starry night sky while drunk. Finally, she squirted green-flamed joy into the carwash of mouths around her dick. When she was empty, the faces withdrew, pulling her balls off her after a half-hearted tug of resistance, followed by pulling layer after layer of dermis off of her finished dick; a stream of magician's scarves unspooling, white to pink to red to nothing. As they left her, she wailed a roaring yowl of labor pains, and recalled accounts of mothers ashamed by childbirth orgasms. The beings gnawed at her disembodied genitals—no, those were theirs now, not hers, not anymore. And the smallest creatures descended on her newest nub, and ate away at the floor of her torso, excavating, sculpting out her new cunt. Like maggots eating away infection, they knew just what was poison and what was healthy, alive, what was her, and when the feast was over, Zoe spoke around a phantom dick down her throat, "show me."

They took her pussy out to do so—not the flesh, not the lips, hood, or clit—just the hole itself, the space where the parasite lived for so long, now a proper void, a cleared sinus. The little flying creatures dispersed the nothingness's weight amongst them, and held it up to her, proud and puckish, patting their little pot bellies full of her torso. She stared into her own nothingness, and saw everything that she was, were, will be.

Rain Corbyn

She was a vast continent, pristine before the colonialism of naming, labeling, partitioning, and trading, which could only lead to plunder and strip mining. Or maybe this was the aftermath of the last war for her precious resources, wiping out all of the meddlesome creatures who dared to live on her and call her theirs. How dare they, she thought, approach me and tell me that my forests ought to be lawns, that my hurricane is only acceptable if it mills their petty grain, that I can be divided into countries, states, and districts, each one named after their most accomplished rapists.

The million alien heads around her bobbed and nodded. As they fell upon her body and shredded it with needle-like mouths, others fed her in return. Ambrosia and honey, desert manna, the first gulp of frosty beer after yard work, foie gras and membrillo, the mundane but sublime stretch of a perfect fried mozzarella stick, strawberry Pocky, green seafood curry so spicy you can't go on but can't stop, champagne lapped out of cleavage, the firm avocado taste of clean cock. But more than anything, they fed her meat after meat after raw, living meat, while they sliced hers away from her with the solemnity of a butcher, the dark humor of a cancer-ward surgeon, the bittersweet tears of a family around a whole roast pig at a funeral.

And her final meat slid into them, and it nourished them, and it became them, until there was no difference left between her and them. Once she was nothing, she could, at last, be anything, could stop pretending not to be everything. She was the cave: no form, no walls, no firmament, just a pristine hole, the grand question answered, a perfect infinite absence. Her void, her entirety, became like everyone else's who has ever died: not gone, not moved somewhere else; just differently everywhere, to be digested forever by those who took her in.

And that is what you have done for me by reading this, digesting it, containing it. Now that my heart is inside you, I can never not exist as part of you, so I can not be destroyed. I am free not to be at all except for what I have stored away in you like a squirrel's cache, for later. I was meat, bone, and hair, and now I am part of your future, a hypothetical that's so much better than any mundane use for my flesh. Take this, all of you, and eat from it. I wasn't using it anyway.

Oh. You're upset at this sleight of hand, and I am sorry, truly.

Alphabet City Anactoria

There were rules to the sort of relationship we had, and you didn't exactly agree formally to a lifelong future together, not consciously, anyway. Then again, you really did have clues that you might consider which genre you were in, whether or not to proceed deeper into the cave. Faeries like me often conceal our names in order to preserve the power we have over you humans, but we do get cocky sometimes, even cocky enough to put our true names into a byline, plain as day. So, in exchange for my true name, the one I chose for myself out of any possible combination of sounds, the one I had to murder my mother's son to step into, am I not entitled to stow a sliver of me away, in you, for the rest of your life, so that we may be together until, of course, one day everything is nothing?

And so now, I must impose one final time on you, and while you can refuse, I won't hear it, because my part of the deal is already over. Because I live within your flesh now, forever and only there, you must promise me, you must, I beg you, if you love me at all—promise me never to die, unless it is to be eaten.

Silicone Toys
Violet Mourningstarr

The first caturday of witchy season,
seven swifties and a bee got drunk on spiked tea,
and shared an uber home.

Lets call her Kiersten, for privacy's sake,
laid in bed wide awake, unable to fall asleep.
But between her legs, it throbs and misbehaves,
until she shoves her fingers in, knuckle deep.

Inability to focus and distraction,
it took her longer to climax, and her body demanded more.
So, she did something she'd done never before,
and found an online store,
to assist in treating her condition.

A cardboard box, plain and brown,
arrived by postal carrier. She pulled the items out,
and set them on the ground.
St★rla, not a new invention,
a doll, anatomically female with auto lubrication.

Violet Mourningstarr

Kiersten's smile grew from both sets of lips, and
she added a pink strap onto her hips.
Without haste or hesitation she mounted her,
new prized possession,
and rode with a sensually painful glee.

After a few times, St★rla lost her shiny new,
and Kiersten knew what to do. She
changed her name. Now a stranger,
she found different ways to use her.

Alex liked sunsets on the beach,
cocktails, with a mouth like a leech.
Daliah preferred to be rough,
pain with every touch, sex wet with sin.
That brought us Jen, and Ken, a set of genderfluid twins,
giving orgasms in multiples of ten.

But dripping her come on silicone
left Kiersten sad and alone.
So, Tinder resumes and
with a swipe right, the doll is back in its box,
and hidden from sight.
But just because you cant see her,
doesn't mean she doesn't see you.
From a gap in the door,
St★rla saw Kiersten's new whore, and swore
a revenge sated in blood.

First, a dead rat in her bag, like a treat
from Kiersten's cat.
Then shoes soaked with toilet water,
and the toothbrush dipped in piss.
But things became much more serious,
when late at night, Kiersten in the bath,
St★rla snuck out and turned out the light.

Silicone Toys

Without a noise, she found the problem.
Bound and gagged, she tucked them away.

"Don't call, don't text.
I don't want to be with you,
I'm back with my ex."

The heartbreak was fast and pure.
The only cure, to numb the aching soul.
She returned to St★rla, hidden in her box,
and rode until her legs burned.
Sitting on her kiss, thick lips opened her slit,
and she pushed her nose in a little bit.
Pumping her pussy, wetness flows,
down her thighs, coating her face,
And St★rla loved how she tasted.
She rubbed her lip against the bud,
then bit so hard, she drew blood.
Red slick iron coats her mouth,
Kiersten shudders.
The hard clit rolled on her tongue,
right as her screaming begun.

By a Thread
Caitlin Marceau

Chelsea smiles against Olivia's lips, loving the taste of herself on her wife's mouth. She pulls Olivia closer, digging her nails into the other woman's skin, flushing scarlet at her partner's excited moans. She pushes Olivia onto the mattress beside her and climbs on top of the woman, straddling her thighs and pinning her hands above her head. Her wife's eyes widen with need.

"Tie me up," Olivia says through heavy breaths. "Please, tie me up."

Chelsea's chest tightens at the request, knowing that this is how their arguments always start now. She smiles down at Olivia, trying to hide her anxiety at the request, and nods in agreement.

She climbs off and makes her way over to the nightstand where Olivia keeps the handcuffs. Chelsea received them as a gag gift during her bachelorette party and would have thrown them away if not for her wife's interest. They're a gaudy set, the magenta faux fur the only thing protecting Olivia from the metal that's guaranteed to turn her skin green. If she pulls at the cuff even a little, the ratchet releases from the pawl with ease. Still, they were the only restraints the couple owned and Olivia couldn't get enough of them.

When Chelsea turns back, she finds her wife in the center of the bed with her hands stretched above her head, writhing with excitement as she waits to be bound to the headboard. Leaning over Olivia, Chelsea secures a wrist in the cuff.

"Tighter," Olivia breathes.

Chelsea tightens the cuff a little more, already knowing that it won't be enough, that her wife won't be satisfied, and that this is the start of a fight even if Olivia doesn't know it yet.

"Tighter," she begs.

Chelsea pushes the metal into Olivia's skin as the ratchet moves deeper past the pawl.

"Fuck, tighter! I want to hurt. I want to bleed," she moans, eyes rolling back in her head.

"It can't go any tighter!" Chelsea snaps, throwing her hands up and getting off of the bed. "The stupid fucking cuff is just going to pop right open if you so much as breathe at this point!"

She turns her back to Olivia, running hands through her hair. She suddenly feels exhausted and the idea of having sex is now the farthest thing from her mind.

"Well, that's the fun part," Olivia coos. "Then you get to hit me for being bad and breaking out of—"

"I don't want to hit you! I don't want to hurt you! I don't want to make you fucking bleed!" Chelsea yells, turning to look at her wife. "I can't believe we're fucking arguing about this again!"

Olivia sits up, rolling her eyes.

"You don't have to be so dramatic about everything. Christ," she says, getting out of the bed, tossing the handcuffs onto the mattress behind her. She pushes past Chelsea and grabs her housecoat off the back of the bedroom door, sliding it onto her naked body and tying it closed.

"I'm not being dramatic!" Chelsea shouts. "I've told you before, this stuff makes me uncomfortable. I hate that you'd—"

"Do you know what makes me uncomfortable? Do you know what I hate?" Olivia asks, crossing her arms in front of her chest. "Our boring fucking sex life. The fact that the most daring thing you've ever done in this bed is rearrange the pillows!" she spits.

"That's not fair!" Chelsea says, her throat tight with emotion. The frustration mounts inside of her, eyes stinging with the threat of tears. She digs her nails into her palms to prevent herself from crying.

"You're right, it's not. You put the pillows back the way they were, so I guess that one doesn't count."

Olivia throws open the door and makes her way down the hall to the bathroom. She grabs her toothbrush out of the holder and squeezes some Colgate on the end before shoving it in her mouth.

Chelsea grabs her oversized T-shirt off of the floor and pulls it on, trying to compose herself before following Olivia. By the time she gets to the bathroom, her wife has already rinsed her mouth and put her toothbrush back.

"I said I was open to tying you up. And I've been getting more into the BDSM stuff you like, but I'm not comfortable hurting you! I'm not comfortable fucking maiming you to make you come!"

Olivia wipes her mouth with a towel and glares at her. "I'm not asking you to maim me. I'm asking you to try something new. Don't you love me? Don't you want me to be happy?"

"Of course I do! But that's not—"

"Then why don't you want to see me fulfilled the way I need to be?"

"I said I'd try, but what you're asking is fucking crazy! I'm not going to—"

"This is the kind of bullshit that made me—" Olivia stops talking mid-sentence, the words unsaid hanging heavily in the air between them.

Chelsea feels like she's been slapped and she takes a step back from her partner with a wince. The tears welling up in her eyes threaten to spill over, and she pushes her nails even deeper into her palm to assuage them.

"I'm going to sleep on the couch tonight," Olivia finally says.

Chelsea wants to stop her, wants to call her back to bed, wants to smooth this whole thing over.

But she doesn't.

Instead, she watches Olivia walk away, trying not to think about her wife's previous affair or how it started with a fight just like this one.

Chelsea wakes up to the sound of the front door closing. She bolts up in bed, heart thundering in panic, and reaches out a hand to wake Olivia.

Only her wife isn't there.

Looking at the alarm clock next to her, she exhales slowly, realizing it was just her wife leaving for work. Clutching her chest, sadness hits her like a brick. The unsaid *I'm sorry* and *let's work through this* tastes bitter in the back of her throat.

Still exhausted, she throws off the covers and gets out of bed, her body aching from a night spent tossing and turning with worry and guilt. Her sore shoulders need a massage and once she's done working on them, she begins rubbing some life back into her thighs when her phone vibrates on the nightstand beside her.

She leans over to see who it's from and spots Olivia's name flashing across the screen. Picking the device up, she hopes for an apology or even just a good-morning text, but her heart sinks when she reads the message.

> I have a thing after work tonight, so I'll be out late. Don't wait up.

Chelsea's face burns hot, her cheeks flushing red with humiliation and anger. Her mouth dries and her jaw clenches as she thinks of what to text back. She looks down at her phone long enough for the screen to fade black, her eyes staring back into their own reflection.

Eventually, she settles on what to write.

> Okay.

Later that night, when Olivia gets home and stumbles into bed, Chelsea pretends to be asleep.

By a Thread

When she wakes up the next morning, Olivia's side of the bed is empty, again. She runs a hand over her wife's pillow, smoothing out the wrinkles in the cold fabric as she ignores the pit of despair growing deeper inside of her. Although she's glad her wife is still home—she can hear Olivia tinkering with the coffee machine downstairs in the kitchen—she can't help but lament the warm kisses and soft caresses she usually wakes up to.

Is this my fault?

She knows it's an unfair question to ask herself, but she can't help but ask it anyway.

She sighs, forcing herself to get out of bed, and makes her way downstairs.

In the kitchen, Olivia taps the back of a spoon lightly against the wooden cutting board as she waits impatiently for the coffee to finish brewing. Her to-go mug sits on the counter beside her, the sugar jar and an open coffee creamer carton flank it.

"Morning," Chelsea whispers from the entrance.

"Morning," Olivia replies, not bothering to turn around.

The silence between them grows and expands, threatening to swallow the whole room. She waits for Olivia to say something, to say anything, but she remains silent.

It's eventually Chelsea who breaks to speak first.

"It's a Saturday."

"What?" Olivia asks, finally turning to look at her wife.

"It's a Saturday. You don't work weekends, so where're you going?"

Olivia turns back to the coffee machine and slides the pot off the burner, pouring the scalding liquid into her cup.

"I'm going on a hike."

"Alone?"

"No, with a friend," she says, shoulders squared and tense.

Chelsea can't help but imagine them freckled with kisses in the shade of another woman's lipstick.

"From work?"

Olivia gives an exasperated sigh, like she's already exhausted from a fight they've yet to have.

"Yes, from work."

Chelsea waits for her to continue, to explain who the mystery friend is, but Olivia doesn't offer any more than that.

"Oh. Okay. Do you think you'll be home in time for supper? I was thinking we could try that new—"

"I don't know. Probably not," she interrupts.

Olivia's eyes focus on the coffee cup as she turns to face the other woman, knuckles white as she tightens the already-too-tight lid on her drink.

"Look, I've been thinking… Maybe we should try being poly."

The question takes Chelsea by surprise. Whatever she expected her wife to say, it wasn't this. She stares at her spouse for a long time, opening and closing her mouth over and over again as she tries to find the words. It feels like all the air has been sucked out of her lungs, like a fish that's been reeled in and left to die, choking on air.

"What?" It's all she can manage as memories of her wife's affair play on repeat at the back of her mind.

"I think we should try being poly," Olivia repeats, her voice loud and clear as she finally lifts her chin to meet Chelsea's gaze. "It's obvious we want different things in the bedroom. I love you, I do, but I love myself enough to find someone willing to give me the sexual gratification I need. If you're not going to try and meet me halfway on this one, then I deserve to find someone who will."

Chelsea doesn't know what to say. Part of her wants to grovel and beg for Olivia to see that she is trying to meet her halfway, that she's desperately trying to understand her wife's needs and support them however she can.

The other part of her wants to scream and cry and rally against the unfairness of what's been said.

"This way," Olivia continues, "you get to be involved. You'll know who I'm seeing, and who I want to have a physical relationship with. If we're poly, you get to be part of the conversation this time."

This time.

The words make her feel small. They make her feel like a child who's been told that they get to make an important decision, but only if they make the right one.

She almost says as much, but doesn't.

"Am I not enough?" she finally asks.

At the question, Olivia looks away, her face turning red. She moves past her wife, exiting the kitchen, and making her way to the front door.

Although Olivia has the decency not to reply, Chelsea feels the answer hanging between them.

No, you're not.

Stony-faced and resolute in her decision, Chelsea powers up the computer, and opens an incognito tab in the browser. She runs her fingers along the keyboard, the smooth plastic cold against her skin as she breathes a couple of deep, calming breaths. Debating what to type in the search bar, her face reddens with each idea. Like a teenager discovering porn all over again, she blushes, ashamed as she watches the actresses explore each other's bodies.

But back then she only pretended to be ashamed.

Tonight, she's filled with self-hatred and disgust.

Deciding the longer she waits, the worse she'll feel, she gets to work. She types in the URL of a popular tube site, hits enter, and tries to ignore the pit in her stomach. Clicking on a menu, she selects "categories," and scans through the list until she finds what she's looking for.

BDSM

She clicks on the word and waits as the site brings her to a new landing page, this one filled with thumbnails of people in ropes and chains and strapped to machines Chelsea's never seen before. Dragging her finger along the trackpad, the cursor hovers over a video until she finally hits play.

Chelsea watches nervously as a woman in sheer panties is bound with a thick cord. The man stands behind her and kisses her neck as he ties her arms behind her back, weaving the rope gently around her wrists, around her chest, and even between her thighs. She moans as he touches her, deft hands working her as much as he works the rope.

Chelsea watches the video with rapt attention, her chest tight as she observes the couple on screen. She wishes this was all Olivia demanded from her because she'd happily obey. The idea of her soft hands roaming her wife's body, the cold contrast of her touch to the biting confinement of rough rope, the power she'd have to make her lover tremble and pant and come endlessly.

But this isn't what Olivia wants.

She doesn't want Chelsea's warm hands, soft kisses, wet lips.

She wants the weight of her body fighting against gravity, the sting of rope cutting into her skin, and the heat of her blood dripping on the floor.

Is this how you let that other woman fuck you? Did she need to tie you up to get you wet? Did she hurt you to make you finish? Was Vicky enough?

Chelsea closes the video to look for another, settling for one with the thumbnail of a man with wet eyes and running eyeliner. After only a few short minutes, she knows this also isn't the right one. The man is bound to a wooden beam with a leather leash and heavy chains. He gags, tears rolling down his face, as his partner thrusts himself deep into his open mouth.

Although the other man is rough and unrelenting, the way he laces his fingers through his partner's hair and runs a thumb along his wet cheeks is too intimate and tender for what Olivia wants done to her.

She closes the video and puts on a new one. She does this again, then again, and again.

She stares at the computer screen late into the night, pretending each clip isn't breaking her heart a little more every time.

"You could have called!" she yells, waving her mobile in front of Olivia's face before tossing it onto the butcher's block.

"I told you, my phone died."

"Then you could have used your friend's phone," Chelsea spits, getting more worked up with each passing second. She's like a train gaining speed and doesn't know how to stop.

"I don't know your number!"

"How the fuck do you not know my number?"

"Do you think I just memorize everyone's fucking contact info when I put it into my phone?" Olivia says, rolling her eyes with annoyance.

"I'm not everyone!" Chelsea screams. "I'm your wife, or did you forget that too?"

Chelsea slams her empty wine glass onto the counter next to the fridge. She opens one of the stainless steel doors and grabs a half-finished bottle of white, quickly screwing off the lid and pouring the cheap grocery-store alcohol into her glass. She puts the bottle back and slams the refrigerator, the bottles of condiments and glass Tupperware rattling inside.

"Oh my God, what do you want from me? I already said I was sorry about the phone."

"It's not about the phone, it's about you—"

"If it's not about the phone then, what? You're mad that I didn't drink and drive?"

"No, that's not—"

"I'm sorry I spent the night on my friend's couch," Olivia says, voice dripping with honeyed sarcasm as she plasters an exaggerated frown onto her face. "I'm sorry I was responsible. Next time, I'll be sure to get behind the wheel of my car when I'm loaded. God help me if you're lonely for even one night."

Chelsea doesn't mean to slap her, but she does, and the harsh sound of her palm striking Olivia's face fills the kitchen. Red blooms across her cheek as she stares at her wife, dumbfounded.

Something stirs in Chelsea. Her face flushes and warmth builds between her legs—she knows it's not from the wine.

It's from the violence.

Her wife opens her mouth, but closes it when Chelsea slaps her again.

This time, Olivia doesn't stare at her with shock, but with arousal.

Chelsea pulls her wife close, nails digging into her skin, and crushes the woman's mouth beneath her own, the action heavy with need. She pulls at Olivia's clothes, wishing they were already off so she could fuck her wife in the middle of their kitchen.

"Go upstairs," she whispers against the woman's mouth.

Olivia obliges, taking the steps two at a time making her way to their bedroom.

Chelsea breathes heavily and takes out the toolbox she keeps beneath the sink. She riffles through the metal container, wondering if she'd already thrown the spool of fishing line out when her fingers brush against cold plastic. Smiling, she takes it out, checks to make sure there's enough to bind her wife with. Aware of the risks, she'll have to be careful with nylon string, but she knows Olivia's desire to hurt.

And right now, just for right now, she wants it to hurt Olivia, too.

Chelsea heads to the bedroom, the fishing line, work gloves, and scissors piled in her arms. A desperate need for release pulses between her thighs when she sees Olivia. On the edge of the bed, her nude body is on display, her legs spread wide as she touches herself, moaning, giving her wife a show.

Her gaze trails up Olivia's legs, eyes mapping every mole, every freckle, every place she wants to kiss. She frowns, noticing three slivers of red on her wife's thigh. It takes her a moment to recognize nail marks etched in her skin.

"What are—"

"Fuck me," Olivia begs. "Please."

"Get on the bed and put your hands behind your back," she instructs, voice low.

Olivia obeys, lying face down on the comforter, legs splayed wide.

Chelsea slips on gloves and pulls a length of fishing line from the spool, cutting it with scissors. Climbing onto the bed, she crawls towards Olivia's prone form, heart racing. She admires the gentle curves of her wife's body and the way the light falls across her back.

She looms over her partner and keeps one knee pressed firmly between her thighs, smiling at Olivia's compulsion to gyrate her hips, grinding against her. Her wife flinches as she runs a hand over her shoulder. Chelsea notices hints of blue and purple budding across her skin, fresh bruises waiting to bloom.

As she grabs her wife's hands in her own, her resolve falters, the sharp rage felt in the kitchen, now just a dull ache.

"Make it hurt," Olivia breathes.

Annoyance flares inside Chelsea at the request. She roughly wraps the fishing line around her wife's wrists, pulling the nylon tight enough to push into the flesh but not through Olivia's skin. Using the same knots her father taught her when they used to fish, she ties the ends together. As she secures the last loop, a phone vibrates nearby.

She sighs, pulls one of the work gloves off with her teeth, and reaches out a hand to pick her phone up off of the nightstand.

"Leave it," her wife urges. "I need you. Now."

Her fingers find only the smooth wood of the bedside furniture and she frowns, remembering that she left her device on the kitchen counter.

"You said your phone was dead."

"It is. Babe, please, I want you inside m—"

"My phone's downstairs," she hisses.

Olivia stills beneath her.

Chelsea gets off of the bed when the phone vibrates a second time. She pads across the floor towards Olivia's purse, pulling her other glove off, letting it fall to the ground. Picking up the bag, the phone buzzes again and she realizes that the noise is coming from the pile of discarded clothing on the floor.

"Babe," Olivia says, rolling onto her back and sitting up on the sheets, "come back to bed."

Chelsea doesn't hear her, she's too focused on the sound of the phone. Each buzz feels louder than the last, like a hornet's nest coming alive, ready to attack.

She finds the phone in the back pocket of Olivia's jeans, the battery substantially drained, but not dead. She touches the screen and the display comes to life, rekindling her earlier rage.

MESSAGES now

Caitlin Marceau

> Vicky
>
> I missed you... is it too soon to say the L word? lol

MESSAGES now

> Vicky
>
> I wish you were back in my arms

MESSAGES now

> Vicky
>
> Seriously though, I was sad things ended between us. I'm glad we found our way back to each other.

PHONE 2h ago
Chelsea
Missed Call

PHONE 8:17 AM
Chelsea
Missed Call

PHONE Yesterday, 11:04 PM
Chelsea
Missed Call

PHONE Yesterday, 9:56 PM
Chelsea
Missed Call

PHONE 1d ago
Chelsea
Missed Call

Chelsea tightens her grip on the phone. She's not strong enough to crush metal and glass with her bare hands, but that doesn't stop her from trying to squeeze the device as hard as she can. The rounded edges dig into her hand, the pain helping stabilize her and keep her grounded in this moment.

"Babe, please," Olivia halfheartedly tries again. "Come back to bed and make love to—"

"Vicky," she whispers. "You're fucking Vicky. Again."

Chelsea looks over at her wife, eyes seeing through Olivia to the truth she ignored. The nail marks on her thighs, the handprints on her back, the perfume that clings to her hair, the smudged makeup... it's all like the last time.

Vicky has branded herself onto Olivia's body and Chelsea wants—needs—to excise it from her wife.

"It's not my fault."

"What?"

"It's not my fault," she repeats. "I told you what I needed. I told you over and over again that—"

"So you're saying it's my fault?"

"No, I'm just saying that I was clear with my needs and you wouldn't fulfill them. I mean, what was I supposed to do? What did you expect? This isn't my fault; it's a failure in our relationship."

Chelsea feels too hot. She's sure her body will burst into flames and reduce to ash at any moment. The metal of the phone digs deeper into her hand, but she refuses to loosen her grip, as if yielding to the device means yielding to Vicky herself.

Caitlin Marceau

The phone vibrates again.
MESSAGES now

> Vicky
>
> Screw it. I know we only dated
>
> for a few months before this, and
>
> even though it's only been a few
>
> weeks back together, I'm saying
>
> it. I love you.

"Babe, I know this is hard on you, but this is a good thing. It gives us a chance to work on our marriage. To work through all your baggage and find common ground," she says, her voice level and patronizing. "And, honestly, this is just as hard on me as it is on you. It's painful for me too."

"But you like pain. You enjoy it. That's the entire problem, isn't it?" Chelsea asks, working herself back into a frenzy. "You're mad that I don't hurt you, that I don't want to make you suffer, right?"

She stares at Olivia, eyes wide and brimming with a hatred that she never knew she could have for her wife. She looks around the room, spotting the spool of fishing line discarded on the bed. Her chest tightens, and hand aches around the solid phone, palm stinging as the device vibrates once more against her skin.

She doesn't bother to read the message.

Olivia opens her mouth, but Chelsea speaks first.

"I guess you're in luck, Babe. Because I think I'm finally ready to do it."

"To do what?"

"To do what you wanted. To hurt you."

Chelsea whips the phone hard across the room, smiling wildly as it crashes into the wall behind the bed. Shards of metal and glass explode in every direction and Olivia doesn't have a chance to scream before Chelsea tackles her back onto the bed, knocking the wind out of her.

As Olivia struggles to breathe, Chelsea rolls her on her chest and pushes a knee in her back, holding her in place. She grabs the roll of nylon with one hand and her wife's bound wrists with the other.

"Does it feel good?" she asks, winding another length of fishing line around Olivia's hands.

This time, as she pulls the nylon, she relishes the scream her wife makes as it digs into her flesh. It splits her skin like a hot knife slicing through butter as Chelsea yanks the spool taught, her knees pressed firmly against Olivia's back as she makes the binds as tight as possible. She wraps the line up her wife's right arm, wrenching it deep into her forearm, past her elbow, and up to her shoulder. She moves the spool to the left arm, this time working the filament from the shoulder down to the wrist.

Chelsea pants and sweats as she tugs the line tight, struggling for a good grip on the plastic cord slipping between her fingers. Looking down, she notices it's because it's coated in her blood, the nylon cutting deep grooves into her palm and fingers to the bone.

But she doesn't mind. If anything, the pain helps her focus on the task at hand.

She thinks back to the videos she watched, the unending barrage of porn she'd subjected herself to in the hopes to better understand her wife. She tries to remember the intricate ways the actors used the rope, how they'd expertly maneuver the soft cord to suspend their partner or bind them in compromising positions.

She continues to weave the fishing line around Olivia's body, drawing it tightly across her chest, between her thighs, around each breast, across her hips, until she finishes with a few loops around her wife's neck.

Chelsea smiles to herself.

"Wait right here," she tells Olivia earnestly, pushing herself off of the bed.

She sprints downstairs, her socks slipping and sliding dangerously on the hardwood floors, leaving streaks of red in her wake. Across the kitchen, she grabs her toolbox from under the sink, then runs back to the bedroom.

"Is this what you wanted?" she asks, talking loudly over Olivia's cries. "To make you hurt. To make you bleed. That's what you asked me to do, right? Have I delivered?"

Chelsea grabs the chair from the corner vanity and moves it to the center of the room. She opens the toolbox and retrieves a stud finder and pencil. Standing on the chair, she marks the stud, and goes back to the box. This time, she takes out a drill and metal hook before getting back on the chair, and screwing the silver instrument into the ceiling. Bits of drywall and paint rain down on her.

"I know I should probably use two hooks and an offset board, but I don't have time for that. I'm too busy making you come," she tells Olivia. "I mean, that's what I'm doing, right? This is what you need to get off, isn't it?"

She gives the hook a hard tug, making sure it can support more weight than just that of a potted plant. When it doesn't budge, she gives a little whoop of excitement and gets down from her perch, putting her tools back and pushing the box out of the way before heading back to Olivia.

"Have your needs been met, babe?" she asks, voice dripping with sarcasm as she drags her wife off of the bed.

Olivia screams when she hits the floor, but Chelsea doesn't hear it. All she hears is buzzing from the dead phone, an imagined onslaught of texts from Vicky that only part of her knows aren't really there. The woman she was that morning, the woman who loved her wife, is gone and in her wake is the cruel caricature of what Olivia wanted.

She drags her wife's marred and bloodied body to the center of the room. Taking the spool in one hand, she gets back on the chair. She runs the line through the hook and pulls it tight stepping back down. The nylon slices deep into her hand, but it doesn't hurt: it feels good. Olivia shouts in agony as she's lifted ever so slightly off of the ground.

Chelsea continues to wrest the fishing line.

Olivia continues to scream.

Between the struggle to hold the slick nylon and skeptical the hook would come undone, Chelsea moves slower than she wants. It takes her forever to lift her wife entirely off of the ground, but when she finally finishes the sight is magnificent.

Olivia's eyes bulge from their sockets and her mouth hangs open, tongue lolling. It's an expression of anguish Chelsea mistakes for ecstasy. Were it not for the nylon caught in the rivets of the woman's spine, Olivia's head would have come clean off from her body weight pulling down on the razor-sharp cord. Red seeps from her skin and pools onto the floor, the fishing line slicing her clean to the bone. In the dim light of the bedroom, the plastic thread looks invisible. It gives Chelsea the impression her wife hovers above the floor like an angel suspended in air.

She stares at her partner, admiring her handy work, surprised to find herself aroused at the sight of Olivia like this.

"I get it, Babe. I get why you needed this," Chelsea says to her wife.

She takes a seat on the nearby chair and spreads her legs, slipping her fingers below the waistband of her jeans.

"Who'd have guessed that I needed this too?"

Hunger, the Sea
Charibdys

The tip of Sievon's filet knife slid from the gills into the soft belly of the mackerel with a yielding ease, parting the white flesh with a needful tenderness that left the guts unsplit. He let his thumb rest on the notch of the wound, the intestines just visible in the slit, plump and stained with blood like wine, pale parted lips of flesh. The way the muscle gave under him, the hint of sea in the smell, filled him with desire: the need to give, to take, to press his mouth against the slit and run his tongue along the thinnest separation of the belly; to taste the exposed muscle and fat, peel the veneer of skin back, let the oil smear his lips.

The heavy bottom of a pot clacked against the cutting board at the station next to his.

"Sir?" an assistant said, their voice hesitant, as though they were afraid of interrupting him. He couldn't remember their name. Human faces had always blurred together for him. "Are you all right?"

"Fine," Sievon said, his thumb still pressed into the pale meat, watery blood trickling through the creases of his knuckles. Had the assistant noticed he was always covered in odd bruises, always wearing long sleeves and collared shirts? The assumption was usually leather, but those days were behind him. He picked up his knife and slid it

Charibdys

through the uncut gills, then beheaded the fish with a crack of the spine. The guts slipped out, jewel-toned. Again he was thankful that the stiff kitchen aprons hid his obvious signs of arousal.

"Is something wrong with the fish?" the assistant ventured.

"No." What would convince the assistant to leave him alone? The constant scrutiny of being head chef was exhausting; all he wanted to do was feed people; share the textures, the flavors, the sensations available at the tip of a knife.

"I'm fine," he repeated. Certainly he had nothing to share with this assistant, regardless of how long they had worked the kitchen. He lifted his head and offered the other chef a wooden smile, all too aware of the dismembered fish on the cutting board. A delicacy, prepared correctly. A gift from the ocean herself.

He had never been accused of being an approachable man, but whatever the assistant saw in Sievon's half-hearted smile made the younger chef scurry away. Well enough; that was as much small talk as Sievon had ever been able to muster.

Today was one of the slow days: no mid-week tourists in this quaint fishing town to devour the fruits of the sea, and everyone else was too broke to eat the local delicacies regularly. Sievon couldn't concentrate, anyway. He had the staff close up early and leave so he could anticipate his visitor in peace. His excuse was always that he stayed late alone to clean and reorganize, bathing the cramped kitchen with the smell of bleach and hot water. A perfectionist, his staff called him. An old-fashioned control freak. To have his responsibilities distilled to lunch-break accusations made him laugh.

When he was finally satisfied with the gleam of the counters, he took a bucket of fish heads and other offal out to the old fishing shack. He could count the minutes until midnight.

The brisk scent of ocean wind announced his visitor's arrival before her three-meter bulk stooped through the door of the shack. Her shell glistened with mother-of-pearl, angled body sculpted by the pressure and the unyielding darkness of the deep sea, fractured eyes clustered into the facsimile of a face over her domed head. Her mandibles worked over each other, toothed, delicate, and he felt himself harden at the sight of her. A mermaid, a monster: any description of her was insufficient. She was the sea itself and the rocks turned by it. In her many arms she held a net tangled with fish, still twitching. A gift, for him.

Sievon's body ached for her touch. But it would be irresponsible to waste a gift, so he gutted and stored the fish with the deft hand of a professional while she stood close behind him, the pointed tips of her fingers prying and exploring the movement of his muscles as he worked, his shoulders, back, ass, until he was done.

Her arousal was different from a human's, if no less fickle. With the cold blood still coating his fingers, he turned to her and she moved up against him, backing him into the counter. She had to lean forward to meet his gaze, her own eyes chrome and unblinking. He ran fingers over her chest, her abdomen, her undershell, down to the slit tucked between her lower legs, already flowering open for him. Her hands seized his upper arms, tugging at the fabric of his shirt, his hands, hard enough that it would leave a mark, and pushed him to his knees, trapping his head between the counter and her own angular body. Sievon submitted easily, bracing himself to bury his mouth against her slit, tasting saltwater and naked skin, slick with desire and plump against his mouth. She didn't voice noise—not that he could hear, not in surroundings so thin as air—but her gills shivered and her mandibles clicked, limbs buzzing with audible pleasure.

It was not her fertile season—she was empty—but the taste of sea-salt and oil saturating his nose and mouth brought with it the memory of a similar position, her pinning him against the counter, pointed armored fingers yanking at his hair, filling his mouth with her unripened eggs—an offering of her own being. There was so little he could offer her of the same weight.

Perhaps satisfied—or dissatisfied—with his tongue and lips against her, she lifted and set him on the counter, spreading his legs to free his own stiffened genitals from his trousers. Sievon leaned back while she stripped him, ran her pebbled claws over his thighs, his sides, stretching his legs to fit around her, enjoying her careless strength, the way her plated body and sharp joints pinched his skin.

She dipped her head and pulled at the soft skin and fat of his thigh. His breath went ragged with need. His hand closed over the

Charibdys

handle of the fileting knife. To consume, be consumed, offer oneself for preparation…

He thrust the knife into his belly and opened his flesh for her. He peeled back the skin and yellow fat, exposing his own guts, the same color as a fish's, deep reds and purples, healthy and plump with blood.

All he felt was the blood in his head and in his crotch and the tug of her many hands on his body, a prelude, a relief. He dropped the knife from slick fingers as she lowered her head into the hollow of his belly and took him into her mouth. Weakness which was pleasure in and of itself spread through his hips and legs as she nuzzled, licked and sucked at his coiled intestines, her gills fluttering against him torn open and vulnerable. She did not bite down but worked along each section tenderly, as if to clean him, pulling him to her to bury her head deeper. He drove his hands into the gaps of her shell and the tips of his fingernails left narrow scratch marks, pushing the flush of blood through thin gaps of skin.

He tightened his legs around her, hot and wet with blood and seawater, erect against her chitin. She shoved deeper still, hollowing him out, widening the slit up towards the cage of his ribs. He moaned. She worked slowly, softly, savoring his taste, his delicacy. Her jaws and the wedge of her head were well-spattered with his bright blood, but the fluid only made her shell slick and easily move against his malleable flesh. He felt his organs against his skin, slipping out of himself, prickled and pulled and worked by the deft tools of her mouth, curled and clutched against her, his vision a tunnel only filtering through the cold moonlight of her eyes. He was barely aware that she moved his knee to ride against, but in his haze he was glad for her to use every part of him as she wished.

He thought of her bearing down, cracking him open, sucking his flesh and marrow out from emptied bones, and that thought spilled him over, seizing his flesh and spattering himself and her shell with a chain of white. His last hold on consciousness went with it. He knew she juddered, came around him as well, but his body may as well have been jelly; he felt her shiver, slacken, and withdraw. She delicately tucked his intestines back in with the proficiency of a veterinarian, pinched his seeping fat and skin together and kissed it with her mandibles, as surgical as an ant's jaws. His body rippled with luminescence drawn from the abyss; a healing radiance, a different sort of relief—the shaky post-adrenaline rush of survival, a wound escaped.

Still too spent to move, he gazed up at her strange silhouette and glimmering eyes as she petted his soft body, lingering on his chest and belly and thighs, all of him but tender flesh that yielded under her harboring shell.

The Roses of Heliogabalus
Sofia Ajram

And when the most excessive gluttony and fucking became mechanical, inconsequential, a rote obsession; like a flame dying of asphyxiation—in short, a bore—the emperor Heliogabalus sought the grander pleasures in life.

His calendar metamorphosed into the tender loam soil for him to seed his depraved desires: First, new whores every day. Then, splendid and vulgar gatherings with beautiful boys and nubile maidens. Through both young blooms or those impudent creatures ripe to the decadence of his sex, one name reigned supreme, resurfacing time and time again: the skilled poet and lover, Abu Nuwas.

News of this man flowed around the emperor Heliogabalus like streams and rivers. Like a freshly learned word, the ceaseless frequency of his name dribbled out the mouths of many, clergymen and courtesans alike: *Abu Nuwas, defamatory professional; mercurial hedonist; licentious dreamer; who could recite ten thousand ancient poems by heart; Abu Nuwas, who smelled of peppered fragments of the Old World; whose cock was as long as a fishing rod and as thick as a mast; Abu Nuwas, whose cheeks spread in glory like the Ishtar Gate.*

The hetaera described him as having dark, dangling locks and babel eyes.

Babel eyes.

What could that mean? the emperor thought. He did not want to ask the council; unlearned nepotists and dusty old imbeciles. The only answers they divined were from their intellectual ancestors, distilled down into stores of aphorisms, spewed up to club beauty to death with their stupid maxims.

His babel eyes.

Meant it that the poet transcended all languages; was all-knowing —worldly? Meant it that he looked to heaven—ambitious; too high-reaching, proud enough to want to build, to climb that spire to God?

The exoticism of a Bedouin, of opium and odalisque, of hidden treasures of the Old City, of Royal tigers and of Oud, brought from the East, and oh—! the tales of such a brash and beautiful man! Heliogabaus had to have him. Wanted Nuwas to sing his praises. *Needed* him to delight in their bodies pressed together, this champion of vigor.

When Heliogabalus dreamed of this man, covered from his dark hair to the delicate arches of his feet with constellations of rose petals, he woke with a start, pressing softly into his loins.

His spirit is stalking me, he thought.

This man. Who had traveled from the capital of Abbasid Caliphate, a rare diamond in pursuit of pleasure. Orally skilled, in all senses of the word, a flower whose scent could only be matched by his own. Sometimes the most innocuous flowers carried the most beautiful scent.

We will see, he thought, and fetched for him to be summoned like a pail of water.

Abu Nuwas stood at the center of the throne room, gathered bright as a burning sun, his feet bare against the marble. His linens were embroidered with brightly-coloured stripes of indigo and rich verdant that pooled around his wrists and waist. A single thread of gold wove through the fabric, around the nape of his neck and down the front of his tunic. Thin gold rings adorned his lobes.

The Roses of Heliogabalus

Heliogabalus plucked a fruit from a bowl. The ones the servants picked, just for him to watch softly rot. He took a bite and the juices burst out over the pout of his lips, its succulent pulp sliding in between his ivory teeth.

He asked the poet of his background.

"My mother was a seamstress and I do not know my father." Nuwas said, observing the emperor. "And what of you?"

What of me?

Heliogabalus' face twisted into a fierce snarl. How had this lowly court poet not known the extravagance of his cruelty; the extraordinary depravity of his sexual behavior—so debauched he could make the lowliest slaves blush; the child-god who, in defense of becoming tamed, lived a life of decadence and opulence, whose rage rarely found its low tide, where his exquisite reefs of generosity would expose themselves. What was real and what was rumor mattered not. Such salacious tales were made to trail in his afterimage like a signature; but this man, this Abu Nuwas, had not heard of his diverse legacy just entering its bloom of adolescence. Perhaps Nuwas was goading him. He was, after all, a defamatory professional.

Heliogabalus let silence be his response, and stood back a pace, instructing the poet to commence his readings.

Nuwas began reciting the Quran.

"*No*," interrupted Heliogabalus with a raised palm. He fluttered his fingertips. "Give me yours. Your witty verse…your pretty poems."

The stranger looked at him. A slow, strange mirth overtook his eyes. He nearly strangled with laughter.

"The *poems*," the emperor reprised.

Nuwas nodded and began his recitation.

His voice was liquid gold; and out of him flowed a drifting, evanescent rhythmic verse with seductive tempo. Words of roses, cascading lomatia, and violets unraveled from his lips in literary synesthesia. They unfolded as the gentle petals of a butterfly unfurling its powder blue wings.

Heliogabalus closed his eyes but was too enamored to keep them closed for long. With or without sight, the poem enveloped his senses. It was as though he were strolling along the alpine meadows of the

Carpathian Mountains, watching, as honeybees carried the ripe fruit of flowers to their capricious mistress; as though, plucked from flight, he had put one in his mouth and the hum-buzz of its wings was vibrating down his throat and into his belly. The sensation bloomed and decanted into him like a fine wine, a sumptuous floral feast.

He breathed deeply of it as all the scents of the world floated up. Nuwas, reciting poetry; and for *hours*, he recited poetry. *Such stamina!* thought the emperor.

As the poet continued, the emperor's spirits enraptured and ascended in sublime applause. Nuwas' musical cadence awakened in him his aching mind and burning loins, and he could not help but to stroke himself.

Where had he come from; this anachronism, this man who punctured time? This planet, whose gravitational pull might only be matched by his own? Himself, an expansive solar mass confined to the body of a man. The emperor wanted him to want him. Being on the receiving end of desire, thought Heliogabalus, was the closest any man could ever reach to immortality.

When the poet fell quiet, the emperor dropped the peach core and stepped toward him.

"Again," he said. "Something new. For me."

The next poem moved more slowly, fragments of flowers like desert grains of sand bestrewn by soft winds. The emperor circled him, watching with growing desire—this fey boy whose intensity in his eyes, befringed by dark lashes, was only upstood by the softness of his mouth, set in a frame of dangling locks.

Heliogabalus gorged himself on it, feeling himself throb, half-hard beneath his robes.

Suddenly and precariously, Nuwas felt the emperor embrace him from behind, lacing his fingers through his hair and tilting his jaw gently to draw him into a kiss. The poet trembled deliciously, continuing his poem like a creature reaching blindly for words. Hesitantly, unsure at first, then growing in command.

Heliogabalus placed his lips on the poet's neck, and the skin there pulsed. He circled round and pressed Nuwas down, down, down, until his back arched against the steps.

The Roses of Heliogabalus

Nuwas reached up, still reciting, as though half in a fever dream, his melody of spoken word sometimes broken, sometimes altered by kisses, and used his hand to gently squeeze the emperor's cock through his clothes. Heliogabalus fleetingly wondered what made a man such an expert in sex.

He drew the robes down off Nuwas' shoulders and revealed freckles that bedecked his skin, both lovely and unorthodox. He trailed his lips along each one, joining constellations with the honeyed sap from his lips, ensuring he did not miss an asterism between them. Perfect. Who had the hubris to rearrange the stars—gods? Or men?

Nuwas reciprocated, unfolding Heliogabalus from his robes like the spathe off a lily, revealing the swollen spadix enclosed within. His desire ripened as the poet's hands followed the curve of his spine, cupping his ass.

His touch was sublime—truly sublime!

When they were content, Nuwas stretched and lounged alongside him like a cat half-dozing in a bed of roses, lighting an opium pipe.

The emperor loved which sexual and surprising textures the poet anointed his words with; the poetry dripping from his mouth like wine, ushering in seasons of new scents: orange blossom, saffron flower, and rose, like a forbidden garden.

As they lay, the moon climbing to its seat in the heavens, Heliogabalus gazed skyward and could not help returning to the poem, again and again. A few words stuck to him, some syrupy ambrosia. Of dilated eyes and flushed skin, of sacrificial offerings, and honeyed milk and roses, bruised at their edges, cascading from the sky in unbroken waves.

It unfolded before him an irreversible destiny: roses, an orgy; opening to him a new kingdom, where he knew with it what he might do.

With excitement, Heliogabalus abated to sleep beside the radiating warmth of the poet, and when dawn revived him, he knew what he must do.

Sofia Ajram

Each plebeian was to contribute the unadulterated blooms of ten thousand roses. New rulings came into effect where water was precious and scarce: all natural resources were to be redirected from the town to water these fresh gardens. For a time, Rome inhabited the economy of roses. Solely roses, their resinous aroma filling the vestibule of the palace and city streets.

Rose hedges were grown all across the capital. Climbing roses, their canes woven in and out, crawled through the basilica and across building arches. Fortifying walls were built, enclosing the city to shield them from drying winds. Horticulturists were employed to show the regional farmers how to extend their blooming season to even January.

Heliogabalus demanded every space between trees, buildings, and baths be filled with roses, lilies, and violets. Pleasure gardens were encouraged, spread around temples with offerings of roses for the goddess Venus.

Cattle were slaughtered and the viscera of those with favorable omens were used for their high nutritional value to fertilize the roses. When this was not enough, townsfolk were brought in to perform sun dances for genial weather to the Arab-Roman sun god, Elagabal, before they, too, were dispatched. Their blood, a libation; he, their god. And all gods loved the power to give and take life.

Older roses were preserved by being coated in olive oil sediment. Gardens which grew unscented roses were tilled and turned again. The emperor Heliogabalus wanted a perfumed medley; hundred-leaved cabbage rose, and Eglantine imported from Western Asia, grown wild enough to overthrow small buildings.

A beautiful grey-blue foliage enveloped the city walls, dappled with sublime pink and white, their clusters surrounding the corona of beautiful golden stamens. At dawn, roses were cut before the morning dew on their petals could dry.

Designs of roses were to be worn; embroidered with golden thread across scarves and tunics. Fabrics and yarn were dyed pink as the beaches of Crete, and across Rome, it became the season of the rose.

The Roses of Heliogabalus

Which cardinal vice could possibly represent the highest form of excess? Heliogabalus wondered. Lust; gluttony—? Sloth—?

Yes.

He would draw Nuwas into the hedonistic trinity of all three. A man such as he was already a great distance from the heavens; he did not have far to fall.

The emperor gifted the poet ornamental jewelry with which to adorn himself; erotic chains that draped over his abdomen and down between his proud cheeks. Soon after, it would be time.

Within his bedchambers, Heliogabalus snipped at the curls of blonde pubic hair that peeked out the corners of his dress. For the day of the festivities, he wore dainty garlands of gold around his wrists and ankles, a voluminous silk robe, which tied low at his hips and fell open, revealing a soft, hairless abdomen, and a beautiful crown of thorned roses, crafted from thin sheets of metal, petal-thin and set with quartz and lapis intaglio flower buds.

The villa where the festivities were to take place was an open-air theater, like an immense garden rotunda. Arched columns, which seemed to defy gravity held a pink-stained linen veil, which sighed across the room overhead in watercolor frescoes, as a gauzy canopy, or a cloud pregnant with rain. The air ached with fragrance, holding a curious scent, gourmandise, of fresh pepper and floral jam.

It was home, on this night, to as many as it could accommodate; over a hundred guests. The ones on the fringe flocked to the alcoves, crushing rose petals underfoot, urgent to see the wild and drunken revelry. Sultans traveled from far, bearing gifts, knowing a rare entertainment would soon take place.

The real architectural marvel, which dominated the landscape, was in the main court. Amazonite pillars in striking cerulean green, watery with veins, speared overhead. Towards the Far East, where the sun would rise, was ornate, patterned furniture, detailed with carved horses and nacre cherubs; marble columns and hand-stitched rugs and down-feather cushions strewn across the wide open grounds.

Languishing at its center, like flocks of birds, lazed the social elite, the exhibitionists, sacred courtesans and finest sodomites, draped in scarlet and violet clothes of Coan silk.

Sofia Ajram

Their elegant host looked upon it all from a chaise lounge, consuming milk from a crystal horn, and smiled at his own generosity. Such an atmosphere of gratitude; why depart to heaven when he could move heaven to come to him?

At the banquet, they would eat, sleep, wake, and eat some more. The festivities would begin in the middle of night and reach their climax when the sun entered solar noon.

The banquet table was the heart of gastronomic excess. Mouths full of feast; sweet lamb, pheasant, and venison. Canapé of oysters from the coast of Carthage. The udders of pregnant cows, rich, bubbling, consumed together with wine and milk as fair as moonlight. Overflowing vats of shimmering pomegranates and raspberries. Rose syrup, crushed with shaves of mountain ice, combined to make sorbets.

At the center of the revelry was the raven-haired court poet, Abu Nuwas. Anointed with rosewater and adorned in flowing robes as blush as a pressed desert rose and braided with golden thread, the sleeves of his robe cut short, where, spiraled up his arm, serpentine and tight against the muscled tissue, was a gold viper whose teeth crowned a red-black bezel garnet. Baroque pearls, like fragments of light, jeweled along his lobes from hoops of gold. They swayed beneath his black curls, as though caught in an infernal storm.

He looked beautiful, seasoned with divine ingredients, his lips and wrists still bruised from the previous night's passion.

Night grew thin and melted to dawn, a pleasure-filled gathering which sprawled their collective bodies across one another, while others sat, weaving lemongrass into circlets, as though staging an extravagant tableau.

A lavish courtesan lay by Nuwas' feet, covering her supple breasts gingerly with an ivory ostrich feather fan. Reams of quicksilver hair unraveled down her back; soft curls, rich and vivid, as otherworldly twilight with Venusian undertones; chaste, save for a coquettish wildness in her eyes.

As the sun rose, Heliogabalus gestured and Nuwas began his composition. He was to recite the poem which he had created the night of their first congress.

The Roses of Heliogabalus

Together, he and Heliogabalus had refined the poem. Nuwas gazed at him with brilliant, clear eyes. As he rendered the poem, one by one, the bodies began abandoning their garments, shedding their robes like membranes.

Din rose to a dissolute madrigal, dipping in and out of hypnotic harmony; kissing, moaning, tossing their heads in Bacchic frenzy.

A hand glided up Nuwas' calf and twisted like a python around the meat of his thigh as he looked down. The silver-haired courtesan, like a fine horse reined with lace and rose garlands, smiled up at him. His eyes held her body; moon-pale and trembling with an excitement that seemed to spread itself with wild contagion into him. He felt a hand clutch at his back, and another grope his ass. The courtesan ran her hands delicately under his tunic in search of an opening between silk and skin. He had finished his poem, and so, he smiled and assented, sinking to his knees.

Her flesh seemed to dissolve like pearls in wine beneath his fingertips; a caressing deluge, petal-soft and flower-mouthed. So hypnotizing, Abu Nuwas could not resist.

He allowed himself to be drawn down and fell on the luxurious embroidered silk pillows over her reclined body. He sensed a crowd of voyeurs enjoying them and precum sugared the front of his robes like a glittering stain.

The courtesan opened herself, eager to receive, her swollen curves enfolding around him. His tongue danced over her abdomen and he parted her legs enough to reveal the soft downy hair that lay there. Aroused by her desire, he nestled his face into it, stroking the blushed edges of her lips with his thumb. She writhed, curling like a leaf beneath each stroke, until finally, restless enough to move her hand to touch herself, he sucked at her clitoris with such ecstasy-awakened desire, tasting the deep, rich musk there—the scent of a seashell, and with it the songs of the ocean—that she came like a thunderclap. Draping necklaces of cum decorated both their skin like satin; hers, marble-smooth. Once Nuwas had committed to memory the taste of her seashell sex, he raised his head from her groin to begin his poem anew.

The sound of his verse was swallowed by the swell of moans, but still, every time he looked up, he saw Heliogabalus, whose eyes fixed on him. A main dish, a plate Heliogabalus was savouring, craving to finish. And for a moment, there was only the ache, hot and hard and humiliating.

As a hand sheathed Nuwas' groin within its palm, his face warmed and his mouth opened in a small mewl. He tilted his hips as the hand pumped him. It rolled the sleeve of his cock, elation filling his body, spreading out like a stain, like a burst of exploding stars behind his eyes and in his loins, where his pearl seed spilled out and swirled with sweat between the fingertips.

A man's hands held him firmly in place, while the proper amount of hands and mouths wanting and touching, grabbed and sucked all the parts simultaneously. The one sliding into him, fucking him raw, released a song of moans to welcome every thrust. He could feel the finger glide the rest of the way in. Pleasure ran through him like an electric shock. He opened his eyes, half-lidded with ecstasy, and the Roman orgy whirled before him.

He saw one woman reach out and trace another's breast, its pebbled nipple. The recipient arched her back up into her touch. He saw the crushing of silk pillows beneath the coterie of weighty bodies, heavy with desire. His body became a palace, the rooms of which these strangers seemed familiar with; the texture of the walls and columns built of copper skin, sinew and bone. Yes. The glorious Gates of Ishtar. That's what they all said, wasn't it?

Staring in the same direction and reclining on the chaise longue, Heliogabalus gathered his hand beneath his robes, keeping himself engorged. Each time Heliogabalus approached orgasm, Nuwas' eyes, animal-wild, would raise and the emperor would cease his pleasures. His gaze was a startling, wordless exile, sweat plastering his hair across his forehead and cheek. Desire clouded his eyes. Desire made him beautiful. He had the stately charm of a sculptor's creation. *His* creation, Heliogabalus thought.

The bodies moved with feverish urgency. It incited within the emperor a kind of primal fury. Undeniable. They looked so beautiful together, the bliss on Nuwas' face, the courtesan's palm cupping his jaw, her thumb rubbing just beneath his earlobe.

The Roses of Heliogabalus

Bruises blossomed across Nuwas' limbs and ass. He sensed a milky-hot resin pour over the top of his foot. A hungry mouth leaned down and lapped the salt between his toes. A moan resounded in him in deep resonance like a strummed instrument.

The emperor, pleasuring himself beneath his robes could not resist. He stood and wove forward, kneeling before the poet and dusted his fingertips over Nuwas' lips like a candied succade. Limbs sprung like thick vines from around him. Bodies engulfed them, spilling across the floor. The emperor's mouth fell upon Nuwas' throat. And pulling back the poet's robe, off and down his shoulders, oiled with sweat, mouths and tongues lapped at the slit of his cock. Nuwas parted his lips, gasping against the courtesan's neck. The emperor caressed his legs, gently cupping his palm across his ass and kissed whatever skin he could reach.

Soft moans of pleasure faded out, an exodus reduced to a ringing in Nuwas' ears like a lone finger on the edge of a crystal chalice. His senses dilated as in a reverie.

Nuwas had felt this way before. There must've been opium or some sort of hallucinogenic in the wine or olive oil. Perhaps one. Perhaps both—studded or laced in with the amphorae stamped with the emblem of Heliogabalus' profile; the mark of the sun-god. He could name a list of delicacies the emperor had not laid his hands on, which had been passed around the room.

With such an immense feast, Nuwas' own body had taken to it slowly, distilled it into his blood so that he felt shipwrecked within his own senses. A refugee of desire, hungry for touch.

Again, Heliogabalus murmured, breath hot against his ear. The poet felt some kind of pull to obey.

Nuwas began his third recital, the words a spell. This poem in excess, repeated three times, as though to summon, though their speaker blind and inattentive; aware of only the concerto movement of bodies against his skin. The sensation of touch lit his veins aglow. Every stroke was more sensual than anything he'd ever encountered across his travels. He felt warm, not suffocated, but filled with light. Like he was a small satellite planet drawn in to kiss the surface of the sun. And it made him feel bold and beautiful that it was kissing him back.

Nuwas reached out a hand, to kiss and caress the center of his heavens, and the emperor stepped back as though to refrain from filthy lust; as though provoked by some mood; as though to say: you, the sphere to which the stars revolved; you: the temple of my desires; you: a holy instrument tuned by god;

you: my favorite.

Heliogabalus receded against his chaise longue and watched. Like the sea would lap at the moon, so, too, would these rising tides lap at his feet; he, the phosphorescent sun; and they, the soft, roiling ocean of skin. At that, he would have all that he could stomach: the bliss of a mob, reaching for him, granting him the infinite paradise of love.

Yes, he thought, watching them. Chaos was poetry realized. And he was there to revive the permanence of chaos. As the garden, before the fall.

And upon this mantle, he performed the sacred gesture. As Nuwas reached that final line once more, and concluded his poem, the group reached the acme of lust.

Nuwas was too far gone to hear the bell sounding to open the veils beneath the sky. He had forgotten that they had been holding that mystifying sea of rose petals.

A sudden golden sunlight streamed through the veils. He winced as the vault of heaven wheeled above him, but he could not keep his eyes raised for long. Plumes of color spread like fireworks behind his eyes, and as the sun crested to its zenith, burning like a celestial fire, a new pigment bloomed forth.

Pink;

in all its flush hues, no longer behind, but in front of—all around, and covering his golden-brown shoulders and hips, and across his obsidian hair. They moved tenderly, falling in graceful motions across the bodies writhing in ecstasy. A baptism of petals, the purest of decadence, in ravishing blooms of padparadscha.

A delicate foam of petals covered them, falling more and more. As he sensed them blanket his skin, a vertiginous feeling overtook him. He opened his eyes but it didn't help. Too much color and movement.

The Roses of Heliogabalus

Smears of pink wavered at the edge of his vision, a cornucopia of petals.

His arousal was suddenly tinged with fear.

What—

The word choked in his throat. He could no longer move his body, he thought, with sudden alarm.

He lay prostrate as petals blotted out the sky, warming the air around them. When he opened his lips, they filled his mouth.

Petals fell and fell, cascading in whirls, showering down and blanketing the enraptured revellers. Puddles formed around bodies, as volcanic soil, creating new islands; a breast here, a raised hip there, the small curve of an ear as a hidden island reef.

And then they grew: to lakes, to oceans, enveloping everything like a rising tide, an endless sea of roses, guests choking and gasping for air. Petals entered their lungs; petals played at their mouths. Cavities of flesh filled with flower upon flower in floral carnage.

Petals misted the air; so much so that when Nuwas inhaled, they would fill him with their bedewed essence. They fell in exquisite sublimation, from the one to the many, blessing them in currents of fragrance.

Sweat, blood and oil jeweled the bodies, so that, elate with mania, Nuwas could not lift himself from the deluge of skin. He tried to raise himself, then fell and broke, slipping in what he thought was semen, before looking down to see a bloom of red rush in and tint his vision.

Wild thorns were raking his skin, blushing like a fever, blood racing across his stomach. Undoubtedly, the emperor had left some with their thorns, verdant green to divide the pink, spreading like blood clots.

One snared his ankle, tearing away a wet strip of flesh and Nuwas cried out. Petals dissolved their cum to dawn-coloured jelly. His body haemorrhaged starlike and pollen-thick particles between the stipple of beauty marks along his skin.

As much as he tried to clamber to the top of the bodies, he found himself incapable. Billows of soft tissue pulled him down, mouths consecrating him with honeyed kisses, as hands transgressed into his body.

Sofia Ajram

He felt delirious, like a soul burrowing through the womb's lining to directly bathe in the earth's atmosphere. The petal waves frayed the edge of him, making him into a soft sculpture, smaller and smaller, to fit in the palm of Heliogabalus' hand. He felt at the emperor's mercy.

When Nuwas looked up, he could see no raging or thrashing. He only saw twisted expressions, impossible to read. Difficult to divide pleasure from pain, cries of delight from those of terror.

He witnessed Heliogabalus in blazing infernal magnificence, watching with passive detachment; death, tonight's entertainment. Eyes verging on burnt gold. Nuwas could neither read his expression—boredom? Indifference?

What had the emperor expected from the banquet—that their screams would be excessive? Was this the quiet consequence of decadence; this apogee of beauty?

Perhaps Nuwas understood. Death, the ancient antidote. Beauty and death and gluttony and lust; Heliogabalus had made it so that Nuwas' tongue—the language of the poet—would distill to its essence and combine with the beauty of the masses. Like this, Nuwas, too, would be loved. Adored. He would be beautiful.

Let no season run truly empty, he thought. *Let there be roses for always.*

Heliogabalus gathered them before they could spoil. Distilled them into an oil; mashed all the corpses together with the roses, extracting the most saccharine perfume, his prize to be won.

A sieve of people passed through a thousand times until what remained was a refined purity of souls.

Here, reduced to aspic, to oil, they would occupy compressed space. All the worship and sacrifice. Pulverized and effervescent. Reminiscent of a diamond. For whatever could sate the gluttony of a god?

He uncapped the vial and inhaled deeply of the scent. Through all the rose, he could still smell it, then. The aromatic note of Nuwas' saffron skin. The smell of it alone made his cock throb and swell. He

The Roses of Heliogabalus

knew then, for centuries after, that the crushed petals and oil from the mouth of the poet would be sold on the black market as an aphrodisiac; high value, like all the most rare and lavish things. The sweetest fragrance.

He dabbed it on his wrist, then sealed the glass cap onto the vial, and returned it to the shelf amongst the dust-covered others.

The Leatherman
Darren Black

Jesus faced
Faced down
Down-low
Low as a moan
Moans a word
Word like fate
Fate the twist
Twist in wind
Wind of lash
Lash to back
Back and forth
For the effect
Affects his heart
Heartfelt flow
Flow to spine
Spine to bone
Bones of hips
Hip to thigh
Thighs to calves
Calves bulge boots

Darren Black

Boots to ground
Grounded he waits
Weight of his days
Dazed with bites
Bites of the whip
Whip snake wraps
Wraps him afraid
Frayed at the nerves
Nerves he unwinds
Wine of his blood
Bleeds with tears
Tears to atone
A tone he knows
Knows from the sting
Stings out the grief
Grief he now sings

Little Saddleslut Grows Up
Avra Margariti

There were once three sisters spinning flax, and they said, "Whosoever spindle falls, let us kill and eat her."

I was not the girl who got eaten, but the girl who ate. The girl who devoured, despite my early resistance to the meat crossing the threshold of my mouth. Maro, they called me in my village, and the shit-filthed saddle where I once lived through my grief. Stachtomaro, Stachtomaritsa, Little Saddleslut.

But I am that girl no longer. All grown up now, running away from my village, my mother's bones, my sisters' remains, the church that to this day still mourns them and my monstering.

I have gotten myself a decent apartment, a data entry job in the city, a good reputation among my colleagues, even a long-term girlfriend. Nektaria, she is called, sweet as the nectar of her name. Yet, whenever we kiss, all I can imagine is her blood bathing me like a russet absolution.

In our queen-size bed where the silk sheets smell of lavender fabric softener, Nektaria writhes in ecstasy, not knowing my predicament. How my mouth longs for her flesh like a toothache begging for relief. How her supple body against mine rouses something primal in me; it summons the ocher-painted Lascaux caves, the saber tooth tiger chased by the prehistoric hunter. And more images still: figures run through the forest past the city borders, predators chase prey through pine needles and coily ferns.

The musk of my memories surges through my bloodstream. I am alive and an animal, floating out of my head with need. So intense that, when Nektaria exposes her unmarred neck, I bite down on instinct, and draw blood.

The sisters I cooked and ate, the maternal bones I worshiped, the past immortalized in scarlet-scrawled fairytale pages—everything rustles a red tune in my ravening belly. *You will never be free of this need, the dowry we left you and your beloved.* The stories got this part wrong—the body count. How hunger will always beget more hunger. How, for victim to turn victor, one must give in to the sweet meat-song.

Later, after I have cleaned Nektaria's neck wound while she kissed my apologies away, I lie awake between the cooling bed sheets. I look at my sleeping Nektaria. The girl who found me when I was fresh in the city and lost through its glittering labyrinthine streets; who took one look at me and said, *you're not from around here, are you? You're strange—I think I'd like to keep you.*

She curls around me in sleep, so trusting and pliant despite my biting earlier—my *monstering*. I brush the curls away from her face, tuck her in as she sighs sweet as elderberry wine. *No harm done,* her last words before sleep.

But the harm is done. The harm is inside me, and it wants out. No longer am I the girl who eats the ones closest to her. I do not cower on my outdoors saddle, covered in ash, bird shit, and gold woven like flax out of mother's bone marrow.

The bite mark glistens on Nektaria's neck, beneath her flaxen hair. I look away.

Phone turned on protected mode, I seek the apps where girls with strange appetites go to find those with compatible desires. Little forests of depravity etched in a vast city of need.

Nektaria and I love each other. So what if I want to bite and she does not wish to be bitten, chased, hurt?

For her sake, I will find someone who will let me.

Little Saddleslut Grows Up

I try the clubs first. Underground dungeons with a steel-and-leather mouthfeel permeating the incense-perfumed air. The public floors and private playrooms are strewn with wooden crosses, riding crops, and other implements and devices where body fluids have seeped through the materials over the years. The women's faces blur together. They adopt names like Amelia, Lorelei, Cicely, Pandora. They smile at me coyly, artificial sweetness unlike my Nektaria's honeyed radiance. And under the girls' veneer of innocence, their own hunger thrums pulse-like and subcutaneous. A hunger calling to mine like a crimson-writ song. A meat-song.

We go over the basics. Do you want to be hurt? How much? Where? Will you let me?

I don a pair of vampire gloves, supple kidskin leather covered in tiny spikes all over, like a rose garden decided to lend me its thorns in order to prick beautiful maidens' skin caught in my ropes.

I wonder, do these girls picture someone else in my place, the way my mind conjures my unwitting girlfriend? Do they wish their own partners could learn to shed shame and repression enough to give them the relief they crave, the exaltation through pain?

I bring my spike-gloved palms down on unmarred expanses of skin. Watch blood vessels burst, bruises and pinpricks of red raised to the surface. My teeth follow, worrying at the marked flesh until it transforms from a dawn-pink cirrus to a caliginous cumulonimbus.

My mouth fills with it—the thunder-steel aroma. The red-meat taste.

I remember being younger, back in my old village. How we wove flax for meager coin, and my hungry sisters said, *let us eat*. How mother dropped her spindle from her arthritis-aching fingers, the first to lose our cruel game, and I said, *no*. I screamed: *Please, not her!* My two elder sisters ate of mother's body anyway, crooning through flesh-filled mouths, *she is old, she's only holding us back*. I had no choice but to follow, then to harm my sisters in turn. Oh, I remember still the taste of mother's bones as I suckled them like a teething babe, gorging myself in the filth of my own grief and guilt.

Avra Margariti

Little Saddleslut, Little Saddleslut.

"Maro," the girls all say afterward, held perfunctory in my arms during our wind-down session. "Let's do this again soon."

I look at them. Amelia, Lorelei, Cicely, Pandora. But not my Nektaria. My girl who doesn't know what past I run from. That I am fleeing still, and always will.

"Yes," I say, stroking with cool hands the flesh I marked. "Let's."

Already, I can tell I won't be returning to the clubs. The bounty they offer is not enough to sate my hunger.

Next, I find the encrypted ads. Girls asking for someone to roleplay with them in an immersive setting. They want to be Red Riding Hood and I, the Wolf, chase them cross-country through the woods. Catching them and straddling them against the underbrush. My mating bite on their shoulder turns them into wolves themselves, liberated from decorum. Others are more sensitive cases. Girls who had once been stalked or kidnapped, needing to recreate their harrowing experiences on their own terms. Those near-final girls want me to wear an old boyfriend's flannel shirt and cap, or brandish a dead uncle's hunting rifle.

I am up to the task. I can chase and catch those girls begging for their blood to be tasted, their limits to be tested. Afterward, the women plan therapy sessions about how best to deal with the trauma re-visited in our play.

But what about my own bad memories? The forest that stretches so deep and dark and similar to the woods encompassing my old village?

I come back to Nektaria's bed with my taste for blood sated, but my memories unsettled. After nights spent running in the woods, my emotions are like a frayed nerve, an open wound.

Little Saddleslut sat in her filth, Little Saddleslut spun marrow into gold, Little Saddleslut will never outgrow the feel of familial flesh between her teeth.

"You smell of the forest," Nektaria mumbles as I slip into bed beside her. My body is cold from my outdoor shower—my vain

Little Saddleslut Grows Up

attempt to erase the women and the blood and the trauma. Yet, Nektaria still smells it all: the smoke and leather, the blood and fir.

She burrows her drowsy head into my neck, where my pulse thumps like a feral thing under her lips. I cannot tell if it's due to perpetual fear, or leftover exhilaration.

I kiss her forehead, tasting her sweat's succulent salt. It's a comfort I doubt I deserve.

"You keep running away from me," Nektaria murmurs.

Before I can think of a reply—where I go, what I do, does she hate me?—she has settled against me, falling into trustful sleep.

The girls I chase can be sweet and fun. They can text me, *get home safe*, after our nights together despite them knowing what I'm capable of. They can make me feel like a useful monster, after I've given them the growling catharsis they are after. But they can never *be* her.

They can never be my girl.

And so my hunger is not sated, but multiplied.

This is my family's inheritance—a dowry of meat and need, woven flax-like through my genetic code.

I can only trick my hunger to save my girl, whose pulse calls to me like the sweet nectar of her name. Falling asleep around dawn, I dream of city and forest and need.

In my dream, my sisters order me to eat our frail, old mother. Though I resist at first, I do not resist for long. In my dream, I lie in my saddle's filth and weave all the frayed threads and broken fragments within myself into gold. In my dream, I hack my sister-torturers to pieces and cook them over the fire. I flee into the night with my bounty of shit transmuted into gold, yet I cannot weave this hunger into quenching, only a quickening of my core.

I wake up drenched in sweat, my drool dribbling over Nektaria's bare shoulder, as if I'm seconds away from devouring her in sleep.

Moisture sticks my underwear to my skin. My core throbs and dilates, like it's giving birth to my hunger. A need, spindle-sharp and spinning, spinning me out of control.

Nektaria startles awake. I am about to apologize, choked by the dregs of my shame, when she smiles under a mantle of moonlight.

Her thumb caresses my cheek, circles rhythmic and concentric like a tree's primordial rings. "You're not running again. Tonight, you're taking me out on a date."

When I hesitate, she pouts. "Say yes."

And I do.

I go numbly through the motions of everything I once adored doing with Nektaria. Getting dolled up for a night out in the city, her in her velvet dress and high heels, me in my three-piece suit and blackened boots. Another memory: back in my old village, the priest's son had tried to force my hand in marriage, claiming I had left a shoe in his house. He shoved my dirty, bare foot into the shoe and claimed it fit me perfectly, now he must marry me, to push the pagan out, and purge my hunger.

Nektaria twirls before the mirror, round and round while the mossy notes of her floral perfume assault my nose. A forest scent.

I did not eat the priest's son, the one who thought himself a prince riding in to save me from my depravity. There was nothing palatable about his arrogance; his spoiled-meat musk could never have quenched my hunger.

Nektaria pulls me in front of the mirror. At least this time, I don't have to pretend when my arms encircle her soft stomach, squeezing her tight enough to comfort us both.

"You never talk to me anymore, Maro," she sighs. More grief than grievance.

"It's hard," I say. "I don't want you to hate me."

"How could I ever?"

And still, I swallow my words the way I once swallowed my sisters' cruel, wagging tongues.

On our way to the restaurant, Nektaria holds my hand in the cab's backseat. Our pulses mingle in a pas-de-deux that has no right making my gums throb like heartbeats.

She looks glorious under candlelight, the way it glints off the diamond ring I bought her after my latest promotion at work. Dainty, even as she digs with gusto into her steak dinner. Nektaria's pretty, red

Little Saddleslut Grows Up

mouth forms words, but I can no longer hear her voice. My teeth tear into my own rare steak, as deliriously as a mangy dog gone unfed for far too long. My fingers slip wet with blood and succulent juices as I grip the steak, ripping flesh from bone, and sucking on the marrow until it coats my tongue. A rumble starts in my throat and traverses my being, incandescent.

I jerk out of my fugue state to realize every patron and waiter in the restaurant stares at us, wide-eyed at my wild manners.

Beseeching, I turn my gaze to Nektaria. I flinch away when her clean hand tries to touch my dirty one.

"I'm sorry," I say, my voice gone to guttural growls. "I'm so sorry, I can't do this anymore."

You don't deserve this.

I push my chair backward so hard that it clatters to the ground. I scramble away from our table, my girl, and the restaurant that was supposed to rekindle our affections.

"Maro!" she calls after me.

Stachtomaritsa. Stachtomaro. Little Saddleslut.

I run panting into the feral night that swallows me, and I do not look back.

My ramshackle hotel room is home to bug detritus and waste barely scrubbed clean. The walls look scabrous with it. In a way, I am back where I began. Back on a saddle dressed in filth, mourning the bones of my mother cradled against my chest, then inside my stomach. Eating my sisters, not to keep their remains as a memento mori inside me, but to rid the world of their inner filth even as their skin stretched unmarred and pristine. The perfect little church ladies to my heathen corruption.

I do not think about Nektaria back in our apartment, searching the rooms for clues of my wrongness, or perhaps being angry enough to erase all signs of me from our lives. I do not return her calls, for how do I explain a past of flax and bone even I don't fully understand?

Perhaps coming to the city had been a mistake. The forest calls to

151

me still. While my hotel neighbors are fucking and the bedbugs are fucking and my fucking broken heart feels about to explode in a burst of red, red meat, I visit the apps again. They're the only thing left to soothe the pain in my gums that pulsate like a teething baby's. Yet nothing can soothe that other, deeper agony inside my chest, the one that urges me to abstain from sweetness if I cannot have Nektaria. To only live bitter and sour, to sate the base needs of me but never seek inner peace.

In the apps, I look for a girl who wants to be bitten into like steak, wants to be chased by a feral, mangy dog with a taste for flesh, wants to be caught and fucked, no questions asked.

A girl who will wear my teeth-marks with pride come morning.

My breath frosts the pre-dawn air as I wait in the forest fringes. I'm still dressed in my dapper suit from dinner—an accidental departure from my usual hiking boots and running gear. Soon it will be time for the chase. So why not shed this city-skin of civility I first donned when I moved here? Nothing good has come of it; nothing good stays. I know this now. So I undress myself despite the chill nipping at my heels. I drop down on all fours, then roll around in the dirt until my bare skin is thoroughly coated in soil, animal waste, and the forest's rot of decomposition.

It feels purer, this filthy new skin. More authentic than anything I have tried to wrap myself in since trading village for city.

I take my phone out of my clothes bundle to read the app's encrypted messages one final time. The girl with the username *sweetsinphony_* told me not to check in with her before our game of prey and predator. Once her rabbit-white dress came into fleeting, fleeing focus, she said, I should give chase.

And I do.

The air whistles sharp in my panting mouth. The forest twigs and stones break my skin as if trying to bloodlet me. Purify me into something brand new. In the advancing dawn light, the girl is fast and

Little Saddleslut Grows Up

sure through the forest. She runs with a wild abandon none of my previous play partners have ever matched.

She smells so sweet, perfume mixed with musk and rising adrenaline. My core is wet with it, moisture streaming down my legs like morning dew as I run. I catch glimpses of her, hummingbird-quick. A high giggle crests her chest, lost in its own exultance. Her face is concealed under a Venetian mask of scarlet velvet. Her flaxen hair drives my addled brain incandescent with need. There is a peculiar grace to this girl's movements, one I find almost familiar through my meat-crave haze. The slobbering of my gums.

The girl vaults over verdure, twisted tree roots, and paths choked by pine needles. Then, she stops amid a purple-flowered glade bathed in dawn. My meat hunger and elevated heartbeat are both forgotten for a second. The girl wasn't supposed to stop until I caught her, those were the rules.

I wonder if there's something wrong. If it would make me a true monster to keep going now without checking in.

"Well?" the girl says as I pant, only for my breath to be snatched by birdsong coalescing into her familiar cadence.

In the vanishing act of adrenaline, my skin chills. My sweat sours. "Nektaria… It's you?"

"Aren't you going to catch me?" she asks, slow-twirling in the glade like a dancer in a music box, her Venetian mask fallen to join the wildflowers.

She looks serene and smug, my girl, this woman I thought I lost through my wickedness.

"I'm sorry," I say, and the earth shifts under my shame. "I'm so sorry. I never meant to hurt you—"

"Oh, hush," Nektaria says, and suddenly she's the one taking control, tackling me to the ground. I have been caught at last, there between the wildflowers. "I've always wanted this. You would have noticed, if you weren't so busy running away from me."

"I wasn't running from you." Despite my hunger, my lips only kiss her forehead, licking the sweat of her brow. Not biting yet, even as she straddles me, poised to grind against my groin with a mischievous tilt of her chin. "I was running from myself. My past."

My sisters and mother and the flax we had once spun together, in a village a lifetime and a fairytale away.

"I must tell you…" I trail off. Must explain. Must keep her from leaving me. Yet I was the one who left, and she, the one who found me once more.

"Later, Maro. When you're ready. I can be patient, for you, only for you."

She brings my hand to her throat, directs my teeth toward her sweet-thrumming pulse.

We are animals then. We are nibbling and nipping, rolling like a mated pair in the grass, tearing at each other. Nektaria sheds her dress like a second shredded skin until she is bare before me. She sighs for more, *more,* while the soil mixes with our sweat, and the forest turns to mud with our need. It streaks her sticky body, and mine.

Little Saddleslut, they called me, lying in my saddle's filth of familial grief.

Yet I am not dirtying her, I realize. I am setting Nektaria free, the way I was too self-pitying to notice she craved all along. We are not so different from each other, after all.

The forest smells of chlorophyll and sex. Nektaria moans sweet as loam and birdsong. I grind up against her with animal heat, animus need. My teeth sink deep into her shoulder, to lap at secret inner wounds. The dew on the grass evaporates only to be replaced by the libations of our bodies as the sun rises to bless our union. Everything is out in the open now, a bleeding relief laid bare. A dark fairytale budding between us—palimpsest of scars from stories past.

I touch her golden hair in the afterglow. It flows like flax spun between my fingers. Memory stings still, but it is now tempered; a sacred pain.

My girl smiles at me, sweet as the nectar of her name.

I kiss her again and smile back as I grab hold of her flaxen hair, and tenderly *pull.*

White & Wolf
Marisca Pichette

White.
She is vicious. White teeth parade across her face, a plaster skin mask, seeing-holes black pits with a glimmer of something like sky on the inside. Her bones pitch the angles of her body like tent-poles. She leans.

Wolf.
Her tongue tires of lolling. It retreats into her throat to taste leftovers, regret. She fills herself on foolishness, her stomach crowded by the delicate foot bones of so many wrong feet. She rolls off the bed, her grandmother's fur strewn across the floor in matted tufts, and takes the sheet in her mouth. Its corner carves a path in the dust.

White.
Sharpening the knife over her knee at the kitchen sink, her hands knotted with tension, paled by scars. She has never eaten so much, never purged so little. Poppies and cornflowers on the wallpaper,

Marisca Pichette

magpies perch on the sill. Black eyes watch as she removes her mask, laying it on linoleum to stay clean as she skins the next limb.

Wolf.

Keeping the perimeter empty is her task. She wears a path around the cabin, her feet disturbing rotted leaves as she circles, circles, circles. Five-gallon buckets shed plastic chips on the dirt, stacked in a wall behind her. Stretched skins cast near-human shadows in the afternoon, drying into something White will use, something Wolf will want.

White.
The seventh skull is finally picked clean. She places it in the cupboard next to tins of tuna and baked beans. Untying her apron, she readjusts her mask, plaster rough against scarred skin. Her hair is gone, burned away. She sits in the evenings with a needle, carefully felting a wig from grandmother's fur.

Wolf.

She eats apples for dinner. Sometimes White carves them into a pie, adding honey and bread. The meat she turns to stew, and Wolf tries to forget the pieces bobbing in its depths, broth brown like the churned-up waters of the pond behind the cabin.

White.
On a clear day she sees the charred ruins of the castle, stricken masonry bones one hillside away. A finger of forest separates the cabin from the past. She thinks about the matches in her hands, the door she

White & Wolf

didn't expect to be locked, blocking her escape. Revenge came at the price of her face.

Wolf.
She found White after, burned, starved. The cabin was a refuge for them both, but it was not empty.

White.
Seven men stood between her and the future. Between her and Wolf. White lost her beauty, but she still had her knife.

Wolf.
She made the mask for White. Molded it over the skull of the first of seven men White killed so that she and Wolf might have a place to live. The first man tried to rape White. The second killed grandmother, wore her skin to bed. The final five were like the people of the castle: necessary.

White.
At night she lies in bed, wearing her mask. Through the seeing-holes she watches spiders weave webs between beams. Wolf lies beside her, each breath keeping her moored to time. Without her, White would be adrift, melted hands wrapped around an empty stomach.

Wolf.
The night White cooked the rapist, Wolf found her kneeling over the toilet

> bowl. Wolf flushed his memory away and unearthed plaster in the basement. Her touch left streaks in the white, scratches.

White.
She finishes her wig sitting outside, her feet crammed in steel-toed boots stained with oil and blood. Wolf stalks the edge of the cabin, apple in her jaws. White positions the wig on her head, warm and soft as Wolf's body beside her in bed each night. She looks at Wolf. Wolf bites the apple in two.

> Wolf.
> Grandmother hides in the corners of the cabin, clumps dropped from the murderer's coat as he tried to escape White's knife. Everywhere her scent remains. Wolf sits beside White and smells her. Plaster, sweat, fur. Something of her memory is lost, pushed aside to make room for a deeper present.

White.
She leans on Wolf. They walk back inside, limping into something that might endure. Wolf thins, White fills out at last. When they reach the kitchen, she draws the curtains over the sink. Pale and soft, worked from the finest skin. She sets her knife aside.

> Wolf.
> She walks with White to the fire. White sits as she stirs the coals to life. She has not touched fire since the castle, just as Wolf has not touched meat since her grandmother lay with a man and never awoke. She coaxes

White & Wolf

new warmth from the embers, a poker pinched in her jaws. When flames rise again, she sits back with White, head cradled in her lap.

White.
Wig, mask. She has never been more of herself than she is now. As the fire warms her feet she takes a cake from the purse she sewed from his skin and breaks it in two. She feeds one half to Wolf and takes the other for herself, savoring the taste of honey.

A Kiss with Thorns
K. M. Carmien

1

Everyone knows how the rose-rot kills.

Smell, first. Everything stinks of the flower, heady and sweet, from rotting meat to your true love's hair.

Second, hunger. The victim eats everything: dirt, their own flesh if deprived too long, and cannot be sated. Some try to starve the sufferer, like one sweats out a fever—it only kills faster.

Third and last, if they live so long: they seek the castle. The rot's birthplace, so it's said. The ruin sits at the air dome's edge, just on the border of the blasted wastes, where the atmosphere is too thin for any but the rotted to breathe; it spears the sky alone and foundering in its thicket of briar roses, blazing red and rust. And the rotted make their pilgrimages, for no reason they can tell.

Nobody ever mentions the dreams.

2

Vanya dreams of an impossible lake, here where water is dearer than diamonds, and pale sand painted in wavey streams of red and violet and burning orange by the seven-banded moon, and her.

Princess by the shore, mirage, daemon lover. Her red hair falls like a curtain around them as she bends to kiss Vanya, blocking out the moon and the pinprick stars, and their mouth opens under hers as easy as a rout. They hook a leg through hers and hold her closer, yes Vanya just like that Vanya yes.

It isn't real, they know it isn't real because the water smells of itself and the princess smells of petrichor, and they can inhale without tasting rose.

They lie back together, when they're done, her head pillowed on Vanya's shoulder, her hand resting over their heart.

"Promise me you won't get lost," she says. Her fey, fever-bright eyes are glassy and unfocused, like someone thinking of something far away. "So many of you get lost."

"I won't," says Vanya. They don't ask so many of who. Asking her questions in this mood never works.

(The first time they dreamed her, after they put the rose-spores under their tongue so they could reach the castle and burn out its heart, she said, it's been so long since anyone has been here, how did you get here? and they said, where? And she laughed, a laugh like bells, the sweetest sound Vanya ever heard.)

"And I have to ask you one more thing. I know I ask you so much already, but I must, truly. I wouldn't if it wasn't important. Will you?"

"Of course."

"Remember—" She leans in, so that her mouth nearly brushes the shell of their ear, and murmurs three syllables. A name. The whole of it, the shape, slips away—but not the syllables. "You must, Vanushka."

3

Waking, Vanya walks the old road, the king's road, beneath the merciless eye of the sun. Their stomach twists inside them. The hunger passed the point of pain three mile markers back; now, a live thing, it tries to tear itself from Vanya from the inside out. But they can't eat yet; they need to save their food. This close to the castle, it isn't safe to enter villages for supplies. People shoot the rose-ridden on sight here, and Vanya can no longer hide their infection.

The king's road stretches long and straight, from the city where Vanya was born to the castle.

Once upon a time, a shuttle could have carried Vanya the entire length in a matter of days, but the last of those machines died long ago. The road would stall a shuttle now anyway; the black surface warps and bubbles up, here sunken, there crumbled away entirely. The guard-posts stand empty, animals nest in the refueling stations. Scrub pushes up through the cracks.

And Vanya walks, and walks, eyes fixed on the red mountain in the distance, while behind them a pyre of the infected stains the sky with smoke.

"Vanya," she says—not by the lake, this time. Steel and glass and a strange, vertiginous blue sky; leaning gray towers like broken teeth marching endlessly away on a plain of green-scudded water.

Broad-leafed vines climb the towers, but nothing else seems to live there, nothing moves but Vanya and her. A warm, heavy breeze buffets them through the broken window. "How long has it been?"

"How long since what?"

"Since we opened the door."

"I don't know what you mean."

She bites her lip and looks away. She looks so small, here in this huge arched room. Vanya feels small. Feels strange, and lost, an insect rattling around some incomprehensible machine. "I don't mean to be ungrateful," she says quietly, "This is better than being dead. It's only—"

4

They put a hand on her shoulder, carefully, as if she were a wild thing who might run. "Maybe," they say, "You don't have to be grateful. For whatever it is, I mean." The words feel inadequate, utterly clumsy, but they can be, can't they? It's just a dream.

(Isn't it?)

"No?" A nameless expression ripples over her face. Something of pain, something of amusement, something sweet and aching. "I don't want to talk about this anymore," and her fingers tangle in the front of their shirt and drag them in to kiss her, and the pair of them tumble gracelessly onto the concrete. Vanya doesn't care about the tooth-rattling jolt as they hit, doesn't care about the rough scrape against their palms or the cold, only kisses back, and nothing, nothing else matters.

Two mile markers later, Vanya cracks.

They kneel at the side of the road to take a drink of water, just one mouthful, but their fingers find the hunk of mushroom bread instead, and as if the hand belongs to someone else, bring it to their mouth. They gulp it in one bite. And—

Can't stop.

The wild thing of their hunger rears up, tears through the loose mushrooms, sucks down the mushroom powder, the cricket bars. They snatch up fallen crumbs and dirt from the road itself, a stray millipede, flecks of gravel. Their teeth tear a hunk of brittle nail from their finger and they eat that too and suck down the blood. It all tastes of rose-scent.

A Kiss with Thorns

Vanya collapses on their side in the lengthening afternoon, chest heaving, vision blurring, and hungers still.

An older dream, the third or fourth time they saw her, they don't remember:

5

A garden run wild, gray-white stone walls and pillars crumbling under a riot of green, and flowers, so many flowers, dozens of shapes but every one red. They sit under a vine-strangled dome held up by columns carved with blurry faces (screaming, or laughing; the eyes move if Vanya looks too long), and on a long bench beside them lies their lover, feeding them berries. The berries stain her fingers red as her lips, and taste of air.

"I know it isn't fair," she says, "How far yet you have to go, what it's doing to you."

"It isn't so bad yet," replies Vanya.

She shakes her head, and gives them another berry. "You won't say that later. You'll regret this."

"That's what my mother said," they answer without thinking. *You're going to die and for what?*

You think you alone can stop this? You think you'll be a hero? That's a story, Vanya! The bite in her voice, not quite sharp enough to hide her tears. Her hands in pale-knuckled fists. *You stupid selfish child.*

"Your mother." She pronounces the word like it's in a language she doesn't know. "What's she like?"

"She's—" Vanya shuts their eyes a moment. "She's stubborn. She cares so much, about everything, but not in a soft way. She won't stop, ever, when she's doing the right thing."

"I don't think she would like me, then."

"Why?"

Her mouth twists into something like a smile but empty, a thin sardonic curve. "I'm the most selfish person alive, Vanya. I'm selfish, and fickle, and I haven't ever done the right thing, not once."

"That's not true!"

"Should I be flattered you think well of me, or angry that you called me a liar?" Vanya sputters, and the not-smile dissolves into a peal of laughter. "Oh, you're just the loveliest thing, I so hope I get to keep you forever."

6

And the time after that:

"Is this real?"

"Mm, wrong category, my love. Real, dream—" She holds out a hand and tilts it from side to side. The white sheets, some smooth shining material she called silk, slide down around her shoulders, bearing the purple marks of Vanya's love bites on her shoulders and green-veined throat. Around them, the walls are pale and fuzzy, unfocused. "Those aren't words that apply."

"Yes, but."

"You can touch me, can't you?" She drops her hand to Vanya's side, trails a nail down to the curve of their hip. They shiver. "See? Why does a word like real matter?"

Oh, it matters, it matters more than almost anything—but Vanya is too lost to say why.

Almost three mile markers after they eat everything—hard to say what the jagged, broken spear of rock leaning at the side of the road means —four shadows cross the road.

A moment later their masters follow, clubs and scavenged plastic shivs at the ready. Two in front. Two behind. Vanya should have noticed—should've heard the birds fall silent, should've heard the footsteps—but the blood roaring in their ears and the stink of roses blinkered them. They rock back a half-step, raise their hands. The pale afternoon sun shines right in their eyes at this angle.

The one who seems like the captain, a rangy woman half a head taller than Vanya, smiles an empty smile. "Give us that pack. Nice and slow. Nobody gets hurt and we can all go home."

A thin, shrill laugh prickles at the back of Vanya's throat. Because they can't, of course, not ever; wherever they go, whatever happens, that road is closed forever. And if they lose their tools—the

7

machete, real metal; the city-made matches; the kerosene—then they might as well die here. Their journey comes to nothing.

Slowly, slowly, Vanya puts up a hand to shield their eyes. "Please," they say, not because they expect begging to help, just to buy time. There's a gap between the captain and the man on her left. If Vanya's fast enough, sure enough—

They break left.

Too slow.

A club catches them in the back of the knee and they go sprawling. They grab for their machete and one of the bandits slams a bootheel down on their hand with a sick crunch that spears up their arm; a kick snaps their head sideways, and the world flickers black and light-spotted. With their good hand they haul themselves to the edge of the road. The bandit captain's knee slams into their chest, pinning them in the dust, and her fist flattens their nose. The snap fills their head.

Choking on blood, Vanya thinks, *not like this*, thinks, *Mother, I'm sorry, I'm sorry.*

Thinks a name.

Their mouth shapes each syllable, soundless. A prayer. If it's the last thing, a good last thing, her green eyes, her fingers in their hair, her smile, her voice.

And their throat burns and heaves and roils, pain stabbing across their palate, their tongue. Bulges, cutting off their air. Can't breathe can't scream, can't think, can't move—

A rose sapling heaves itself free of Vanya's mouth in a spray of crimson and bile.

Whippy branches, scab-color blossoms, finger-length thorns burying themselves in the captain's arm. She screams and throws herself back, too late, too slow. One of the other bandits hacks at the roseling with his shiv and it clamps another branch around his wrist and tears, spraying blood hot and rose-stinking into the dirt.

What did they do? What did they do?

8

Vanya runs.

The moon throws down multicolor branch-shadows. Vanya, curled in the nest of scrub and roots they crawled into when their legs gave out, gnaws weakly on bark, too tired to properly bite, too hungry to stop even though it stabs at their tongue. Their whole body throbs. Every time they close their eyes they see again the rose, their rose, open a vein. Hear the bandits screaming.

What did I do?

But they know: they called for help. Help came.

"Of course," she says, and she cannot be real, cannot be here, but they hear her clear as clear. "I may be fickle, but do you think I'd let anything happen to you? You only have to ask. All of you only ever have to ask."

Vanya doesn't open their eyes. They don't want to break the illusion.

"I told you, those categories aren't important." Warm fingers stroke their forehead. "Look at me, Vanya."

A Kiss with Thorns

They look.

Half in shadow, half painted in moonlight, she kneels beside them. The moonlight makes her eyes flicker red, paints her teeth bloody, throws a pale balefire flicker over her hair. Vanya tries to ask, "how?" or, "am I dying?" but their torn tongue and ragged lips won't obey.

"Hush, poor thing." The world judders. Blink once on scrublands. Blink again on a white-paneled room, and she lifts a glass of water to their lips. They drink greedily, in wasteful gulps that splash it down their chin, almost choking in their haste, not caring how it stings their lips and mouth.

"Careful."

Blink a third time, and they're in an arch-windowed bathhouse, looking out on a sky full of all the wrong stars. A humid breeze ruffles the water and her unbound hair. She peels their ruined clothing

9

off, pushing their hands away when they try to help. "Let me," she orders them, and they do; her touch is gentle, her fingers sure, as if they've done this together a thousand times. She guides them into the water and rinses the blood and road-dust and sweat from their skin, itching at the bruises, at the cuts across their face and mouth, at their ruined nose. The pain fades away under her hands. Their nose, their knee, their throat—so long ago, now. Nearly healed; on the dream-timeline. "There you are, my brave Vanya. Better?"

"Yes." They could float here forever. In the way of dreams, the water runs clear again, and the cool of it soothes their muscles, holds them up. They feel new. Except for the hollow drumbeat in their belly. That stays.

But they forget it, almost, looking at her perched on the bath's edge, her dress clinging to her legs and belly, one slap striding off her shoulder—and they should be too tired, too spun out from the weight of what just happened (what they did) for this pure surge of need at the pit of their spine, the way it sings in them, the way their cock hardens, but it's only a dream. They stand and reach for her.

She smiles, and bends to them, and they pull her into a kiss. It arcs all through them, lighting up their skin, crackling wherever they touch her. They fumble with the buttons of her dress, and she laughs and rucks her skirt up; Vanya presses a kiss to her stomach, just above her mound.

They think, through the haze of desire and the sweet throb between their legs, all?

"Did you think you were the first? Do you begrudge me that, the others?"

Vanya flicks their eyes up to her face and catches the wariness there. "No," they murmur, of course they don't, they never could, and they bury their face between her legs.

She's wet already, and they know just what she likes, how hard to mark her thighs with their nails, how to lick into her so that she gasps and pulls their curls hard enough to hurt. When they slip a finger inside her, she makes a tiny low noise that goes straight to the base of their cock. When they add

10

a second and curl their tongue just so against her clit, precise and eager, she jerks in pleasure so hard her heel catches them in the shoulder, and they both have to stop to laugh.

"Up here, come up here," she manages. Vanya hauls themself out of the bath, easy the way moving in dreams is, the tile rearranging itself obediently, the water streaming off them. She pulls her dress over her head and, tossing it aside, straddles them, warm and soft, her slick wet on their thigh.

Vanya kisses her again, hungry, so hungry for more of her. One hand finds the curve of her waist; the other cups her breast, their thumb playing over the tight little bud of her nipple. "Oh, just like that, yes, there, good, Vanya." She slides a hand down between them,

A Kiss with Thorns

to Vanya's dripping cock. "Tell me what you want." Her thumb plays over the head of their cock and every vein lights up, they can't think to answer, couldn't get enough breath if they did; they let out a whimper, their hips bucking.

"Words, my love."

"Cruel," they rasp, and kiss the dip where her shoulder meets her neck. She chuckles. The sound thrums down her throat, vibrates under their lips, blood-warm and inviting.

Vanya bites.

Sugar-sap blood bursts over their tongue, a sweet hot trickle with a tang of sweat-salt underneath, and they want more, ache for it, all they have to do is bite again—

They wrench themself back so hard their skull bangs into the tile. No. No.

She catches herself on their shoulders, too close, her hair hanging around their face and the blood dripping over her collarbone to spatter onto them. They push at her—have to get her away before they do worse, and they will do worse, their stomach pulses, they're salivating, they want, they want—but she grabs their wrists. "I'm sorry, it wasn't meant to hurt you so, it wasn't."

"You have to let go, I—"

"Vanya, Vanya, I can make it better—do you understand? All you have to do is let me. Say yes. Please, say yes."

11

Drowning in the hunger, the need—they'll die if they don't eat, they'll die if they don't come, they'll die if she stops touching them and they'll die if she doesn't—they gasp, "Yes."

She smiles, relief, triumph. A thorn bursts from her wrist. Still atop them, still wet, she carves them open from the collarbone down, parting muscle and bone easy as air, the lightning-strike of pain so sweet it takes their breath away as she levers the heart from their chest.

"Mouth open. That's right, my love, there you are," and they come

171

ruinously hard as she pushes the dripping, twitching heartsmeat between their lips.

And after, awake, the journey in too-short flashes: the sun, the road, their aching legs.

Emptiness where their hunger should be.

Now here they stand at the castle, and the castle fills the sky.

A faint breeze, chill and rose-sour, lifts Vanya's sweat-soaked curls and sends a musical rattle through the roses. Palm-size red blossoms, thorns like blades, live growth layered over tinder-dry dead, the scent so strong it sits like a paste on their tongue, too-sweet and cloying. Metal streaked with rust winks through the growth. Bones show yellow-white in the dirt—not half so many as there should be, but the riot of growth and color, the tides of scent, tell where the rest went clear enough.

(Do you begrudge me the others?

No.)

Vanya draws their machete and circles the castle. No break in the red larger than a handspan, seemingly no difference in the castle itself. Except—there. An outward bulge, under a patch of dead brown growth, maybe twice again Vanya's size. Behind it, only shadows.

They can't shake the feeling that they were allowed to find this. That it's bait. So take it, they tell themselves, You have a quest to finish, and swing the machete. It hits the stem with a thunk and sticks.

Vanya works it free and swings again. And again. And again.

12

The calluses on their palms crack and rip, a little muscle down in the small of their back twinges and burns. Their lungs heave. They grimace, and it tears the thorn-slashes across their lips open again. Sweat drips stinging into the cuts. They grit their teeth and keep going. Keep swinging, as their vision flickers and blurs, narrows to the flash of the blade.

A Kiss with Thorns

One last strike, so much effort their entire back screams in protest, and with a crack, the last branch gives way and the machete blade snaps at the base. Vanya tosses the useless hilt aside and stands there a moment, gulping down the thin odd air. They face a double set of metal doors, one that opens up and down, one that opens left and right, forced apart by a vomit of woody stems big around as Vanya's waist, and dark.

Vanya takes a steadying breath and climbs through. Black spots dance in front of their eyes as their boots clunk on metal, and their knees wobble; they catch themselves on the wall, and rear back as if burned when their hand brushes wood. The world swims. They shake their head to clear it. It takes a moment for their vision to make something out of the blot of shadows. Ahead of them stretches a metal corridor, age-stained, grown over with branches. There's another set of double doors, a sign in flaking letters they don't understand; some strange grayish stuff they think might be real plastic makes two big circles from floor to ceiling under the growth. An airlock. A real one.

Soon. The thought rises up on its own—but she's not here, she's not real, she was only ever a mirage, something they made up to ease the road here. (No matter that the roseling came when they called her name. No matter that they felt the warmth of her skin, how she lay in their arms and stroked their hair.)

The hall flickers. Golden light blinks on, off. They shut their eyes against it and a breeze tugs at their hair, a ghost-kiss marks their shoulder. Not real, not real. They cling to the smell of rotting petals.

That is real, that is the truth, there is only the castle and what they came to burn. They fumble for the

13

kerosene. All they have to do is spill this everywhere, and—what? This place is so much bigger than they thought, and will it even all burn?

But what will they do, give up? They sacrificed so much to hunt down the rot's heart.

Vanya sloshes kerosene onto the wall, onto the roses, and limps along, following the branches.

The castle, depthless with shadows, creaking with age, swallows them.

They measure the length of the walk by the level of kerosene and how the light fades. Half the jug gone, three-fourths gone; almost too dark to see now. The halls curve all the same direction, the signs incomprehensible, faded with age and half-hidden under rose-stems. (They imagine the rose-vines winding around them, thorns kissing their pulse points.) Their boots leave prints in dust nearly an inch thick; their footfalls send echoes racing up and down, falling into the dark. They turn a curve and nearly trip on a man-shaped thing—but it's only a suit of armor crumpled on the floor, the faceplate burst open. Only that.

And before them, a huge hole that must have been another door, vomiting blossomless, thorn-studded rose stems. No light reaches the inside.

A clunk sounds above, sending a violent start through them that wakes the fire in their back anew, and weak white light spills down. When they step forward, another clunk, and the light behind them dies. Vanya clutches the kerosene jug tighter, fingers sweaty on the handle, and squares their shoulders. If this is a trick, they have no other options. They step through.

The light's even weaker here, blocked out by stems and dust. But it shows the bed in the center of the room.

It shows her.

Laid out as if in state, hair tangled with filth and dead blossoms. Dust limns her profile, the arch of her nose, her eyelashes.

Roots split her open from chest to navel.

14

They pulse slow, so slow, lying in curls around her, over her hips, her arms, her chest, framing her face like a painting. The jug slips from Vanya's numb fingers and tips over. Rose-stink fills the air as the rest of the kerosene spills.

A Kiss with Thorns

No.

But they would know her anywhere—every laugh-line, every eyelash, the faint curve of her smile (higher on the right side, lips slightly parted), her upturned palms, her ring-fingers long as her middle fingers. How she lies with her left foot pointed a little outwards. The fingernails grimed, so that she's a little less than perfect, marred enough to be true.

Vanya sinks to their knees at her side. So still, so waxy and sallow —but when they touch her face, half expecting her to crumble under their fingers, they feel her breathing. Some unnameable tearing feeling roars inside them, batters against the cage of their ribs. It howls in their ears. The rose-scent is so thick they're dizzy with it, or maybe they're just dizzy. They can't, they can't, they can't.

You're helping her. You're saving her from the rot, that's why you dreamed about her, so you could end this, so you could set her free. The right thing, the kind thing. Save her and everybody else, with a book of matches and a gallon of fuel. It doesn't sound true.

Vanya leans in, for one last look, just one, to steel themself. Their blood drips into that perfect mouth. Three drops, hot and copper.

She opens her green, green eyes.

No, oh no. No, please.

"Vanya," and they hear it with their bones, their sinews, from inside, "You came for me."

You can't be, I told myself you weren't, not here, not real, no, oh god, no.

But they know the name for this feeling, now, this savage, screaming, shredding thing pushing at the edges of their self, their skin, and what else have they ever wanted so much? What else has ever filled them to spilling with this kind of joy?

15

The rose-stems marionette her hand up to cup their cheek. Her fingers are limp and fever-hot and soft. They lean into the touch as if pulled. "I told you I'm selfish. This is how selfish. I should have let them destroy me when I could still be destroyed, before I could infect anyone else, but I didn't want to die. And I should have left you where you were, but I was so tired of being alone."

The rose-ridden. Her. It doesn't make any sense, and it does, a nightmare-logic sideways sense; Vanya can hear the story behind her words, rising up like a beast in the dark, feel its breath hot on their neck. "You're killing people."

"You kill each other all the time."

"You eat them," but they can't call up the bones outside anymore, or the rib-thin infectees, or the pyres staining the sky with smoke. Not here before her leaf-bright eyes, her smile just for them.

"All things must eat." Her thumb traces their torn bottom lip. The contact shivers all the way through to their jawbone, lighting electric down their spine. "Don't tell me you came all this way just to burn me. You'll break my heart."

All they have to do is move fast enough. All they have to do is pull away, and strike one match.

"Vanya," she murmurs again, "Look at me, my love," and Vanya sways forward, and kisses her. Kisses her graceless and hungry and with a mouthful of blood as she twines around them.

She tastes of dust and roses, roses, roses.

What They Don't Tell You About The Mummy's Curse
Anton Cancre

Dear Archaeologist's Digest,

I never thought it would happen to me. But, there I was. Down to the root in a desiccated throat while cracked-skin fingers rammed triple knuckle deep up my corn mine. A dream cum true for a humble soul like myself.

But, let's back up. It's worth giving you time to grab the lotion or water-soluble lube and slick that fist or Mr. Fister. I get where many of you need that slippery-slick smooth motion. Personally, I crave the friction of dry scrapes. I desperately want to feel skin slough off in rough trade against unforgiving leathery dryness. You do you and I will do me.

So, I'll admit that I am not an archaeologist. Never had the money for school. Did have the love though. I always dug old shit. History and stuff. Wanted to know where I came from and the like. So, yeah, couldn't get the degree, but our local museum needed people with strong backs. I spent my youth tossing hay bales and picking stones. I knew how to bend and I knew how to lift and I didn't tire so easily.

Some of y'all talk shit on country boys, but let me tell ya: a job needs done, we do it. Won't stop 'til it's done right, neither. Say what you want from your concrete towers 'til you need a bit of spit 'n polish on something, then we'll talk.

So they hired me to unload crates. Move boxes from point A to point B. Always talked down to me like I couldn't read a damn floor plan, too. Not a one of 'em knew how to work a pallet jack, but I was the idiot.

Sure. Whatever. I got to see all'a them bits o' history. Not just the shit y'all get to see, neither. All the boring stuff ain't no one wanna take a look at. You got any idea how many ancient relics I've rubbed my rock hard cock against? No, you don't. And you don't wanna. That's not mentioning all of the time smoothed ornaments I've rubbed up on my gooch. More 'n a few gems been dipped deep inside my ass. Several you seen on display, too. Maybe dulled a bit from whatever scraped off onto 'em, but that is just between us girls, right?

What matters is this: Big ass case came off a truck. Late at night, too. So, I was the only one there. Driver didn't even step over to piss or nothin. Just backed up to the dock, then high-tailed it the second I unloaded the one damn crate. I assumed he had other pickups, since he left with an empty truck.

Now, don't you go lookin at me weird for openin' it. Needed to know where it needed to go. 'sides, it was just a regular box. Plain boards. No special markings. No stamps sayin' *Handle With Care: Old Dead Egyptian Fucker*. So, I popped it open, like I woulda anything else.

Musta jarred it enough to pop the top just a bit. The sarcophagus. Maybe he was already ready to go. Trust me, that particular Staff of Rah was enough to move its fair share of wood. Open just enough that cinnamon and anise filled my nose. Cumin, too. I can cook like a motherfucker, so I know my spices. But my stomach wasn't the thing stirrin' in me. That undercurrent of aged meat, thick and rich. A little sweet. Popped my cock up like a steel pole.

Okay. So every movie in the history of ever should have prepped

What They Don't Tell You About The Mummy's Curse

me to run when the slow, soft creak of the lid moving started. There's possession, bugs under the skin, strangulation, curses, all of the like in line for those situations. But, I was curious. I wanted to see. Fuck that. I wanted to feel.

That leathery, wrinkled hand that reached out from the deep black inside. Fuck, did I want to run my tongue along the grooves and ridges of ages. Every part of me wanted to taste skin that had been cured by sand older than anything I could reasonably conceive of. Was the sun even the same sun when he walked under it?

Stuck in those damn dumbass meandering thoughts, I missed seeing him rise up, whole, from the sarcophagus. I looked up and there he was. reduced by time to the leanest flesh possible. Ropy muscle and tight tendon. Ridged. Bulging. His joints poked out at sharp angles. All of him, naked and beckoning.

Though none as much as the fuckin hog jutting out from his hips. Look. I'm no size queen. Nine inches is usually my max. But I have to admit that there was something to this beast rising from a dense bush of pubic hair. Like the fuckin four pack tube of tennis balls I get for my pitty just aimin' straight for my face.

Before I knew it, his fingers laced into my hair. Fucker was stronger than there was any reason to expect. No way to fight back against that pull. Of course, there was no fuckin way I was going to do that, noways. I've rimmed dudes behind the dollar store for a pack of Salems and a smile. No way in hell I wasn't gonna miss the chance to suck cock across centuries.

Sure, it was dry. Dry as west Texas wind in August. The second my lips touched the folded edges of his foreskin, ready to pull it back to get to that sweet, sensitive skin beneath, they stuck. Every bit of moisture pulled out of them.

But I'd been drooling from the moment I smelled him. My mouth overflowing with fluid. My tongue did what it needed to. Slid out between teeth. Edged itself along the inside of my lips. Nudging the raw, cracked and leathery skin of his cockhead. Like an old boot that had seen serious work in the angry sun. Dirt. Dust. Dry, dead skin flaked off into my mouth. And I sucked down every morsel.

I had to stretch my jaw just to fit his head past my teeth. He pulled my head in closer. Thrusting into my mouth. Trying to fuck my face like I'd never worked a dick before. I wrapped my right hand around his shaft and pumped. Yeah. My hand was dry, too. He was the one who didn't give me a chance to spit on it. Don't judge me.

I cupped the wrinkled flaps of ballskin in my left hand. Undulated my fingers to move his balls around in there like those Chinese medicine balls. All the while working my middle finger along his taint and up to his asshole.

It didn't give and I didn't have any lube, so I just pushed on through. Hell, I was pretty sure he woulda shoved his giant cock all the way through my skull if I hadn't taken control. Skin split. Cracked open. Parted for my finger. It scraped and pulled itself through. In and out. Dragging pieces of him along with it. Given the moans and mutterings he spilled in whatever fuckin language he spoke, I'm pretty sure he didn't mind.

Didn't take long, but don't you start talkin' shit over that. YOU go ahead and wait a few thousand years between nuts and tell me how long you hold out. I felt the muscles in his ass clench 'round my finger. His balls pulling up in my hand. His cock pulsing against my tongue and lips.

I didn't know what to expect. A puff of dust to choke on? Lame, angry, and bitter old semen drooling like oil onto my tongue. A single, oversized sperm wriggling its way through an overstretched cockhole before squirming down my throat.

Ended up being a pretty standard hot load. A bit saltier than I prefer. Dude could've used some more fruit in his diet. Can't really think of any fruit that grows in the desert of Egypt though. Dates? Indian Jones had dates. Fucker coulda eaten some dates. I ain't no bitch though. Sucked down every damn drop.

His fingers loosened their grip on my scalp. Cock wilted in my mouth. Floppy, cracked skin deflating in my hand. Motherfucker tried to back away. Like this shit was over now that he had his.

Look. Pharaoh. King. God. Street rat. I don't give a fuck. You don't nut in someone's mouth, then just wander off.

Reciprocation, my man.

So, yeah. I stood the fuck up. Grabbed him by his shoulders and

What They Don't Tell You About The Mummy's Curse

pulled him back toward me. Looked that ancient son of a bitch in the eyes and made sure he saw what was up. Made sure he knew he wasn't the only one gonna get their nut that night.

A quick glance down, my eyes tracing the direction for him, was all it took. He went down on his knees in front of me. His breath, hot against my stomach. My heart tried its best to pound out of my chest. It finally hit home. I sucked a mummy's cock. Slurped down its cum. Now, it was gonna taste mine.

I'm sure someone is reading this, getting all red in the face and triggered over the "desecration of ancient artifacts" or some bullshit. I respect history. I respect the shit in museums. Their unique, important place in our understanding of who and what we are. How fucking fragile they are. How a wrong scrape or brush of air can completely destroy them.

But, when you got yer hard cock pressed up against a pair o' dust-dry lips, ready to slurp it into the soft palate of ages, thoughts like that tend to float to the background. You go ahead and respect history with your mind and your morals. I respected the fuck outta history with my dick.

His lips were cracked. Much worse than the wasted, ashy-lipped shitface in an Atlanta alley back in '18. His teeth, too. Broken and sharp. Like fangs raking along the ridged skin of my cockhead. Tongue like sandpaper. Not cat-tongue sandpaper, but *sandpaper* sandpaper. High grit tore my skin and every nerve was on fire.

Clearly, manicures weren't a thing back in his day. Nails were ragged as fuck. Wrinkled and crusty fingers forced themselves into my ass. Agony bloomed like a fuckin orchestra. Do orchestras bloom? I don't fuckin know. Do I sound like the kinda person that goes to the Met? Fuck you.

There was a lot going on. Ecstasy, too. Nerves screaming back and forth. Confused. Overwhelmed. Even the memories are jumbled. Dice shaken up in a cup.

I didn't last long, neither. Shot my jizz down the throat of long history before you could count to ten. My brain, my heart, my soul lit up like the Fourth of fuckin' July. Explosions and neon electricity. I thought, for a moment there, that I saw into the center of the sun.

Anton Cancre

Definitely felt my heart turn lighter 'n a feather. Even if it was just for that second, damn did that second feel fucking amazing.

Would you believe that asshole just got up and walked away?

Yup. Just wandered off, naked as anything. Maybe he had an ancient love to find. Maybe there were old grudges that needed answerin'. Maybe he just wanted some better ass than this wasted piece of shit.

I just know I'll never find a dick like that again and the scars on my cock are all I'll have to remember him by.

With drained balls and soured dreams,
D.Z. Knutz

MOTEL POZITIVE
j ambrose

A single shitbox car populated the lot between a seedy gas station and Triumph Lutheran Church, marquee board questioning *HOW IS YOUR LIFE WITHOUT GOD?* An interrogation that went ignored by the only nearby soul: the shitbox car's driver, with his sweatpants and boxers in a puddle around his ankles. One hand thumbed through new notifications—two from his roommate Mikey asking *Where the fuck are you* and *Btw you didn't lock the door after you left*, three from Grindr, one from DoorDash, and a spam email—while the other cradled his half-hard cock. Soft rock crackled through the radio that worked only when forced to via percussive maintenance. The church and its inquisitorial words continued to loom, intent on an answer.

Evan didn't consider himself unsaved, nor in need of saving. He knew what he wanted and didn't deny himself the pleasure of attainment. He cruised parking lots, gay bars, and the occasional hiking trail until his jaw went numb and half a pack of breath mints couldn't stifle the lingering aftertaste of cum. Wherever his cock pointed, he ventured—a simple method of living; enjoyable too, when he wasn't met with abject disgust from the good and pure and nonjudgmental townsfolk. He figured a life with God must make you an uptight bitch.

His phone chimed—more texts from Mikey that he didn't see and, like clockwork, another Grindr notification. Nameless except for a mushroom emoji.

Ten feet away.

A body blocked the dwindling rays of the setting sun. Evan kept his eyes on his phone. A cerulean line appeared in the chat: *I have something that will change your life.*

"Never heard that one before," Evan scoffed, turning to look the stranger up from shin to collarbone. His car provided taller people with the luxury of full anonymity, to the benefit of both parties ninety percent of the time. But now a temptation to take a peek at their face and puncture their artificial mystery took hold of his limbs until their hands, adorned in tattoos and bulging veins, cut such an idea short.

He didn't protest. The stranger smelled too good, otherworldly even, a cloying floral cologne masking the intoxicating stench of sweat and something that was probably weed. It smothered his initial fear, turned his brain gooey. He inhaled hard, and the stranger chuckled.

"You need what I can give."

"I need what you can give," he echoed breathlessly as desperate fingers unzipped their jeans, pulled them down with their boxers just far enough to release their erection and something else: a biohazard symbol tattooed above the root of their cock. It stared him down, ink spreading across the whole of his vision to engulf him. It was harsh and angry against the stranger's milky skin, yet it entranced him with a soft, unspoken promise. Of what, he had no idea.

"What is it?" His head was stuffed thick with arousal like he hadn't fucked in weeks. Jesus, what was it?

"A gift, a blessing, an honor, one that people like you, *us*, spend our whole lives looking for without even knowing." Their voice sounded strange. He couldn't place the accent, nor decipher just why the cadence twisted so serpentine around his eardrums, but he knew he needed them to keep talking. He wanted to swallow every inch of their tantalizing cock until he sucked out every word through its soft pink tip. The stranger kept his neck static even as he strained against their grasp, toward the tattoo beckoning with its six horns and single all-seeing eye. An acute sense of being edged.

"I need what you can give."

He was bent over in the backseat, his cheek smushed flat against the window that fogged with each whimpered exhale. However he got there was unremembered and unimportant. A hand cradled his throat, too sweaty to tell where it ended and his skin began. Someone moaned and Evan thought it was him, but honestly he wasn't sure, he didn't care—the stranger pumped into him with a trance-inducing rhythm, treating his body like an instrument meant to be played. Their lips muttered an infinite stream of expletives intermixed with something almost akin to a nonsense prayer. *Infect* and *offering* and *defile* splattered onto his exposed back until Evan dripped with ritualistic incantations. *Transmit* and *rot* and *new life* and *oh god it's coming, take it, take it into every cell.*

Climax flooded Evan to the brim and beyond, wiping his mind blank. Distantly, he felt the hot cum ooze through the sore muscles in his sphincter. And ooze, and ooze. Only his chest moved, heaving with the effort of catching his breath in the balmy heat, as he felt every inch of his innards electrify. It wound through his intestines and into his stomach, up and up his esophagus while burgeoning across the plains of his lungs, and slipped into his heart until it exploded in every vein. His body shuddered with a sensation halfway between an orgasm and the urge to vomit as it tickled the back of his throat before nestling deep in his brain folds. It settled down there, and he collapsed into a soggy puddle of fucked out flesh.

The hand around his neck moved to slap him softly, almost playfully, like a cat toying with a dead mouse. "Enjoy it, friend. Find others to enjoy it with. Enjoy, enjoy, enjoy."

The weight evaporated. A door slammed shut. His cock twitched pathetically against the sweaty leather seat.

Evan thought he'd had life-changing sexual encounters in the past. His first time with a trans man, for example, who exclusively used tentacle-shaped strap-ons—so of course he came back for a second, third, and sixth time, or his hook-up with the leather daddy in the cemetery across from the bank who made his legs shake at the faintest memory. But this…there really wasn't any words for it. He could make an attempt if he put his cock-drunk mind to the challenge. A subtle possession, an obsession made manifest, his arousal and filthy whims reified into a squirming, perhaps living, thing that asked only for the opportunity to thrive as he thrived: on the stench of sex and thrill of willing conquest.

He needed others to experience it. There had to be more people out there like him, who would receive it with open arms and holes not knowing exactly what it was, but that they needed it as he needed it. Not yet though, not yet. He wanted to wait, sit with himself and this blessing for a while. What was sex if not exploring uncharted territory, and what were these sensations if not a new landscape to indulge in?

So Evan laid in bed, nakedness spread-eagled across thoroughly sweat-soaked sheets; the thermostat read a brisk 65 degrees, but that didn't dissuade his leaking glands for a second. His cock cast a long shadow onto his stomach in the full moonlight streaming through the window. It strained with each deep inhale of the treacly aroma hanging heavy in the air—the same pungent sweetness that had clung to the stranger's skin and drove him wild. When he closed his eyes and let every muscle in his body go still, he felt the alien sensation tingling every cell like a second, omnipresent heartbeat. Like a thousand heartbeats, all ever so slightly desynchronized that they created a festering network of rhythms. His original pulse beat only a fraction harder than the rest. He sank into its depths, wanting to lose himself in it, dissolve and merge with it.

His phone buzzed him back into reality, an incessant noise that drowned out any attempt at drowning. Mikey. Always has to be Mikey. He answered with a groan.

"Good to see you, too. Did you get my texts?"

Another groan, eloquently communicating that he hadn't. His cock stiffened despite the interruption. Mikey just had that effect on him, and any morsel of attraction was heightened to the point of overstimulation by whatever was now mingled in his bloodstream. "When are you coming back?"

His laugh revealed his teeth and wet, warm mouth. "Miss me

already? I told you, something like a week depending on whether or not Sebastian bothers to show up for his scenes this time. Are you—? *Evan*."

He couldn't help himself. The pressure just kept building, aching for release. His hand worked furiously.

"You're such a little degenerate," Mikey teased before sighing. "I've gotta go, Kim says drinks are on her tonight and I'm not missing out on that. You enjoy yourself, but no orgies."

Enjoy, enjoy. Oh, he certainly would, certainly *was*.

His whole body shuddered, bent back away from the mattress as an orgasmic wave crescendoed and crashed over his head. Oh god, *oh god*. It wouldn't stop. His eyelids screwed shut, as he gasped for breaths that only gulped in more of the overly floral stench. For a moment the stranger's hand was back around his neck, choking him. Pleasure bordered on pain. A hunger pervaded the heartbeats and Evan felt grasping fingers rooting around inside his veins, searching for somewhere to go until a nuclear bomb erupted in his groin, exploding behind his shut eyelids until the room, the mattress, his body evaporated momentarily. He found himself in the aftermath, panting through a crazed smile. Words evaded him.

After he recovered in what could've been minutes or hours—he might've fallen asleep, he wasn't at all certain either way—Evan pulled himself to a sitting position and stared in disbelief at what greeted him. In the cum pooled on his stomach swam hundreds of tiny golden spores, each barely larger than a single glitter fleck. They glowed in the moonlight, a vast smattering of stars lighting up the milky galaxy of his jizz. He rubbed his eyes, but the tiny spores persisted. He laughed to himself, a disbelieving chuckle that spiraled into howling. It was madness. He was going mad—and he couldn't get enough of it.

He couldn't get enough of his own arousal either. He welcomed the way this blessing consumed him from the inside out. In a way it was no different from how he previously lived his life, only now his infinite libido became corporeal. There was a duty now, towards this thing that was so intrinsic to his nature, yet thoroughly distinct from anything he'd known before. His days shifted into a cycle of masturbation punctuated by periods of post-nut clarity—the body's desperate cries for mercy. For all its omnipresence, the writhing warmth was not omnipotent and Evan remained bound by his physical ability to produce enough semen.

But he found meaningful ways to fill the waiting time; scrolling Grindr until pins and needles tingled in his fingers. He proselytized to anyone who would listen which, to his confusion and dismay, wasn't many. Those who didn't ignore the initial offer were quick to block once he attempted to explain what exactly was in store for them if they agreed. Repeated fuckbuddies evaporated. Even Justin—infamously even more unorthodox in his tastes than Evan, and no stranger to any bodily excretion, fluid, or urges—said he was busy. *Sure.* He'd never been too busy for sex a day in his life until now. Frustration ached in Evan's chest. His cock swelled for round four, and every drop of stress dissolved into that familiar blissful haze.

Safe to say, he exhausted Grindr's possibilities, but that was the mere tip of the iceberg. He squeezed himself into every filthy internet crevice he was familiar with, quickly developing a copypasta manifesto of sorts, equal parts advertisement and proclamation.

SHROOM POZ TOP SEEKING HOLE FOR PRECIOUS GIFT. YOU NEED WHAT I CAN GIVE.

Included among the cobbled ramblings were several pictures of his gold-flecked jizz adorning the new biohazard symbol drawn on his pelvis in Sharpie. Only more radio silence interspersed with disgust and accusations of trolling. Evan grew desperate, bordering on panic.

The spores spread, germinated, spread. Golden fungus sprung from his skin, long stalks wrapping around the base of his cock and intermingling with his pubic hair. When he spat into his hand to lube himself—after four or five orgasms, he had to put in real effort to jerk the cum out—more organic stars glittered in his saliva. Even more, a whole budding forest of them, grew from the discarded cum tissues littering his floor in a layer of disease so thick that it concealed the carpet. The saccharine smell congealed into a visible fog.

He was too exhausted to move more than a few feet from his bed once or twice a day to refill a jumbo water bottle. Evan feared his body would succumb to its own weaknesses before given the chance to put out into the world what he had been given, to share this legacy that, despite his anxieties, he couldn't imagine living without. But he persisted, and sent out feelers into more and more obscure places, waiting for a bite.

Of all places, Evan found his heir, or rather, his heir found him, in an occult forum dedicated to sex magick. His ramblings weren't entirely out of place among the pleas for succubi and promises of eternal sexual virility.

"Holy shit, I was beginning to lose hope and here you are, proving me wrong. Thank gods for that." His screen name read, almost stereotypically, vomitlover119. "Mind if I PM you?"

While typing out a quick, "Please do," the seed of another orgasm sprouted against his tender prostate. He choked down the distress building in his throat. Each orgasm grew more painful than the last, a pain strong enough to sour his overwhelming pleasure. Mushrooms emerged from his skin where there had once been fat, patchworking his thighs and stomach and turning him into something nearly more flora than fauna. The angel's choir of heartbeats pulsed through his body with a fury.

Vomitlover119's message was somewhere between a manifesto and a suicide note. In his words, he'd been a leech on society for far too long to go unpunished—but in that time he had tried desperately to repay the world for the oxygen he'd wasted. He'd tried volunteering, tutoring, and gardening and that was all hunky-dory, but there was no self-flagellation in such hobbies. He needed to reverse the roles: be a host for something. He had tried everything to no avail; being a dominatrix's pay pig had worked until his bank account ran dry, and the ceremonial magician who promised to invoke a spirit into him bailed at the last minute. What he wanted was a pregnancy, or the closest thing he could get to it as a cis man. Best case scenario, a pregnancy that would kill him in the process.

"I hope you can see that my life is nothing if I can't bring something better into the world. But if you don't want to go through with it now that you know how much of a loser I am, I'd understand."

"Like I'd judge someone for being a loser." Evan couldn't help but feel they were cut from the same cloth. There wasn't a more perfect person to receive the blessing. As he typed, his chapped lips cracked into a smile and the festering warmth smiled with him, intravenously celebrating the promise of a fresh vessel.

"How soon can we arrange this?"

Now. Now, now now. "Tonight."

"Tonight?"

"Why delay your purpose?"

They met up at the motel room that Sasha—Evan almost balked at the knowledge of his real name, as if it were more intimate than fucking him, breeding him, in a way—had booked for the bailed possession attempt. After clawing his way out of bed with a bathrobe tied around his body, driving there was a breeze. For the first time in days, his cock remained flaccid for more than ten minutes, as if it was saving itself for what was to come. Despite the bathrobe, he felt naked without an erection between his rotting thighs.

Amidst the shitbox car's protests at being pushed over fifty miles an hour came the electronic music of Mikey's ringtone. His hands white-knuckled the peeling leather steering wheel, foot on the gas pedal like he could outspeed the interruption. GPS told him three more miles. In all his many erotic escapades, he'd never been in this part of town. The music came again, somehow louder, and he relented.

"What?" he barked.

"Don't fucking *what* me dude, where the fuck have you been? Try taking less than four days to answer my texts next time. I'll be home in an hour, and I swear to God if you trashed the house or someone left their shit, I'll—" he hung up, chucked his phone into the back seat to rot alongside the used condoms and empty water bottles.

The receptionist said nothing as Evan breezed past the desk. A faded navy blue hat obscured the entirety of their face, and it dawned on him halfway down the hallway that they were probably asleep.

The door to Room 39 swung open just as he put his fist up to knock.

"I was watching through the peephole," Sasha confessed in a voice oddly timid for a man of his size. He stood, slouched and bearish in nothing but his plaid-patterned boxers, and took Evan's existence in with hunger and disbelief, as if he was manna from heaven. "You came —I mean of course you did. Please, come in."

Evan didn't move. He was too preoccupied by Sasha's thick arms, thighs, and fat stomach adorned with a dense forest of hair trailing down into his boxers and sprouting out the leg holes. Oh the things he would do to this man. Sasha didn't move either. The look in his eyes when they finally remembered each other's faces said he thought the same things.

The only lighting in the room came from the motel's neon sign ablaze outside the window, and his nose crinkled at the immediate smell of must. Sasha made himself pretty on the half-made bed in the few seconds it took for Evan to take in the room before he remembered why he came here, and the insatiable desire reignited inside him. He reveled in the look on Sasha's face, the carnality replacing all the awkwardness that previously stained his features, when he dropped the bathrobe. The ripe vine of his cock throbbed hungrily amidst the golden garden of Eden that had become of his body between navel and kneecaps. Sasha's wish made manifest. They were on each other in an instant, a desperate tangle of flesh and fungus.

Sasha straddled his thighs, irresistible belly fat spilling over and pressing his thick cock against Evan's. Pleasure exploded in his veins at the touch, pulse pounding need, need, need in a voice that wasn't his own. The man's body enveloped him as he rutted his face into Evan's hairy armpits, already drunk on the familiar scent wafting up from his skin. His hips bucked against the soft, hairy, welcoming flesh that Evan needed to be inside, needed to infect, and make new.

"Give it to me," Sasha said. "Save me."

Evan was halfway inside him and twitching relentlessly, body and mind overwhelmed by the sensations writhing inside and around him. He didn't have the cognition to pump, but his body didn't need him to think, just needed to move, rhythmically and ruthlessly, like he was nothing but unnecessary weight attached to his cock. A spasming

Sasha rolled his hips. He became the sea, crashing down on him in wave after wave of incapacitating pleasure. His ass sucked Evan in even deeper, and all he wanted to do was drown inside him, in the pleading moans tumbling from that wide open, drooling mouth.

Both men subsisted on momentum alone, two bodies locked in perpetual erotic motion. He needed to fill him up until he watched him spit up biohazardous cum glittering with the heavenly spores that would bless him with a useful existence. Something hot splattered across his chest, and Sasha briefly went limp, sinking down the full length of his cock and pressing a breathless scream from Evan's lungs. He slapped his wire-stubble jaw, put a thumb in his mouth, and that was enough to revive him.

They continued on and on, Sasha's body evolving into a toxic fleshlight for Evan's unrelenting libido. Spores leaked from the ruined cavity that continued to yearn for more and more and he wouldn't, couldn't stop. Each orgasm gripped him with burning fingers, blurred his vision until he didn't know which way was up, only knew that there was a body beneath him begging for the greatest gift he could deliver. He had to ensure successful transmission. So he went until his body collapsed into the sweat-drenched pillow of flesh that was Sasha and he felt no distinction between their bodies. Evan's pulse thrummed in sync with his. Lungs heaved in unison through exhausted whimpers, each other's spit drooled from their mouths. He heard Sasha's gratitude as if it were his own. His cock still hooked inside him, a wilted, shriveled thing inside another. What remained of Evan was content to lie there forever.

Bliss surrounded them, germinated inside and between them, reached out of them with spindly golden fingers. It soaked through the tangled sheets and broken box spring mattress, dripped into the carpet and up the peeling, cigarette smoke-stained wallpaper. Fungal ecstasy infected each room, making no distinction between vacant and occupied, for its only desire was desire itself. Golden spores sparkled constellations down the narrow hallways, bearing a pungent, irresistible aroma—and wouldn't it be nice to find its source? When did innocent curiosity ever hurt? An ache nestled into each guest's groin as slender stalks crowned with tiny caps entwined around every surface, burst through opened windows and doors left ajar, and reached up, up, up and out into the world yet never farther than the cracked pavement parking lot. Balconies flourished and new life exploded from the motel, now a heart of many sorts. Its rebirth was all at once immediate and unhurried. No one spoke a word about it to another soul, each fearing that it was a personal unreality, a side effect of new medication or lack thereof. And acknowledging it, if it was real, would necessitate acknowledgement of the ache and a confession that it whispered sweet nothings to them, that self-restraint took every ounce of willpower, and they wondered why they should deny themselves such a chance at discovery, spontaneous experimentation.

And what they found—those who choked down their desire to appear sane in favor of something that tasted so much meatier, so much juicier—was Room 39, an aureate garden, knee-high from the carpet and inches thick from the walls, blossoming forth from the rich bodies of its hosts, only identifiable as human by their intact cocks and faces frozen in pleasure. Eternal, otherworldly pleasure. Half a smeared biohazard symbol beneath a yellow sea. Of course they couldn't resist the invitation to share in such a revelry, not when the air was thick with the tantalization emerging from every inch of the room, and each mushroom strained to greet them. Nobody had to know they were there, what they did there. A craving satisfied, nothing more. An itch scratched, and scratched, and scratched.

How lucky they had been to chance upon it. How fortunate that the summer wind carried the motel's new delicious aroma.

The Taste of Ash & Blackberry
Clar Hart

Meg sucked on the lip of the crushed aluminum can. No luck. It was dry. The mossy bouquet of her chest screamed for water, the bouquets of chokeberries, grapes, black currants, and red berries had grown parched as she drove through the desert. Outside her car the searing heat evaporated the color of the landscape to a dehydrated ecru.

Her phone was in the backseat where she'd angrily flung it after Julian's call. She kept driving anyway. The hotel was already booked.

Finally, she slammed into the parking lot and stumbled inside to the hotel's bar. She pulled herself onto a barstool as her insides twisted like sand. She ordered a vodka soda and tried not to think about the emptiness of the hotel room awaiting her.

"Here alone?"

Meg turned. A woman dug her fingers into the back of the neighboring vacant chair. She wore black silk that hugged her curves.

"Go ahead." It's not like Julian would take it.

The woman poured herself into the chair next to Meg. Her shirt was buttoned so tight Meg couldn't tell what grew in the cage of her chest.

"Nice dress," the woman said to Meg. It was beige, Julian's favorite color, cut low in the front so the bloom of her chest swelled out and berries dripped to her navel.

"Thanks," She was tipsy enough to follow it with, "Nice face."

"Glad you noticed," the woman smiled, a sharp half-smile that revealed her canines. The woman caught the bartender's eye and waved her hand for a drink.

"What brings you here?" she asked.

"Vacation," Meg sipped her drink. "You?"

"The same. Vacationing to come here, or to get away?"

"Is this anyone's getaway?" Meg gestured at the hotel. The interior was interchangeable with any number of anonymous hotels in indistinguishable cities that existed only because they were between two places.

"Maybe not," the woman replied. "But if you asked, I'd come with you."

Meg tasted the woman's mouth and drank in the heady liquor on her breath. The woman's hands tangled into the tendrils of Meg's chest as she pushed Meg against the hotel room wall. A currant, the flesh of it taut with juice, crushed between them and ran down Meg's waist.

Grasping the woman's hips beneath the black silk, Meg slipped a leg between her thighs and slid her hands up past the woman's firm stomach to tug at the shirt's stretched buttons. The woman brushed her hands away and instead reached for the straps of Meg's dress and tugged it down to the waist. Freed, the harvest of Meg's ribcage poured forth, a cascade of ruby blisters and bruised amethyst fruit.

The woman's lips roved across Meg's neck, down her collar bone, to linger on the brimming bouquet. Lightly tonguing at a crowberry, the woman swirled the bud with the tip, before she took a cluster of blackberries into her velvet wet lips.

Meg arched, a wave of pleasure raced up her spine as she pushed into the slick heat of the woman's mouth. The woman scraped her teeth against Meg's flesh as she sucked the turgid berry skin, over and over until the wave crested and it burst, soaking the woman's tongue.

The Taste of Ash & Blackberry

The woman kissed Meg's gasping lips. Juice dripped into the hot thirst of her throat and Meg savored the woman's taste mixed with the sweet acid of blackberry.

Meg slid off the rest of her own dress, the beige of it stained carmine. She moved to the bed and lay backwards, knees spread, and beckoned the woman in. The woman slid on top of her, her heat burning into Meg's inner thighs, her belly. She touched the woman's buttons again. This time the woman shrugged and reached up, undoing the first button. Slowly, she continued down until the shirt puddled around her waist, its slinky fabric clinging to her hips. Meg stilled, her eyes frozen to the woman's chest.

It was completely hollow.

Where there should have been vines, berries, or flower buds, there was only rung after rung of pure white bone gleaming in the dim hotel room lamplight.

She reached forward and traced a finger along her smallest rib. The finger came away white with ash.

Meg ran her hands along the woman's edges, to the knobs of her spine and back again. The woman's ash fell lightly to dust the fruit of Meg's chest in a soft haze. Meg tangled her fingers in the woman's hollows and dragged her in until her exposed ribs were buried in the lushness of Meg's own. Meg drank the sweet scent of her breath, nipped the soft petals of her lips, and drowned herself in the tide of the moment as it rushed over them.

When it ebbed they lay tangled together. Juice seeped across the woman's ribs and ash dusted the leaves of Meg's curves.

As Meg drifted to sleep, tucked in the hollow beneath the woman's arm, a story trickled into her dreams. Someplace where the sun never reached everyone grew up empty, all shadows and white edges. There was a girl who left and went someplace sun-soaked where the people were lush with fruit, a place to grow and flourish. But the mockery as she tried. The glances. Until the only option was to embrace the nothingness and pretend it was a choice.

The dreams that came after tumbled through darkness into waters so deep Meg couldn't see if they were empty or full. Bones hugged her and fruit drowned her.

Clar Hart

Meg woke the next morning, the space beside her empty. The morning bloomed around her, heady and lush, and she drank it in. On her tongue rested the lingering taste of blackberry and ash.

We're All Family Here
Shelley Lavigne

The results were impressive, Ed had to agree.

James's arm felt strong through the button-down and made Ed think of Superman under Clark Kent's clothes. His thumb lingered in the cleft between a well-defined deltoid and bicep for a moment before letting go.

"Rock hard," Ed said, putting his hands in his pockets instead of hanging them awkwardly at his sides, cooling from James's heat.

"It's just been six sessions! I've never seen results this fast, not naturally," he punched his stomach, flexing abs Ed couldn't see, but could picture. "I can get you set up with a session—friend's discount. See if you like it."

They weren't friends, but Ed was curious. "Yeah, sure."

Peak Fitness was devoid of machinery like most CrossFit gyms but had none of their stark industrial design. The gym felt more like a yoga studio; everything was earthy tones, woven mats, plush beige carpets, natural materials. Rooms branched off and silhouettes swayed behind frosted glass doors. Folks milled about the lobby, wearing identical light gray athletic gear that hugged every muscle.

There was a slogan painted in curlicues behind the front desk: *The next phase of human fitness!*

"Ed!" James waved at him from reception. He, too, wore the gray uniform, showing off what Ed had previously only imagined, strong, defined calves and thighs, pecs and a narrow waist. Ed let himself look, he was after all, admiring the results of his colleague's work, the results of this place which he considered buying into. There was nothing strange about that.

James placed a matching set of butter-soft uniforms in Ed's hands, snapping him back to reality.

"Oh, I'm fine with what I've got on," Ed said. He'd come prepared, in a carefully picked mismatched set of expensive workout gear, something he hoped said confident, casual gym rat.

"You have to use their gear, it's a rule," James said with a shrug.

Ed wanted to play along, but the thought of wearing the painted-on clothes before he'd benefited from Peak Fitness body sculpting lessons seemed unfair. Not to mention, he always hated the comparisons public locker rooms encouraged, the flagrant display of naked bodies. He never quite knew where to put his eyes.

"Welcome, Mr. Edward Kind," the receptionist said from behind James. Her name, Nadia, was stitched onto her gray uniform. "We need you to fill out some paperwork."

Ed took the clipboard from the receptionist, surprised for a moment at the thickness of the stack of papers. He flicked through the pages filled with questions.

What is your full given name?

What is your date and place of birth?

Do you have any previous gym experience? If so, list duration and name of gym.

Do you have any notable injuries that might impact your ability to do exercise (both physical and neurological)?

Are you on any medications?

Have you ever felt shame about your sexual impulses?

His stomach clenched. He swallowed bile.

We're All Family Here

To answer this question would be to give his shame a voice, power. It was a question he tried to dodge as it frequently arose in his mind, especially the why of it and the inevitable flood of questions that unleashed. Naming it would be like chaining himself to shore, powerless to escape the tide's deadly swell of self-knowledge.

"I'm only here for tonight's lesson, do I really need to fill all this out?" Ed asked.

Nadia's smile was bright. "We need to make sure you're the right fit for our regimen."

He looked back at the stack of sheets in his hands, and clicked the pen open.

Closed.

Open.

He wondered for a moment how James answered. Looking around, he found his *friend* chatting up an androgynous woman—not what he thought was James's type. He often wondered what James preferred, losing afternoons to daydreaming various scenarios where he'd stumble across James during a date, and be invited to tag along. James's date tended to be boring but attractive, not quite the match James deserved.

"Fill out the first five questions," Nadia suggested after a moment. "We'll need the rest if you decide to become a member."

He did as instructed.

"Uh, where are the changing rooms?"

"Behind me, but we have solo rooms down that way."

First bit of good news.

The door latched behind him with a satisfying click.

The buttery soft gray clothes were tight, but so elastic he barely felt them once on. He peeked into the mirror and was shocked by how good he appeared. He would catch his own eye in a bar if he looked like that.

He backpedaled from that thought.

"We're going to be late," James said as he opened the door, grabbing Ed by the arm, and dragging him into the classroom.

It smelled of incense, instead of the typical chemical lemon disinfectant smell of gyms. Woven towels laid at regular intervals around the room. Those towards the front were occupied. James grunted before leading them to two cramped mats in the back corner. Ed counted about thirty other heads in the class.

"Take off your socks," James said. "Matthew says that they prevent the flow of energy from the Earth."

"Matthew?"

"He created this gym—Matthew Peak. Former researcher, uncovered some secret to muscle and physiology, but lost his funding because he was too radical for the establishment. Apparently Big Pharma wanted to bury his research, but instead, he opened this gym to share his knowledge with the people. For the low, low price of forty bucks per lesson."

Ed whistled. That wasn't cheap.

"Worth every penny."

There was another tinkling of bells and Ed turned to the front of the class. A man stood on a dais. Matthew was proportioned like the Vitruvian man—generically handsome, blond, blue-eyed. He looked like an action movie star: so sure of his place in the world, and not bogged down by confusing desires. All he wanted was good to prosper and evil to be defeated.

As Matthew's eyes ran over the crowd appraisingly, Ed sat taller.

"Before we start, follow me on a mental journey," Matthew said. His voice was deep, soothing and strong. Fatherly.

"He's so good at this," James whispered with a small enthusiastic wiggle on his mat.

Matthew started to hum. The deep rumbling noise made the hairs on the back of Ed's neck stand up. As it crescendoed, he felt it settle in his stomach, in his groin, a sensation that was pleasant, deep.

Ed's eyes closed.

His phone alarm went off, startling him awake.

He could feel the workout in his muscles—the pleasant ache in his arms, the tightness in his abs, the burn in his ass. Nothing made him feel quite as in control of his body as post-workout muscle tension. He

We're All Family Here

had not felt that way in a while; a couple colds followed by overworking and under sleeping kept him away from the gym. So, when it came time to renew his CrossFit membership, he hadn't bothered. He was too ashamed of how far behind he'd fallen. Over time, he forgot how good it felt to workout.

He thought back to last night, trying to figure out what happened.

His memory was completely blank.

His body had gone through a strenuous workout, but the details of it evaded him. Had he blocked it out? Was it bad?

He looked at his phone as if it held answers. He saw a notification from his banking app and flicked it open to find that he paid $400 plus tax to Peak Fitness at 8:47 P. M.

So, he must have enjoyed whatever it was enough to pay for ten more sessions.

Had he filled out the paperwork? He honestly could not remember, nor could he guess if he had been honest in his answers.

Something else caught his eye. A new app. *Peak Fitness* shimmered at him, a small gray square with white mountains.

"How're you feeling?" James asked, peeking over their shared cubicle wall.

"Good. Amazing actually," Ed said, massaging his thigh. "It's weird though, I can't remember the evening at all."

"Oh, yeah, that's normal. You never quite remember the first sessions," James said. "It's your neurons realigning. It takes a while for the changes to take effect and while that's happening, memories have a hard time forming. Something like that."

"That's never happened to me at any other gyms."

"Sure, but you're not getting results like this at any other gym, either."

Ed thought enviously back to the people at Peak Fitness. The swell of their muscles, their confident postures, the way their uniforms caressed their curves like lovers.

"You going tonight? The schedule is on the app," James said.

Ed unlocked his phone and clicked on the logo. The menu included his balance, a schedule and a grayed-out VIP section.

"Do you have VIP?" Ed asked.

"Sadly no. It's not something you can pay for, Matthew picks them personally. I guess that's just one more way that place is different from other gyms." James flicked through his phone. "Want to join me for Thighs and Ass next Tuesday at 7:00?"

Ed's mind supplied him with a memory of James's thighs and ass in those gray pants. His abs clenched.

"Sure."

Five sessions in, he started remembering fragments of the classes. The grunt of bodies in motion, pushing hard against their limits. The feeling of sweat tracing patterns on his skin. The arrhythmic motion of the spheres. His limbs bending in seemingly impossible ways. Deep bass thrumming. Matthew's face, close to his. "This one has potential."

He woke up the next morning repeating that, feeling buoyant despite the burn in his muscles. His body was a tuning fork, still vibrating from last night's session. He ran his hands over himself. His muscles twitched, as if seeking out his touch. He was filled with a power he never imagined he could possess. He had made his body into a tool which his will controlled; he was no longer governed by impulses and desires he did not want.

He wished he could answer the intake survey again and this time he would say no, no, no.

I am free.

Thank God, I am now free.

When he unlocked his phone, he noticed a notification from his banking app; he had transferred a thousand dollars to Peak Fitness. It hardly seemed a sufficient tithe.

"Hey, bud. I want to talk to you about something," James said as he walked into Ed's cubicle.

"Yeah? Shoot."

"Some of the guys at the gym and I were talking." He hesitated, which was unusual for James. "We've been noticing some changes…" *Wasn't that the whole point*, Ed was about to ask when James leaned in close and whispered, "I just haven't been wanting to fuck. Like, at all. I thought it was just me, but I chatted with a few of the others and they said the same thing." Noticing Ed's lack of a reaction, James shook his head in disbelief. "I just thought you might be having the same problem too and that you might, you know…want to do something about it?"

"But you said you feel so much better. Isn't it worth it?"

"Listen, bud. If you're… you know…There's nothing wrong with that. Not nowadays. I have a cousin who is really happy and lives with his partner and—"

"Thanks for the heads up, pal," Ed cut him off. If James couldn't even put it to words, how could he? This whole conversation was just awkward, painful. It reminded him of the kind of emotional uncertainty that plagued him before Peak Fitness, like the emotional pinch he'd felt when he saw someone scoff at a same-sex couple holding hands, that tug between wanting to join the angry as much as he wanted to join the lovers. He'd since evolved past that. "I have some reports to finish up before lunch, it was nice of you to stop by."

James hesitated for a moment. But after glancing at Ed, he left.

Ed's phone lit up as James walked out of his cubicle. A notification from Peak Fitness.

You've been invited to join the VIP program. Do you accept?

He was chosen.

This was a sign.

He was on the right path.

Shelley Lavigne

"Matthew would like to speak to you, welcome you. Get ready and we'll take you to him," Nadia said when he walked through the doors.

Ed used the communal change room, uncaring of others' glances or bodies. He was giddy as Nadia led him deeper into the gym, into the holy inner-sanctum, following a passageway he'd always seen but never had the courage to enter. Nadia brought him to a door emblazoned with the gym's logo and knocked lightly before pushing it open.

Matthew was more perfect up close. His skin smooth, glowing, his hair in a perfect wavy back-comb. He rose from his kneeling table and gestured at the cushion across from him.

"Edward Kind," Matthew used his whole name as a greeting. "Do you want tea? Water?"

"Ed is good. And tea, too. Tea is good," his nervous laugh followed on the heels of whatever that awkward chatter was, as he knelt a little too hard before Matthew, rattling the cups on the table. The tea was a deep, vivid green, and had an aftertaste that reminded him of asparagus. But it was still good, warm, nourishing.

Ed figured it had healing properties.

"I wanted to thank you for accepting our invitation," Matthew said. His voice enveloped Ed in its warm, loving embrace. "These are trying times for our community and seeing someone like you stick with us over your friends, it just reinforces how special you are."

"Oh, James wasn't really my friend," Matthew frowned, so Ed hurriedly added, "especially after what he did."

"That's great to hear. We need people like you, those who have faith in our mission, who have the strength to persist through adversity. I've had my eye on you for a while, Edward. It's always been clear to me that you are special. I want to teach you how to unlock your endless potential."

Matthew gently placed his hands on Ed's head. A benediction.

Their eyes closed in sync. Ed leaned into the touch, never had he wanted to be this close to anyone nor never did he think that someone would want to be close to him. Ed could smell Matthew's musk under the lemon and incense he wore as an aura. He let it swell his chest, fill his lungs, enter his blood.

We're All Family Here

He wanted to incorporate those bits of Matthew into his body, his cells, his DNA.

When Matthew removed his hands, Ed felt the loss with a chill. Matthew smiled sweetly when he opened his eyes.

"Tonight will be a great night, a historic night. Tonight, I will share my latest findings, and you will join the family."

Matthew helped Ed up and led him to the lobby, now drained of everyone but VIPs. His old self would have been nervous when all eyes turned to him, but he felt nothing but peace, kinship, as they approached.

This really was a miraculous place.

The family of VIPs formed a circle around Ed, hands grazing his skin, combing through his hair, touching his lashes, arms, stomach, one hand cupping his ass. In the warm light of the lobby, it felt like the brush of embryos in the womb, innocent curiosity.

"My dears," Matthew said, and all hands fell away, "I have something important to share, please follow me. There will be time to greet your new brother after."

The VIPs surged forward, trailing Matthew into one of the classrooms. He took his place on a raised step next to a flip board.

"Thank you all for coming tonight, to welcome the newest member of our family, Edward Kind, and to discuss our future. As you all noticed, there are fewer members at the gym today; several former adherents did not share our vision and have decided to abandon our community."

There were growls of disapproval, which Matthew raised his hands to silence. "I understand your discontent, but this is entirely normal. There is always resistance to progress, to visionary minds. We do not need those who question our mission among us, weakening us. We will regrow and rebuild and push our bodies to the next level. See, fitness is not just about physical prowess; when discussing evolution, fitness is a measure of how likely you are to survive and thrive in the current environment. That's what we are doing here, making you the best possible fit for the world with the aim to create a new generation that shares those same traits and views. While reproduction may seem to run against our own tenants of bodily perfection, I am here to say—there is another way."

Matthew flipped the first page over to reveal an image of a bulbous green succulent, with a smaller version growing out of its side. Next to it was a starfish, with each of its limbs separated from its body in a bloodless quartering. Finally, there was a series of geckos, diminishing in size like a set of undone nesting dolls.

"To this day, many animals continue to reproduce without sex. At the cellular level, we do too. Scientists think sexual reproduction evolved to create diverse offspring that may thrive and be better adapted to survive than their parents. But when you are perfect, why would you create offspring that differ from you?"

Matthew flipped the page again to display an illustration of a human body with two torsos sprouting from a single pair of legs. The four arms waved and the two mouths smiled.

At the bottom of the page were the words *Our Future*.

"This will be our next step, this will be the way we grow our ranks, make more of ourselves. So, tonight, let's celebrate the addition of our new VIP, and tomorrow—we change the future of humanity!"

The group's cheer was deafening. In the swell, Ed felt hands press into him, names whispered into his ears, bodies morphing and shifting around his, an anonymous mass of limbs. He was but one cell in the organism. For the first time in his life, he belonged.

Ed's life was changed. He turned down the once coveted invitation to Thirsty Thursdays from the cool co-workers—"I have gym after work" — and was able to walk by the office's Pride Network Activity posters without feeling that pang of guilt and fear and sadness.

Work faded into the background. He was left with snippets of meetings, the taste of reheated coffee, a promise to circle back later. His brain was *realigning*.

He was incorporated into the VIPs; their voices, their smells, the idiosyncrasies of their movements became his own. The only thing that felt real was the gym. The changes in his body. The feeling of possibility. A primordial remembering.

Humans descended from an ancestor that reproduced asexually. He could feel his cells remembering this long-forgotten instinct.

He was on the precipice of great change.

In class, Matthew corrected his form often, his lingering touches burned with the heat of undersea vents where life first emerged. Fuel for creation, but fuel for urges that ran counter to the gym's mission. To Matthew's mantra.

If you follow me, the unwanted will be discarded, you will be remade, perfect.

In his nightmares he drowned in thick, warm semen that felt gritty in his mouth and pulled him down, filling his nose, his ears, his every bodily orifice.

He felt it before he got out of bed, a strange vertical cinching like being pulled in two directions. Swaying—he hadn't felt that awful, that wrong, since he joined the gym half a year ago—he stumbled into the bathroom.

The blinking face in the mirror could not be his own.

A seam split it in two, pink skin pinched where it puckered in. His hands trembled and tingled—nerves or a side effect—and did not quite feel like his own as he tugged off his pajamas. He closed his eyes tight, afraid for a moment that the seam on his face was just a pillow crease, wanting to live in a moment of possibility before he threw himself off the cliff that was the previous limit of humanity.

He peeked.

A line, a soft pink line split him down his middle, bisecting his bellybutton, the artifact of his first birth. There was even a faint pink line down the center of his dick. It too would divide.

The thought triggered in him the sensation of being pulled apart, that moment after a dislocation when a doctor tugs before the bone returns to its proper home.

He was going to prove Matthew right.

He was going to lead humanity into a new era.

The first thing he did was call the gym; he didn't even wait for Nadia to recite her entire greeting.

"It's Edward Kind," he said. "I'm starting to bud."

"Stay where you are, we're coming to get you," she replied.

His observation room was attached to Matthew's office. Its walls were beige and soft like wool. He ran his hands along its surface as he paced the room.

"I'll monitor your progress," Matthew promised when Ed arrived, but he had not been seen all day.

He'd so badly wanted Matthew to touch his new skin, nearly buckling into his embrace when he'd seen him that morning. That had been wrong. Now, he was alone to meditate on his painful transformation.

Ed was slowly being garrotted. A terrible pressure, not sharp enough to cut, just deep, penetrating. A pulse, a sudden tightening, sent him to his knees.

His legs split farther than they had before and a sharp tug rang through his middle.

It had not looked this painful in the illustration.

Was he doing it wrong?

Was he not good enough?

Were his thoughts not focused enough?

Maybe this was penance.

He was lying on the ground when Matthew came in sometime later. There were no windows, no clocks, and Nadia took his phone and watch when he arrived. Time was elastic in this haze of bright light and searing pain.

Matthew untied the sash of Ed's gray robe and assessed his

progress. His earlier desires were replaced by the need to escape the agony.

"You'll be ready tonight," Matthew declared.

Ed looked down before Matthew could re-tie the sash. His legs had split farther, past his belly button, halfway up his abs, his dick split in two like an echidna. The skin between the two was fresh pink. Ed saw two little nubs that looked like large angry pimples where new legs would hopefully emerge.

"Try to relax," Matthew said before another wave of pain knocked Ed unconscious again.

The wheelchair gently shook him awake under the bright lights of the corridor. He tried to beg for drugs, but the seam cut his tongue and jaw and what came out was spit and babbles.

"Are you ready?" Matthew asked from behind. Ed was scared to nod in case his brains tumbled out.

"There's a lot riding on tonight, not just for your brothers and sisters. But for me too. I was laughed out of academia, had to rebuild my fortune, restart my research. Everyone thinks I'm crazy, wrong. But they're the idiots, I'm right. I've always been right. And if you do this, I get to spit in their faces. So, do not fuck it up or I will rip you in half myself."

Ed was too absorbed in his pain to register the threat. Seated, his legs split apart further and the tearing pain seared through to the top of his chest, stopping inches below his collar bone.

He wouldn't—couldn't—let Matthew down.

The asynchronous hearts in his chests beat roughly, swirling blood through his brain and blacking out his vision.

He was on the raised stage now, in the big room where he took his first class, surrounded by brothers and sisters. Most looked at him in awe, smiling as if he was their savior. A couple stood near the doors, pale, disgusted by the future they moved towards. *Unbelievers*, he wanted to brand them, *traitors*. But he couldn't focus on the naysayers, they'd soon be outnumbered.

Matthew spoke, though he missed part of it.

"...his bravery and strength should serve as an inspiration to us all."

Ed felt it then, the split reached his head.

The bones in his skull cracked, his brain splitting in half. Like being shot in slow motion. If he could scream, it would have cleaved the world in two.

The hum started, the tuning fork noise that was the only memory of his first session. It built around him, resonating in his cells, splitting him apart like glass.

His center pinched, as if he was held together by the squeeze of skin between two malicious fingers. His world and body narrowed until it was only that point, the point of division, or meeting.

Then he popped.

He slumped to both sides of the chair and watched in stereo vision as Matthew approached. Matthew ran his hand along new skin, overly sensitive and tender like a fresh cut. It hurt in a way that blended pain with pleasure, heightening both.

"I was right, oh God I was *right!*" Matthew said.

Ed looked at themselves for the first time. Not their mirror reflections, but their true selves. The faces they saw were terrified, unsure about what they had become. But they were also the faces of someone they could love. Had loved, this whole time. Who understood what they went through, who would not judge them when they spoke their shame out loud. Family. True family. True love. Self-love.

A little bit of distance was all it took.

They reached out to one another.

Invitation
Jessica Swanson

I hear the whispers from the hollowed dirt,
great worms slithering up from the silence:
shall we pull it
someone free her
shall we lift it
shall we pull it away.

There is no we, no us,
an ordinary sickle taking an Arthurian cast,
granting immortality, a bloody fountain sprung forth.
The gift of eternal youth: wine freshly uncorked.
This is not an open invitation, but a note gently pressed—
like a rose creased between pages,
or a calling card left in care of the house's mistress.

To you, who stroked my hand and sang of summers past,
who talked about the taste of fresh cream as the fever crept in.
To you, who dabbed away sweat and braided the hair from my face,
hiding the bruised patches with your mother's best kerchief,
stolen from the top drawer because it smelled of lavender.

Jessica Swanson

To you, who thought that perhaps a doctor might offer some help
when the priest refused, prattling on as you changed the flowers
over and over and over and over,
petals falling in great heaps.
Always, you.
Only you, smoothing the collar of my nightgown with your calloused hands.
You, with lips stained red,
fresh with the juice of newly-ripe raspberries, begging to be kissed.
You, soft and smelling of wheat and fear.
You, with eyes like hostile seas
who idly watched your daddy choose
between the sickle and the scythe
saying nothing: you.
Empty promises, like scattered grains
as your mother drove the lock through skin then muscle then bone.
You, who understands the hush that falls across the fields
as the sun rises on reaping day.
You, who feels a throbbing against your palm
from a key that has long-since rusted away.

To a distant ancestor weighed down with unfathomable guilt,
who thinks to herself, *If I pull it, what punishment wrought, what justice served?*

You have my invitation.

Acknowledgments

Thank you to all of the amazing Kickstarter backers who helped make this anthology a reality:

AEB
- AK Faulkner
- Akis Linardos
- Alan Mark Tong
- Alana M T
- Amabilis O'Hara
- Amarah Grove
- Anastasia Kirchoff-Elliott
- Andreas L.
- Andromeda Busch
- Anonymous
- Cam
- Caroline Ugelstad Elnæs
- Casey J Rudkin
- Cat T
- Cindy Phan
- Dai Baddley
- Dead Fish Books
- DrivingMeBonkas
- Em Jeffrey
- Francesco Tehrani
- Giusy Rippa
- H.V. Patterson
- Heather Hall

J Brad
Jay Wolf
Jen Haeger
Jessica Enfante
Joe Butler
John Bowen
Jonathan Helland
Julian Renaud
Kat Day
Katy
Laura Musich
Lekden Davis
Mary
Michael Hicks
Quinn Swain-Nesbit
Rachel Clements
Ruth Pinto
Scarlett Wilkie
Scott Lynch
Simon Crow
Skomam
Spit
Steve Pattee
T
T.G.
Team Dayley
The Underwoods
Thea JN
Tove Sollilja
Tyler Battaglia
W
Zack Fissel

About the Editor

Roxie Voorhees (she/he/they) is an incredible creature with an insatiable love for books in bed. They are the co-editor of MINE and READER BEWARE, and EIC of Book Slayer Press.

About the Authors

Sofia Ajram is a metalsmith and literary horror writer who specializes in stories of anomalous architecture and gay pining. He is the editor of the forthcoming *Bury Your Gays: An Anthology of Tragic Queer Horror,* and the writer of *Coup de Grâce,* a Titan Books novella being released in October 2024. She has also given lectures on contemporary horror films at Monstrum Montreal and serves as a moderator of r/horror on Reddit. Sofia lives in Montreal with her cat Isa. Find them on Twitter and Instagram @sofiaajram.

j ambrose (he/it) writes weird, queer, and filthy stories and poetry. It is an agender creature and professional college drop-out who finds the juiciest inspiration in all works of the flesh. You can find his work in *Vast Chasm Magazine, Hearth & Coffin Literary Journal,* Hungry Shadow Press, or the dreaded thing itself on Tumblr and X @CANINEBRAINZ and his website https://caninebrainz.neocities.org

Roxie Voorhees

Darren Black (He/his/him) lives on Massachusetts's north shore and has served on the committee of the Boston Poetry Marathon. His poems have appeared in *The Muddy River Poetry Review*, *The Saranac Review Online*, and in the *Voices Amidst the Virus* anthology among other publications. His recent poems explore disability status, accessibility, and his own experiences as a queer person living with blindness.

A mass of tentacles and rose vines masquerading as a person, **Amanda M. Blake** (she/they) is the author of such horror titles as *Deep Down* and *Out of Curiosity and Hunger*, dark poetry collection *Dead Ends*, and the Thorns fairy tale mash-up series. For more, visit amandamblake.com.

Anton Cancre's mother wasn't really pregnant with them when she went to see The Exorcist, but they tell people that anyways because it sounds cool. Their poetry collections, *Meaningless Cycles in a Vicious Glass Prison* and *This Story Doesn't End the Way We Want All The Time* as well as their nonfiction book about Silent Hill, *Nightmares of Blood and Flesh*, are available from Dragon's Roost Press. They're also a luddite who still has a blogspot website (antoncancre.blogspot.com). Pronouns: Any/All/Just Not Late For Dinner.

K.M. Carmien (she/her) is a librarian who lives on the East Coast, where she catalogs by day and writes primarily horror and dark fantasy by night (or at any time the words strike). She loves a good cup of coffee, Octobers, and her two cats, Spock and Matilda. If you put a dragon, a vampire, a witch, or a strange and liminal location and/or being in it, she'll probably read it. She has been previously published in Shimmer Magazine. Find her at k_mary_c on twitter, or on a moonless night attempting to befriend an inadvisable supernatural creature.

Charibdys writes a mix of erotica and ero-horror ranging from sweet to bituminous, often touching on monstrous romance. Charibdys's work has been featured in venues including *Slipshine* and *voidjunk*.

Rain Corbyn (they/them) is a queer, Autistic writer and voice actor living on a wooded mountain. More of their writing can be found in *Mouthfeel #1* and Tenebrous Press's Shirley Jackson Award-Nominated *Your Body Is Not Your Body*. They narrate horror as Rain Corbyn and romance/erotica as Richard Pendragon. Their dad-joke portfolio can be found on Twitter @RainCorbyn

JB Corso is a mental health clinician who has worked with vulnerable populations for nearly two decades. They enjoy spending time with their family, writing, and pondering existential questions. They live with their supportive partner and enjoy long car rides relaxing to the Grateful Dead. Their writing motto is "Developing stories into masterpieces." They are a Horror Writer's Association member and a NaNoWriMo winner (2021, 2022).

M. Lopes da Silva (he/they/she) is a non-binary trans masc author and artist from Los Angeles. He writes pulp and poetry. Previously he's been employed as a sex worker, an art critic, and an educator. His poetry can be found in *Eye to the Telescope*, *The Dread Machine*, and *Electric Literature*. Dread Stone Press recently published his first novelette *What Ate the Angels* - a queer vore sludgefest that travels beneath the streets of Los Angeles starring a non-binary ASMR artist and their vore-loving girlfriend - in Volume Two of the Split Scream series.

BlueSky: mlopesdasilva.bsky.social
Instagram: @authormlopesdasilva

Roxie Voorhees

Arthur DeHart (he/him) is a trans poet and writer from the hills of Tennessee. He has a few poetry collections out (*These Hills Still Have Eyes, Mental Hospital Socks; Three Days Worn*) and a horror novel (*The Secrets of Maggie Valley Ranch*). He loves his husband. You can find him on twitter @artjuldehart.

Aleksandra Ugelstad Elnæs is a writer and historian whose work is haunted by all things lost and fragmented. They have an MA in Eighteenth-Century Studies and work in museum education. They are based in Oslo, Norway and can be found on Instagram (@aleksandra1789).

Minh-Anh Vo Dinh (he/him) is a queer Vietnamese screenwriter who focuses on anything that spooks and unsettles the audience. He believes in highlighting the voices of Asian women and 2SLGBTQ+ individuals within horror and how their unique perspectives can elevate the genre with nuances and sensitivity. His writing explores trauma, dysfunctional relationships and belonging while using horror to accentuate the story. You can find him on Instagram: @mavvydee and Twitter @Maverick_Vo

Clar Hart (she/they, ig: @clarhartwrites) is a queer cartoonist, writer of weird fiction and rainy weather enthusiast. They work out of PNW under the supervision of their benevolent overlord, an orange tabby with exactly three brain cells.

Rae Knowles (she/her) is a queer woman and author of dark fiction including The Stradivarius (May 2023) and Merciless Waters (November 2023). Her short work has been featured in Dark Matter Ink, Nightmare, Ghoulish Tales, Seize the Press, Taco Bell Quarterly, and Nosetouch Press, among others. Rae is represented by Laura Williams at Greene & Heaton.

Shelley Lavigne is a purveyor of moist literature, usually queer horror. Their words can be found at The Dread Machine, If There's Anyone Left and others. They live in Ontario where they roam their neighbourhood in search of haunted houses and cool bugs. You can also find them online at shelleylavigne.com

Sapphire Lazuli (she/they), Author of *Our Witchless Flesh* (Coming 2025 via Off Limits Press) and writer/director of *Haunted Houses and Houses That Haunt* and *Those Were The Days*, is an artist whose brush is dipped in weird horror and perverted desires. Their prose is often described as beautifully poetic and adjacent to the reader; Sapphire does not write stories that will hold your hand. Be it cosmic entities appearing as places, gross and erotic explorations of the boundaries of form, deep dives into the darkest ridges of the mind and desire, or even video essays divulging the many mechanisms that construct fear, her horror is bound to allure you.

Twitter: @lazuli_sapphire
YouTube: @sapphicsapph
Blog: www.sapphirelazuli.com

Dori Lumpkin (they/them) is a queer writer and storytelling enthusiast from South Alabama. Their work has appeared in *Diet Milk Magazine*, *Ram Eye Press*, and is forthcoming in many other places. They love all things speculative and weird, and strive to make fiction writing a more inclusive place. When not writing, Dori is most often found reading, playing Dungeons and Dragons, or staring blankly at their laptop. They would like to take this moment to thank their cat, Lilo, for sleeping on the aforementioned laptop at the most inconvenient of moments. You can find them @whimsyqueen on Twitter, Instagram, Tiktok and more, or check out their website: https://dorilumpkin.carrd.co

Roxie Voorhees

Caitlin Marceau is a queer Canadian author and illustrator based in Montreal. She holds a Bachelor of Arts in Creative Writing, is an Active Member of the Horror Writers Association, and has spoken about genre literature at several Canadian conventions. Her work includes *Femina*, *A Blackness Absolute*, and her award-winning novella, *This Is Where We Talk Things Out*. Her second novella, *I'm Having Regrets*, and her debut novel, *It Wasn't Supposed To Go Like This*, are set for publication in 2024. For more, visit CaitlinMarceau.ca or find her on social media.

Avra Margariti is a queer author and Pushcart-nominated poet with a fondness for the dark and the darling. Avra's work haunts publications such as *Vastarien*, *Asimov's*, *Liminality*, *Arsenika*, *The Future Fire*, *Space and Time*, *Lackington's*, and *Reckoning*. Avra lives and studies in Athens, Greece. You can find Avra on twitter (@avramargariti).

Evoking the beauty and power of nature, **Violet Mourningstarr** shines light on trauma endured by people assigned female at birth through their dark prose and verse. They're very elusive, residing in the shadowy places often forgotten and seldom vacuumed. A staunch luddite, and happier for it, Vi cannot be found online.

Marisca Pichette (she/they) covets monsters. More of her work has appears in *Strange Horizons, Vastarien, The Magazine of Fantasy & Science Fiction, Fantasy Magazine, Flash Fiction Online, PseudoPod*, and others. She is the winner of the 2022 *F(r)iction* Spring Literary Contest and has been nominated for the Pushcart and Dwarf Stars Awards. Their speculative poetry collection, *Rivers in Your Skin, Sirens in Your Hair*, is out now from Android Press. Find them on Twitter as @MariscaPichette and Instagram as @marisca_write.

Grace R. Reynolds (she/her) is a native of the great state of New Jersey, where she was first introduced to the eerie and strange thanks to local urban legends of a devil creeping through the Pine Barrens. Since then, her curiosity with things that go bump in the night bloomed into creative expression as a dark poet, horror, and thriller fiction writer. She is the author of two poetry collections, *Lady of The House* and *The Lies We Weave*, both released by Curious Corvid Publishing.

Zach Rosenberg is a Jewish horror and SFF writer living in Florida who crafts horrifying tales by night and practices law by the day. The latter is even more frightening. His works have been published in various magazines and anthologies, including *Dark Matter Magazine*, *The Deadlands*, and *The Magazine of Fantasy & Science Fiction*. His debut books, *Hungers as Old as this Land* and *The Long Shalom* were released by Brigids Gate Press, and Off Limits Press. Follow him on Twitter/X @ZachRoseWriter

Jessica Swanson (she/her) is a writer and librarian currently residing somewhere in Florida. She enjoys cats, cheese, and fancy tea blends. She holds degrees in both Creative Writing and Library and Information Science. While she enjoys horror genres of all sorts, she has a soft spot for paranormal investigations, cryptozoology, and paranormal romance. Her writing has previously appeared in *Hearth and Coffin*, *Voidspace Zine*, *Worm Moon Archive*, and others. Follow her on Twitter at Cooljazsheepie or on Instagram at everystupidstar.

Dragon's Roost Press

Dragon's Roost Press is the fever dream brainchild of dark speculative fiction author Michael Cieslak. Since 2014, their goal has been to find the best speculative fiction authors and share their work with the public. For more information about Dragon's Roost Press and their publications, please visit:

http://www.thedragonsroost.biz

Printed in Great Britain
by Amazon